# EARTH EARLS ARE EASY

Lords of Dystopia
Book 1

## Catherine Stein

ISBN: 978-1-949862-47-8

Book cover and interior design by E. McAuley:
www.emcauley.com

**For notes on content please visit**

catsteinbooks.com/content-notes

"My God, you are all… chaos," Nova grumbled. "Is this an Earth thing? What did they feed you as children?"

"The blood of our enemies," Windborne replied breezily. "You appear discombobulated, Ms. Pratt. Shall we step out for some air?"

"To make it easier for you to knife me? I don't think so."

"Please." He sniffed. "If I'd wanted to kill you, I would have done it already."

The statement rang true. He didn't see her as a threat. Arrogant bastard. Seemed he was just like other earls after all.

"Fine. Let's step outside and have a chat."

They exited the dance floor and stepped through the doors to the terrace. While not as crowded as the ballroom, it was hardly the place for a private conversation. Idle gentlemen lounged against the balustrades with drinks in hand, while ladies overheated from dance fanned themselves. Calculated behaviors in an artificial world. A game with many players and few winners.

If Nova had the opportunity to loiter out here, she'd spend it admiring the view of the stars through the crystal-clear glass panes of the dome overhead. But she was stuck playing the game too.

"Would you be willing to stroll through the garden with me?" Windborne asked. "I believe we have established that I am not a threat to your life. Especially since I'm not armed and you undoubtedly are."

"Very well." Nova started down the steps to the pristinely manicured lawn. The grass had been shorn to a perfectly even carpet of green, every hedge trimmed at exact right angles. She breathed deep, taking in the soothing orderliness.

"What a travesty." The earl placed his hands on his hips. The scowl didn't look natural on his face. It brought back the appearance of awkwardness he'd exhibited during the quadrille.

"What is?"

"The garden. Life isn't meant to be perfect. Obviously all of this is unnatural here, imported from Earth generations ago. But it could at least be allowed to grow free instead of being forced into someone's idea of how things should be." He trailed a hand along the top of a hedge, his brightly painted nails standing out against the uniform green. "The perfection is an illusion, anyway. Look. See how this branch is popping out already? And there in the grass." He pointed at a spot near Nova's feet. "A bit of clover. Someone might come along and pluck it out, but there will be others. Or a tiny seedling will sprout."

Nova kept her posture straight, despite the temptation to bend down and examine the grass for additional interlopers. The illusion was necessary, just as the social order imposed on people was. You played the game to survive. Young Nova had served hours on kitchen duty for "questioning orders" when she'd simply wanted a few explanations. Was it fair? Probably not. But it had taught her how to live within the rules, and that had served her well ever since.

"I'm not interested in your philosophizing." She turned to face Windborne. They weren't entirely out of sight, but isolated enough not to be overheard. "Only in your crimes, Viper."

His blue-eyed gaze turned chilly. "I am very fond of snakes, and of all animals, in fact. It's hardly a crime."

Nova glowered down at him. "Don't pretend ignorance. You, Lord Windborne, are the smuggler known as the Viper."

The earl loosened his cravat, exposing a small patch of his throat. An absurd urge to lick him there shivered through her.

"Call me Wyatt," he said. "Titles are tiresomely formal."

*Wyatt.* The name suited him far better than any lordly address, but Nova knew better than to use it. First names implied intimacy or friendliness that had no place in her mission.

"You admit it, then?" she challenged.

"Admit what? That I'm a criminal? Don't be ridiculous. If I were, I would lie and say I wasn't, and if I weren't, I'd also say I wasn't."

Nova gave serious consideration to lifting her skirts to get at the dagger strapped to her leg. "If you turn this into one of those 'you find three doors guarded by three men and only one tells the truth' puzzles, I'm dumping you into that reflecting pool over there."

He arched his eyebrows. "It's a nice night for a swim."

Of course it was a nice night. The atmosphere inside every enclosure was identical, thanks to the arcanium-powered enviro-generators. Any deviation in gravity, temperature, and humidity would be minimal at worst, and the Duke of Phobos wouldn't stand for anything but an ideal climate. He would have a top-of-the-line generator and constant maintenance. Only people born on Earth spoke as if conditions might change at any moment.

She shuddered. "It must be a horrible place to live."

"This estate?" Windborne asked. "I agree. Too regimented, too wasteful, and filled far too often with people pretending to be something they're not."

"I meant Earth, with all your weather and chaos. And who are you to talk about pretending, Mr. Secret Criminal Identity?"

He looked her straight in the eye and ran a finger languidly down the center of his neon-green waistcoat.

"Darling, I am exactly as you see. I know your world is all about the game, but I play by my own rules."

He spun on his heel and strode away. A moment later, a small drone flew out from the shrubbery and hovered over Nova's head.

"Fuck off." She gave it the finger and stomped back to the ballroom.

# 5

RION FLUNG HIMSELF onto the couch in Wyatt's sitting room and crossed his arms behind his head. "You left early last night."

Wyatt opened the door to the enclosure on the opposite side of the room and waved a strawberry. Flurry flew into Wyatt's arms and pounced on the treat. Wyatt petted the bat's furry head.

"I don't see how you can comment on my comings and goings last night," he said. "You vanished the moment we entered the house."

"Lady Buxley wanted me to lift her skirts in the butler's pantry. I could hardly refuse."

Wyatt rolled his eyes and joined Rion on the couch—which, in this case, meant sitting on his legs. Rion, who had a bad habit of hogging furniture, didn't even flinch.

"Lady Buxley is a widow. What happened to the 'seduce their spouses' plan?"

Rion shrugged. "Got sidetracked. Don't let that flying rat shit on me."

Wyatt stroked Flurry's silky fur. "He's a fruit bat, and he

only voids his bowels in his habitat. He's also very smart, so have a little respect."

Rion chuckled. "You and your animals. How's the zoological garden coming along?"

"Slowly. It takes money and well-trained employees to do everything right. And there's so much to do. So many animals that can't ever go back to their natural environment—if it even exists anymore. They deserve so much better than what they've been given."

"Kinda like us."

Rion didn't mean the two of them in particular. They had money and connections. They were fine and would be fine anywhere. But their people—the people of Dystopia—still struggled under a system that saw them as expendable. Twenty years of work and so little to show for it.

Wyatt sighed. "Yeah."

A weighty silence permeated the air. Flurry must have sensed the discomfort, because he abandoned the strawberry and flew up to hang from one of the many perches Wyatt had scattered around the room for him.

"So…" Wyatt ended the lull before the constant stream of chatter in his brain could carry him off into a river of melancholia. "Why are you here? Not to visit my bat, obviously."

"To find out what you learned from the mercenary. What does she know?"

"Oh." Wyatt shifted uncomfortably, causing Rion to wince. "Sorry."

They both adjusted their positions until they were sitting side-by-side like normal people. Assuming normal people actually existed. Wyatt wasn't sure.

"I didn't learn much," he admitted. "I was… well, I was flirting with her instead of interrogating her."

Rion snickered.

"You know I'm not good at this sort of thing. Aubrey's the spy. I'm much better off sitting at my desk and playing with my drones."

Rion arched a single dark eyebrow. "Is that what the kids are calling it these days?"

Wyatt elbowed him. "Shut your fu—"

The wail of an alarm swallowed up his expletive. Flurry gave a shriek of displeasure and flew back to his enclosure.

"Dammit." Wyatt sprang to his feet and rushed through the door to the office. Red text flashed across all three of his video screens.

"What's happening?" Rion wondered.

Wyatt lunged for the keyboard without even sitting down, pounding out the commands to silence the alarm and bring up all relevant information.

"Critical alert. A shipment has been disrupted. Cargo drone seized outside warehouse fifteen." He tapped out another command. "On what grounds? Where's the fucking authorization? They can't just do that!"

He called up a drone camera from the warehouse and put its video onto the center screen. A man dressed in all black dragged a crate from one of Wyatt's shiny new cargo drones. Scratches and burn marks marred the formerly pristine steel around the hatch.

"Look at this!" Wyatt jabbed a finger at the text on the right-hand screen. "No inspection code. Not scheduled, not surprise, not anything. They tore their way into my ship instead of requesting an open command. Bastards."

It had to be Nova Pratt. Anything this blatantly against protocol could only have come at the instigation of someone untouchable. Someone with enough votes in his pocket to perpetrate any crime without repercussion.

Wyatt sent an override to the cargo drone, directing it to a different warehouse. Flying with the broken hatch hanging open was illegal, but he'd pay the fine if necessary. No way in hell was he letting them destroy his shipment.

As the ship on the screen rose into the air, a second black-clad figure appeared, leaping from the open hatch and executing an elegant tumbling landing. She popped to her feet. The maneuver had yanked strands of her black hair loose from its tie.

"Ah," Rion said. "Your lady."

Wyatt straightened up and turned to face his friend. "Interested in a trip to warehouse fifteen?"

Rion's grin was pure devilry. "Wouldn't miss it."

· · ⊂━ · ·

The cursed camera drone zipped away before Nova could draw her pistol and shoot it out of the sky.

"I hate those things."

"The drones?" Cameron, a skinny, dark-skinned youth on his first mission, regarded her with eyebrows raised. "You must not spend much time downtown. They're everywhere. Delivering packages, directing traffic, sweeping the streets, you know." He shrugged. "Some people treat them like pets."

Pets were another thing Nova didn't understand. Earthlings surrounded themselves with animals, as if they were part of their families. She'd only ever seen animals from a distance or in an exhibit. Downtown supposedly had rats, but thus far she'd—thankfully—avoided them.

"I only come here when necessary," Nova replied. Which now meant twice in a matter of days. So far she wasn't enjoying this trip any better than the last. It was all so... disorderly. Streets twisted and turned, intersecting at strange angles. Sectors sprawled haphazardly beyond their original enclosures. Buildings were built, torn down, or renovated with such frequency that half the city seemed under construction at any one time.

"Good thing they put you with me, then." Cameron gave her a crooked grin. "You need someone who can teach you Dystopian ways."

"Don't call it that," Nova reminded him.

"Right, right. 'No unauthorized nickname for the working district of Utopia shall be used, as it undermines the unity of the city-state and the authority of its government,'" he parroted.

She didn't miss the hint of sarcasm in his voice. Cameron had lived most of his nineteen years downtown, until his aristocratic parentage had been discovered and he'd been sent to the RMC for training. Nova didn't know him well, but she'd already noticed that his upbringing gave him an unusual perspective. One she hoped would aid her in this mission.

"Don't wanna get tossed in the Underground," the boy added, the ironic edge in his voice harder now.

"The Underground is a myth," Nova sighed. "Now let's get this crate opened and see what the Viper is smuggling today."

She ran her hand along the top of the steel trunk, probing gently at the brass hasps securing the lid in place. They didn't budge. A single lock mechanism kept them all solidly in place.

"We'll need a lock-breaker to open this. Or possibly a crowbar to pry it open. Could you check the toolkit?"

Cameron nodded and jogged over to the trailer of the tandem bicycle they'd ridden from the company barracks.

Before he could return, a familiar voice made Nova whirl around.

"Would you like some assistance opening that?" Lord Windborne, again dressed in jeans and a cropped t-shirt, gave her his impish smile. "I assume you are here for an authorized inspection?"

Lord Brandt—tall, burly, and brooding—stepped up to stand beside Windborne. His clothing was military in style, nearly identical to the tactical garb Nova and Cameron wore. Nova scanned him for weapons, but found no bulges in the usual hiding places.

"Maybe Connington sent his mercs for some thievery in broad daylight." Brandt gave her a feral smile. "I'm happy to make an arrest, if you two would come with me."

Nova dug in her pocket for the signed note from her father. She flashed it long enough for Brandt and Windborne to see the signature, then tucked it safely away. "His Grace has granted special authority."

"Pity." Brandt met Nova's gaze and held it. She recognized that look from the merc squads. He could kill a man sixteen different ways with his bare hands and wanted her to know it.

Wyatt—no, she had to think of him as Windborne— walked casually to Nova's side and reached for the locking mechanism. He blocked his actions with his body, but when he stepped back, the three hasps popped open.

Nova flipped the top open and stared down into the crate, not quite believing what she was seeing.

"Books?" Cameron walked over for a closer look. "Oh, Algebra. Nifty!"

Nova pushed aside the top layer of textbooks to reveal an identical layer beneath. Muttering curses, she dug deeper, tossing books to Cameron and Windborne to move them out of her way.

"It's books all the way down." Wyatt smirked at her. "A charitable donation for schools. If you're satisfied, I'll close this up now so we can get them distributed."

She waved a book in front of his face. "Not until we've checked every one of these to make certain they're not hollowed out and full of opiates or gunpowder."

Lord Brandt rubbed his chin contemplatively. "Book full of gunpowder. Hmm."

Windborne dumped the pile of books he held back into the crate. "Very well. Enjoy yourself. I'll send someone around with the addresses of the schools where you can take the books when you're finished."

He gave her a polite bow and walked off.

Nova watched her adversaries leave, her mind turning over what she'd learned. Something was off.

"Hey, there's an error here on page twenty-five," Cameron said, not looking up from the book he was perusing. "We should contact the manufacturer and let them know."

Nova rubbed her temple, still grasping for a thought that hovered just out of reach. "Wasn't this drone supposed to be carrying metal? Or ore? Something from the asteroid mines?"

She stared for a long moment at the untidy pile of books. Paper books. Made from wood pulp. Imported from Earth.

"Dammit!" She smacked her palm against her forehead. "The books aren't hiding anything. They *are* the contraband! He's evading the paper tax."

Cameron cocked his head and frowned at her. "Who smuggles maths books?"

Nova could only shake her head. If she seized the crate as illegal cargo, she would deprive hundreds of students of the books they needed. Which would go directly against her pledge of service to the Utopian people. If she didn't seize the cargo, she'd be shirking her duty.

The Viper had struck again.

"I hate him," she groused, grateful she was adept at scowling. Because what she really felt wasn't hatred anymore. It was suspiciously like… respect.

# 6

Nova stood at attention in the center of Commander Connington's spartan office. In his late fifties, with an athletic build and a thick mane of salt-and-pepper hair, Connington regularly caused both civilians and his mercenaries to swoon. Nova had once thought him gorgeous. Now, though, all she could see was his glacial stare and the harshness of his frown. Whatever she did, he found her lacking.

He drummed his fingers on the table, daring her to speak out-of-turn.

Nova remained still. Obeying orders was easy. Comfortable. A respite from the churning in her belly caused by her lies of omission.

"This report is sparse, Ms. Pratt," Connington said at last. He still wouldn't give her the privilege of a rank, though she'd been doing an officer's duties for years. Only his chosen few ever got an official promotion.

"I had little to report, sir. We did not find the contraband we expected."

He sniffed. "I had good information on that particular drone. It was seen emerging from the E-A splice before proceeding to the A-M splice."

"I cannot speak to the origins of the cargo, sir." Her gut clenched. Thank God for her training, because it was the only thing holding her steady. "But we found no illegal goods, no drugs, no alcohol, no weapons, no…"

"Yes, I understand."

"I did speak briefly with Lord Windborne, who only wished to see that his cargo was intact. But I know he is the Viper."

"And yet you provide no proof," Connington scoffed. "Let me be clear, Ms. Pratt. Just because your father specified you for this assignment doesn't mean I agree with his choice. If you do not do better, I *will* replace you. Phobos and his Chamber will never vote to convict Windborne without clear and irrefutable proof. Until we have that, he will run free. Do you understand?"

*You mean, do I recognize a threat? Yes, 'Commander,' I am perfectly capable of reading between the lines of your none-too-subtle contempt.*

She gave him a curt nod. "If there is nothing more, I will return to my work."

Actually, she'd go find her friend Irene in Medical and commiserate about Connington's assholery for a bit. Then she'd get back to work. Honestly, she did want to uphold the law. Wyatt—no, dammit, she had to think of him as Windborne—couldn't be allowed to dance around doing whatever he liked. That way lay anarchy.

"There is something more, before you leave," Connington said. "Windborne sent the drone you were investigating and the remainder of its cargo to a different warehouse. I want you to go there—tonight, under cover of darkness—and search everything inside. I will send a technical expert with you to circumvent any security."

Nova's jaw dropped. "That's completely illegal."

Connington waved a hand nonchalantly. "I'll have your father sign an authorization."

Nova composed herself, but couldn't stop her jaw from clenching. Not even a duke was supposed to approve such things without going through the proper channels. And she couldn't imagine her father interrupting his evening to do such a thing on short notice.

Damn the man and his meddling! Political machinations were nothing new, but his involvement in this mission made her skin crawl. It felt personal. She knew he disliked the "upstart Earthlings" and their political views, but this was a legal matter, not a vendetta against the Third Chamber.

"I will do my best," Nova finally answered.

*I will do what's right.*

Even if it meant going against orders. She would not ignore the increasing sense of wrongness permeating this investigation. If she had to expose her father along with Lord Windborne, so be it.

The intercom crackled, jolting Wyatt from the state of near-sleep he'd fallen into only moments ago. He shot straight up, blinking rapidly and fumbling for his glasses on the bedside table.

"Begging your pardon, milord," the doorman's voice said. "There's a Ms. Nova Pratt here, demanding to speak with you. Says she has orders from the Duke of Deimos." The sound of spitting followed this proclamation.

"Ugh." Wyatt rolled out of bed and stumbled toward the closet, tapping the intercom button as he passed it. "Tell her I'll be right down."

He grabbed the first pair of trousers and shirt he could reach and pulled them on, then stepped into a pair of sandals he usually only wore if he needed to shower at a gym or the swimming hole. If his slovenly appearance bothered her, she would have only herself to blame.

*As if she gives a damn what you look like, Windborne? This isn't a social call. You're not going on a date.*

Wyatt plodded down three flights of stairs that led from his apartments to the factory floor. Nova waited for him at the visitors' entrance, her path barred by Chet, the nighttime doorman. When he spied Wyatt, he eased his wheelchair away from the door and returned to his desk, though his stern gaze remained on Nova. She'd disrupted his usual routine of accepting packages from delivery drones and reading illegal revolutionist publications. Wyatt could sympathize with Chet's irritation.

Nova regarded him with detachment. "So you do live here. Above the factory."

He raised an eyebrow. "Is that a joke? Haha, silly Earthling lives in a tiny apartment?"

The now-familiar scowl formed on her face. "I wasn't mocking you. I thought maybe only your offices were here."

"You bugged my office, but you didn't know that it's literally connected to my bedroom?"

If she'd wanted to know where he lived, she could have asked any random person on the street. Everyone in Dystopia knew the Lords lived above Central Manufactory. The building was taller than most others around it, and easy to reach from any part of downtown.

Nova folded her arms across her chest. "I didn't plant the bug. The technical division does that. And of course they don't *enter* a building to do it."

Wyatt had to shake his head at that. She didn't have the first idea of how to infiltrate his world, and she was far too honest to make a decent spy. Her odd naivety enthralled him. Despite a lifetime of training, she didn't understand life outside of her carefully ordered bubble. He wanted to take her hand and walk her through his world—show her everything she'd been missing.

*Not. A. Date.*

"Why are you here?" he demanded. Best to send her on her way and go back to bed. Alone. To sleep.

"I have a new special authorization from His Grace, the Duke of Deimos. I am to search one of your warehouses. I thought you might like to know."

"What?" Wyatt stared at her as the words tumbled around in his head. No matter how he considered them, they made no sense. "You what?"

"Shall I wake the others, your lordship?" Chet asked.

Wyatt waved him off. "No, no. I'll handle it. Ms. Pratt, would you care to step outside and explain yourself?"

She pushed the door open. "I'm needed at the warehouse. We can talk on the way."

Wyatt followed her outside. One of his drones zipped to his side, and he gave it a pat.

Nova turned her scowl on the hovering machine. "Do you always have to bring those things with you?"

"Always."

He touched a finger to the spot below his collarbone where the implant rested beneath his skin. The subtle vibrations buzzed inside him as the implant cycled through its settings. Fifty yards. Twenty five. Ten. Five.

Wyatt lifted his finger. His companion drone beeped in acknowledgement. If it was disabled, or if he strayed from the safety zone, the closest drone—of any variety—would fly to his aid. His network wouldn't let him down.

"Which warehouse?" he asked.

"Seven."

Where he'd sent the broken cargo drone. She wouldn't

find anything. He'd already distributed all the smuggled books, and various other contraband, in anticipation of this exact thing.

"And why are you here telling me about this?"

Nova began walking, expecting him to follow. Warehouse seven was more than a mile away, but she appeared content to walk. "It's only fair."

"Fair." Wyatt fell into step beside her. "I didn't realize we were playing fair."

Nova took a quick glance around to check that they were alone, then gestured at his drone. "Does that thing have a camera? Audio recorder?"

"Yes, but they're not on." If she wanted fair, he'd give her fair. No lies.

"Okay." She closed the gap between them, stepping close enough that Wyatt's pulse sped up. Lustful crushes were nothing new to him, but Nova was the sort of person who intrigued his brain as well as his body. And that made her dangerous.

Wyatt liked danger. He leaned closer.

"I have reason to believe the authorization I was given may be illegal," Nova explained. "I cannot in good conscience use it against you. I will defeat you, but I will do it honorably. And I'm not letting this case get handed off to the DPST. You know they shoot first and make excuses later."

She wasn't wrong. The Downtown Police and Security Team was comprised entirely of bullies considered either too foolhardy or too insubordinate to hold positions elsewhere. Rejected mercs, mostly. Everyone hated them, and a majority of the time, they didn't even come when called. Nova was absolutely right to keep this matter away from them.

*Damn.*

Her warped sense of honor only made Wyatt like her

more. "I would expect nothing less from you. Thank you, by the way. Those schools can't afford vidscreens, and books are precious to them."

She turned her head away from him. He would have bet fifty guineas she was blushing.

*Nova Pratt, mercenary. Secret softie.*

"Not. A. Date," he muttered under his breath.

Nova picked up the pace, but Wyatt's long stride matched hers easily. They fell into a silent rhythm, only the sound of their footsteps contributing to the low hum of the city at night. Nova didn't take the fastest route to the warehouse, keeping to main streets and right-angle turns, but Wyatt didn't correct her. He wasn't here to give her a tour of Dystopia.

The streets surrounding the warehouse were dark and quiet when they arrived. A young man dressed all in black stood by the door lock, tapping helplessly at something on a vidscreen. As Wyatt approached, the interior lights turned on and the lock clicked open.

The boy jumped. "I… Did I do that?"

"Good job. You can leave now."

The kid blinked at Wyatt, then looked to Nova for confirmation. "Who's that?"

"Name's Hartford," Wyatt replied. "Internal Security." He jerked a thumb toward his companion drone. "I'll take care of all the cameras."

"He's got this," Nova confirmed. "You're free to go. I'll give you good marks in my report."

The young man frowned at his screen again. "But I'm not sure what happened. Something's wrong. It could be a trap."

Nova nudged Wyatt. "That's why Hartford here is going in first."

"Right. Um… bye." The boy clicked off his screen and darted away.

"Look at you, lying to the kid," Wyatt teased. "Is that a chink I see in your paladin's armor?"

Nova gave him the finger. "Inside, Windborne."

He held the door for her. "Ladies first."

She rolled her eyes, but walked through. "You know I'm not a Lady. All mercs are by-blows."

Wyatt followed, closing the door behind him. "We've been trying to get the inheritance laws changed so that any children, regardless of gender, legitimacy, or biological parentage, can inherit titles and property. But a certain duke keeps paying his lackeys to vote no."

"Yes, yes. I know my father is a twat and you're not entirely evil." Nova turned in a slow circle. "Where should I start looking?"

"Anywhere. Point at a box and I'll open it for you. But you should know you're not going to find anything illegal."

"Then I'll simply have to enjoy being nosy and admiring the cleanliness and organization of your facility."

Wyatt laughed. "If I'd known my warehouse was so alluring, I'd have brought a bottle of champagne."

"You think you're cute, don't you?" Nova had her hands on her hips, but the curve of her lips was definitely—albeit slightly—upward.

"Pretty sure at least one of us does." Wyatt grinned back at her and gestured toward the nearest stack of crates. "Let's get to work."

# 7

Nova bounced in time to the Earth-pop sounding from Wyatt's hovering toy. Maybe she'd taken one too many blows to the head during sparring practice, because after two hours of uptempo beats and cheerful voices, she had begun to enjoy the music. Or maybe Windborne was brainwashing her with subliminal signals.

He hummed to himself as he danced his way to the next set of carefully stacked crates. He was rumpled tonight, dressed in baggy clothing. His partially dyed hair lay flat and damp after a recent washing, and his blue eyes peered owlishly from behind a pair of large, round glasses. He was obnoxiously cute this way.

"These are all exports," he informed her, like he'd done for everything they'd searched thus far. "Crafted by some of our most skilled iron wrights. Beautiful pieces. They'll be used in the new housing developments at our Jovian mining operations. I'm quite thrilled by the support we've received for the community improvement projects. The miners and their families are safer, happier, and more financially stable now. Even your father voted for the latest upgrades."

"Did he?" Nova opened the crate and peered down at the sections of ironwork railings. Wyatt was right. They were expertly crafted: both functional and beautiful. "And here

I thought the only thing you and the duke had in common was a casual disregard for the law."

"Actually, we're both obscenely wealthy. Do you know how difficult it is to give away a massive fortune? You have to make sure every step of the process is done correctly, that the money's not being wasted somewhere along the line. It needs to get to the people who need it, fund the things you want it to fund. Some projects need an ongoing source of income. And you have to watch for the potential economic impact of flooding the system with large chunks of spendable money because if you devalue the currency, then the money you've given away won't be enough. I think I have a reasonable plan now, but it's a good thing I have a lifetime to do it."

Nova had never heard of anyone giving away a fortune before. It simply wasn't done. The money went to the heir, who passed it to his heir, and so on. "You don't want to keep it? Ensure the family legacy by saving it for your children?"

Wyatt slammed the crate closed with such force that it made Nova jump. "I refuse to have children until Brandt's Inheritance Act passes. I could easily marry someone unable or unwilling to bear children, and I will not stand for any offspring born via a surrogate or adopted into my family to be treated as lesser." He shrugged and his voice dropped from angry to wistful. "So I might never have anyone to leave a legacy to in the first place."

Nova moved on to the next crate, letting the conversation drop. Lord Windborne didn't want money, but he did want children. He wanted the kind of family Nova had read about in storybooks as a girl, where everyone was loved and wanted. She'd spent hours reading those books, imagining herself part of such a family.

Adult Nova didn't bother to imagine anymore. But

Wyatt still believed, and her heart gave a strange twinge at the thought of him wanting something impossible.

Before she could think better of it, she laid a hand on his arm. "These crates are all more of the same? We can move to the next area, if you'd like."

He looked down to where her fingers rested against his bare skin, then back up to meet her eyes.

Nova yanked her hand away.

Several seconds ticked by, as they stared awkwardly at one another. Then Wyatt reached for his drone and turned up the music.

"Show me how you dance, ooh!" the singer crooned.

*Thumpa, thumpa, thumpa, thumpa.*

Nova's body began to twitch in time to the beat.

Wyatt started dancing again, settling into his usual happy demeanor. "C'mon. We're almost done, and I'm getting tired, as you can tell by the babbling and the ranting."

She gave him a skeptical look, but followed his hypnotic sway toward a pile of smaller boxes. "Then why are you still dancing?"

He spun in a circle and winked at her. "Because it's long past my bedtime, and my body doesn't know how to process that. So it runs its default code until I keel over and fall asleep."

Nova's whole body shook with laughter. "You are ridiculous! When I get tired I only get cranky."

Wyatt stopped and shook a finger at her. "Cranky is your default state, Ms. Super Nova." His eyes gleamed with merriment. "And yet now you are laughing and smiling. Your scowl is very beautiful, but I'm pleased to see it's not your only expression."

Nova's pulse stuttered. Such an absurd statement, but somehow the most romantic thing she'd ever heard.

Her gaze caught on his lips and stayed there. She could kiss him, easily. One step, a slight tilt of her head. His lips looked soft and inviting. She would wager they tasted sweet, like lollipops or bubble gum. Wyatt Hartford was a carnival ride, and she wanted to take a spin.

The tip of his tongue traced his bottom lip. "Damn. You're either going to eat me alive, or eat me alive. Not sure which I'd like better."

Oh, yes. She would wreck him. Make him scream her name and…

"Fuck," she muttered, spinning away. He was her enemy—or a rival, at least. It didn't matter that he was fun and adorable and wanted to help people. This was an inspection, not a date.

"I think we're done here." She fixed her scowl back in place.

*Your scowl is very beautiful.*

Damn him.

The music turned off.

"Yeah." Wyatt's voice was slightly breathy. "I think I'm getting a little loopy. I'd better go to bed."

"And I have reports to write." She started for the door. "Goodnight, Lord Windborne. I will see you again soon, I'm sure."

"Nova."

She froze at the sound of her name and looked over her shoulder. Wyatt hadn't moved from his place beside the small boxes, but all his attention was on her.

"Why are you doing this?" he asked. "Why investigate me? I know you're a good person. You want to do good. But this isn't it."

"Why do you smuggle?" she challenged. "It's against the law."

"Sometimes laws are wrong. Other times, they are reasonable, but in some cases need to be circumvented. Life isn't full of absolutes. All we can do is what we think is right. And I don't want you to wake up tomorrow and regret what you've done."

Nova shook her head, as if that could settle the uncertainty making her insides quake. "Correcting wrongs with wrongs isn't okay. If you think a law is wrong, you should fix it. I can't let you continue to commit crimes, even if you're giving the money to charity. Stop what you're doing, and maybe we can stop being at odds."

"No. They'll keep pushing. I've poked a bear and he's woken up. And I don't even know how I did it. You could handcuff me right now..." He coughed. "Let me rephrase that. You could walk me to jail right now, and it wouldn't be over. And I think you know that."

Nova turned away, her stomach sinking. Was there anyone in her life who wasn't an enemy in some way? Even people she liked, such as Cameron and Jamie, were tied to people she couldn't trust.

"All I can do is what I think is right."

She shoved the door open and walked into the darkness.

# 8

Wyatt settled into his chair, leaned back, and crossed his legs at the ankles. Voting day.

A low rumble of noise from the factory below was the only indication that their Chamber Room was different than those presided over by the other dukes. It had the same paneled wood walls, the same Persian-style carpet, the same straight-backed leather chairs. Leo, Rion, Wyatt, and Aubrey occupied the single row of chairs, in clear view of the cameras mounted high on the walls.

Wyatt eyed the two enormous vidscreens set into the wall. The lefthand screen displayed the camera feed from First Chamber, and the right showed the Second. Nothing remotely interesting was happening in either image. They could almost have been still photos.

In both Chambers, identically-clad men sat rigidly in perfect rows. Marcus was the sole exception, looking dashing in a powder-blue suit, their long hair curled and hanging loose around their shoulders. They smiled at the camera, which probably meant they'd seen Wyatt, so he smiled back in turn.

"Third Chamber all present." Leo's voice was gruff, and he gave Wyatt a look of annoyance. He would look right at home in the other Chambers, with his severe charcoal suit and haughty posture.

*Sorry*, Wyatt mouthed. He'd been monitoring his drones and lost track of the time. He really needed to change his reminder alarms to infinite duration. He tended to miss single—or even quadruple—beeps. And after being up nearly all night with Nova, his grasp of time today was nebulous.

Rion bumped his elbow against Wyatt's. "Nice outfit. Trying to annoy them with the I'm-a-Rebel-Cutie look?"

Today Wyatt wore a neon pink mesh shirt over a black tank top and ripped flare-bottom jeans. He'd painted his nails the same pink and worn his glasses instead of shoving contact lenses into his too-tired eyes.

"I don't dress for them. What are they going to do, dislike me more than usual? Speculate about my sexual preferences? Anyone can guess we're a bunch of chaotic queers simply from the way we sit."

Rion—who was perched on the edge of his seat as if he might leap up and strangle someone at any moment—gave a gruff laugh. "Except His Grace."

Leo shot them both a quelling look as he rose from his seat.

"Proposal from the Duke of Morland." His deep voice echoed off the walls. "Regarding non-landholding citizens and the ownership and formation of businesses."

Wyatt slumped further in his chair and tried not to fall asleep while Leo read out the entire proposal. Every few months, he presented a new version, requesting that people be allowed to form their own businesses rather than franchising with their aristocratic landlords. It never passed. Never even came close. But Leo continued to press the issue, and Wyatt continued to vote for it. As houses like Ashdale passed to younger generations, they'd picked up a bit of support. But nowhere near enough.

When Leo finally finished, the Chambers voted in order, one snarled nay after another. Marcus was an aye, as were two seats in the Second Chamber, but no one else.

"Morland, aye," Leo said, when his turn came.

The camera turned toward Aubrey, who lounged with one leg hooked over the arm of his chair. He took a swig from a metal flask, as if he were the most bored, idle aristocrat on Mars. "Wells, nay."

Wyatt flinched. Every. Damn. Time. For twenty years he'd known Aubrey's voting strategy was designed to make him an enemy to no one and an ally to be courted by all. But every time he voted against his own beliefs it made Wyatt cringe. He'd never be able to live like that.

"Windborne, aye," he declared fiercely, as if he could speak for both himself and his friend.

"Brandt, aye," Rion finished.

The final tally flashed on the vidscreens.

"Thank you for your consideration," Leo said, somehow managing not to sound in the least sarcastic.

A member of the First Chamber rose and began to outline his own proposal. Wyatt got up, muted all the microphones in the room, then sat back down.

"Can't you mute them too?" Rion muttered, gesturing at the screens. "This is the worst bunch of proposals we've had since Deimos tried to prevent us from voting until we turned twenty-one."

Wyatt yawned. "Technically, they can't prevent me from napping, right?"

Aubrey straightened up into a normal-ish position. "Why are you tired? Leo said you went out late and didn't come back for hours."

Rion leaned closer, his eyes widening with interest. "Did you bang her? Please tell me all the sordid details."

Wyatt ran a hand through his hair, mussing the neat spikes he'd styled that morning. "The only banging was from crates opening and closing. Ms. Pratt had orders to search warehouse seven, but was concerned about the legality of her paperwork. She asked me to grant her access. I showed her around, we examined the inventory, that was it."

*And I babbled and flirted like a drunkard.*

"Sure." Rion dragged the word out.

Aubrey kicked him. "Hush. Not all of us want to hear about people's sexual exploits."

"Tell us what you learned, Wyatt," Leo cut in. "What do you think was her purpose for this? It sounds like a ploy to lull you into complacency or to cover up another search in a different location."

"No." Wyatt's reply was immediate and full of conviction. "She was sincere. She's a good person who believes her duty is to uphold the law."

"Hmm." Leo steepled his fingers. "If she's objecting to the crime itself rather than us or our goals, she could potentially be lured to our side. Aubrey, have you learned anything about her?"

"No. Mercenaries rank above servants, but they're still 'the help.' Nearly everyone in my circles ignores them unless they have a complaint. But James—Lord Metus—likes her. And he loathes most of his family."

Rion snorted. "Metus hates everyone. He only goes to parties to look down his long nose in disdain."

"He's shy," Aubrey corrected. "And you would be too, in his place."

"No, in his place, I'd kill my father and take over."

"Murder is one of the few reasons an heir can be disinherited," Wyatt pointed out. "And treason."

Aubrey took another drink from his flask. He probably had something bizarre and innocuous in there, like carrot juice. "That's why it's important not to be caught doing the murdering. It's fine if everyone knows you did it, as long as they can't prove it. Poison is always effective, but you can't go with anything pedestrian, like arsenic or cyanide. Did you know that somewhere between twenty and forty percent of people can't smell cyanide?"

Leo cleared his throat. "Sorry to interrupt such a sunny conversation, but can we return to Wyatt's issue with the mercenary woman? We absolutely cannot let her shut down the Wealth Redistribution Operation. If Deimos had his way, everyone would be too busy worrying about their own survival to fight the system, and we must prevent that at all costs. Wyatt, your primary concern at this juncture should be getting her off your back. I don't care how. Convince her you're innocent. Take her out to dinner and seduce her. Feed her to your pet tiger. Whatever works."

"The tiger isn't a pet. She's a rescued wild animal temporarily sheltered at my zoological garden with plans to reintroduce her to her natural habitat on Earth if at all possible."

"Is that safe?" Rion asked.

Wyatt wiggled a hand in a so-so motion. "The latest reports are that tigers are doing well in uninhabited areas, but there's always a danger of a corporate state encroaching on their territory."

"Windborne," Leo interrupted, his voice sharp.

Wyatt met Leo's humorless gaze. "Yes, yes, I'll do something. Maybe program some small drones to follow her."

"Thank you. And all of you be careful. I don't like anything about this situation."

The room fell silent. Wyatt crossed his arms over his chest and began to tap out patterns. This was going to be an excruciating few hours.

Dammit, why couldn't they keep talking about tigers? Now he was stuck either listening to the monotonous drone of Lord Pinckford and his horrid proposal for a tax on bicycles or thinking about Nova and ways to halt her investigation.

He reviewed his options.

Anything that would harm her—absolutely not.

Convince her he was innocent—impossible. He wasn't and he wouldn't be able to lie well enough.

Seduce her—yes, please. He could invite her to his bed, where they would take turns driving each other wild with pleasure. They would revel in one another's bodies until they both forgot about things like laws and smuggling and why they couldn't be friends.

It was as much a pipe dream as Leo's business reform proposal.

"Bloody hell," Wyatt muttered.

*You're going to try it, aren't you? You stupid, stupid man.*

He could sit here all night telling himself why he should forget Nova and instead invest in greater security or whatever. But even twenty years in Dystopia hadn't quashed his innate optimism. When he woke in the morning he'd see the sunlight outside his window or hear Flurry's happy squeaks and idealistic hope would bloom in his chest. And then he'd ask Nova Pratt, mercenary and daughter of a man who despised him, out for a date.

Fuck.

# 9

THE MASSIVE CLOCK ATOP the square stone building continued to tick further and further past the hour, its exposed gears turning in an endless cycle. Nova checked the time against her wristwatch, but the numbers were identical. As they had been two minutes ago. She'd been jilted.

That's what she got for trusting a criminal. Lord Windborne was probably busily fencing stolen goods while he laughed at her for accepting an invitation to dinner.

He really had seduced her that night at the warehouse. All the music and smiles and rambling confessions had been a carefully crafted ruse. She ought to have known better.

Nova pulled her bicycle out of the rack in front of the restaurant. Fortunately the Vogue Sector, with all its fashionable theaters, clubs, and restaurants, sat at the edge of downtown. The ride back to her barracks was less than two miles. She could wheel home and slip out of her elegant evening attire with no one the wiser.

"Nova!"

She whirled around, automatically shifting into a defensive stance. Her hand dropped to the slit in her skirt that provided access to the knife strapped to her thigh. Her bicycle clattered to the pavement.

"Nova." Windborne ran toward her. His hair was

tousled, his cheeks red. A sheen of perspiration dampened his brow. "I'm so sorry. So, so sorry."

He paused to catch his breath, leaning on the bike rack for support. He'd traded his usual attire for khaki trousers, a pale-green button-down shirt, and a plum-colored waistcoat. Tiny emeralds studded his earlobes in place of the gold hoops. His fingernails had been painted in a rainbow again, this time with tiny white stars at the tips. Currently, those fingers clutched a portable vidscreen.

Words tumbled out of him in a rush. "I lost track of time. I set an alarm, but I was so caught up in a work problem that that thing happened where it goes right in and out of my brain, like I forgot to close a door somewhere and now all the animals are escaping."

"Are you saying your brain is a collection of wild animals?"

His lips quirked into a smile. "Sometimes I genuinely feel like it's full of bees." He bent down, righted her bicycle, and put it back in the rack. "There. I know you like things tidy."

Nova felt her scowl begin to slip and only managed not to crack a smile through force of will. Her own brain was apparently one of those big black birds from her childhood folktales, because every time Wyatt Hartford came into view, she itched to claim him for her collection of shiny things.

She put her hands on her hips and glowered at him. Best to stay angry. "So you're not a jilter, but you have poor time management skills."

"Correct. I keep telling myself to change the alarms, but then I forget about it until it happens again, and then I'm too busy running out the door."

"Lucky you're an earl. In my line of work, you would be thrashed until you learned better."

Windborne took a turn scowling. The expression looked surprisingly good on him. Fierce. Passionate.

"That's disgusting," he snarled. "Corporal punishment should be banned. And I can't 'learn better' because it has nothing to do with learning things and everything to do with how my brain works. Try motivation with less trauma and more strategies for working with what I have."

"I'm so sorry." Apparently they were trading off tonight. Scowling. Apologies. What next? "I never meant to suggest you *ought* to be thrashed, or even that you ought to change. Military life can be… harsh, and I wasn't thinking beyond that. That's my fault. Should we go inside and have dinner instead of standing out here upsetting one another?"

"Sure." He shrugged. "May as well continue the upsetting where there's food and wine."

As he started to walk, a drone zipped up to follow him, as usual. An idea sparked in Nova's mind. "Why don't you tell your drone to remind you about changing the alarms? Or use that vidscreen in your hand to do it?"

"These little drones don't have that capability, and I don't carry around screens that are connected to my network. But it does give me an idea."

Wyatt wormed a finger between the buttons of his shirt to tap just beneath his collarbone.

His brow creased in concentration for a few seconds, and then the drone beeped. He withdrew his finger and gave a brisk nod, as if he hadn't done something extraordinarily weird.

"We'll see if I remember what the hell I did that for." He jogged toward the restaurant's entrance. "Let me get the door for you."

Once inside, they were ushered immediately to a

secluded table and handed menus. Wyatt didn't even glance at his.

"The stuffed chicken and a bottle of Mare Tyrrhenum Gewurztraminer."

The waiter nodded. "Very good, my lord. Does the lady need a moment with the menu?"

Nova shook her head. "Your finest cut of steak, a touch above rare, with a truffle glaze, and a side salad, no dressing, no cucumbers." Why not request exactly what she wanted? It wasn't every day an aristocrat took her to dinner.

"As you wish, madam. I'll see that the cook receives your orders. The sommelier will bring your wine shortly."

As it happened, the arrival of the wine was as close to instantaneous as Nova had ever seen at a restaurant. The waiter had hardly disappeared when a server walked up to the table with a bottle and glasses in hand.

"Thank you, Shelly," Wyatt said.

The sommelier, whose name tag read "Shelly - she/her," poured them each a glass of the fragrant white wine. Nova wasn't even certain Wyatt had glanced at the woman's name tag. Yet he'd addressed her by name without the slightest hesitation.

Shelly bobbed a small curtsy. "Always a pleasure, milord."

Wyatt waited for her to depart, then illuminated his vidscreen and began scrolling through some kind of list.

"You seem very familiar with this place," Nova remarked.

He nodded absently, not looking up. "I own the property. I try to dine here at least once a week, to put some of that money back into the hands of the people who do the work." He tapped the screen and frowned at it.

Nova kicked him under the table. Bringing her here and ignoring her was possibly worse than standing her up.

"Ow."

"Why are we here?" she demanded.

He finally looked at her. "It seems we have to interact. I'd rather it be on friendly terms. Since you accepted, I assumed you agreed."

Why *had* she accepted? It had been an impulsive decision, when usually she tried to think before she acted.

*He's shiny. You're horny.*

Wyatt's attention returned to his screen.

*Although his gleam is fading with every second.*

"Here, look at this." He abruptly pushed the screen in front of her. "Does this make any sense to you?"

She scanned the text automatically. Names, numbers, timestamps. It was a data log, but for what she couldn't tell.

"It's a list of transports passing through the J-M splice," he added.

"Okay." Nova had never been off Mars, or even outside the enclosures of Utopia, so splices were no more than a peculiar theoretical to her. All she knew was that they were places where space-time was warped or folded in on itself, and they were used for fast travel between areas of the solar system. "Um…" She peered at the data again. "Ship leaves Jovian orbit. Ship arrives at Jupiter end of the splice. Ship emerges from the Mars end. Ship reaches orbit around Mars. Those are the four columns for each entry."

"Correct. And the entries at the top are all normal. Consistently fourteen minutes, seventeen seconds between the checkpoints on either side of the splice."

Nova's gaze tracked down the page. "But, wait. This one is different." She tapped the screen and the entry highlighted. "It doesn't arrive at the Mars end until after these next two ships have gone through. That doesn't make sense."

"No, it doesn't. And it happens again here—" He touched

the screen, moving the highlight. "And here. Someone is stopping transports *inside* the checkpoints."

Nova took a long swallow of her wine, then asked, "Is that a smuggling technique? Load or offload cargo where people wouldn't be looking?"

Wyatt began to tap his fingers on the table in a repeating pattern. "I certainly wouldn't do it. It's dangerous as hell. All communications drop out within a certain distance of a splice. It's how they were discovered in the first place. The whole purpose of the checkpoints is to allow only one transport at a time in the area."

"Because if they can't locate each other, they could crash. Makes sense."

Nova leaned closer, the last remnants of her anger washing away. He'd made a fascinating and possibly important discovery and he was willingly sharing it with her. Her! His—sort of—enemy!

"Smuggling isn't entirely out of the question," Wyatt went on. "But there are much easier ways to do it."

Nova arched her eyebrows and smirked at him. "Is that an admission of guilt, Viper?"

"You do know that name was made up by a newspaper that specializes in sensational rubbish?"

"Oh? And which one of your friends owns that newspaper?"

He sighed. "Brandt."

Nova's eyes widened. "Really? I was joking."

"Really. I should properly introduce you to Rion. I think you two would get along. Except for the part where he enjoys breaking the law. But you're both grumpy and stubborn and honorable."

Her skin heated. Wyatt really had a knack for blurting

out honest truths and making them sound like the best of compliments.

Nova ducked her head and stared at the vidscreen. If he caught her blushing, she would have to flee the planet and start a new life under a different name. Hopefully somewhere without men who made her question her morals and go all mushy inside. Mushy was a liability in her line of work.

"Let's consider other possibilities," she suggested. "Could the records simply be falsified?"

"Could what?" Wyatt blinked out of whatever distracted state he'd fallen into. "Oh, yes. They could be fake. But why not make the numbers look real? Unless it's a code of some sort. Again, there are much better ways to send secure messages than hiding them in transport logs. And I think *something* is happening during these times. Let me show you one other thing." He scrolled further down the list. "There."

"The entry is… incomplete." Nova's gaze flicked up to meet Wyatt's. "Did a ship go missing inside the splice? Can that happen?"

"Never heard of it happening. This was one of my transports, carrying hydrogen from the atmosphere mines. When it never reported back, I got an emergency alert."

"That's why you started investigating. Why you were late tonight."

"Yes." He ran a hand through his hair. "I'm very sorry about that. I ought to have warned you that it happens often, so you could have made an informed decision."

Nova's laugh came out as a snort. "I don't think I would have changed my mind, but I might have brought a book."

"You would have stood tapping your foot irritably and glaring at the clock, cursing the Universe for the entire concept of entropy."

"I do like things orderly. And look, here comes our food. They do an excellent job with orderly here. You chose well."

Wyatt glanced at the approaching waiter. "Last thing before we eat." He tapped the corner of the screen, and a new list appeared, this one with various numbers Nova couldn't decipher. "This is a report from another transport of mine. It passed through the splice shortly after the other disappeared. See all those lines in yellow? Those are damage reports. Minor ones, but an order of magnitude more of them than on a typical voyage, and they're scattered all across the surface of the ship."

Nova blew out a long breath. "As if it flew through a field of debris," she whispered. "You think something— some*one*—destroyed your ship."

"Yes. And I mean to find out who and why."

Nova paused to let the waiter present their food. The steak and salad were artfully arranged on the plate, and the smell was divine. Her stomach grumbled. No saboteur of cargo drones was going to ruin her appetite tonight.

"You'll need more information," she said, slicing into the perfectly seared meat.

"I left several programs gathering additional data at home."

"And you'll want to have discussions about next steps."

He lifted a bite of his own food almost to his lips. "With trusted allies."

"Mmm." Nova nodded around a mouthful of food.

Wyatt's fork dropped to his plate, the piece of chicken still untasted. "Come home with me?"

Nova swallowed hard. "To help with the investigation?"

"Yeah." His voice was soft, intimate. "That too."

# 10

Nova and Wyatt arrived at Central Manufactory as the last of the workers were departing for the day. Many of them nodded or tipped their hats as they passed by. One or two added an, "Evening, milord." They all smiled. It was the same phenomenon she'd witnessed at the restaurant: everyone liked Wyatt.

At least she wasn't the only one to succumb to his charms.

"You're friends with everyone, aren't you?"

He frowned at her. "What? No. I'm friends with very few people."

Nova made a subtle gesture toward a blushing woman who had dipped into a curtsy.

Wyatt's expression turned sheepish. "Oh. I'm friend*ly* with most people, I suppose. But none of them really know me. You know, with all my weirdness and animals and drones and whatever. I don't… spend time with many people. I'm quite terrible at being anything other than myself, and some people can't handle that."

"Well." She linked her arm with his. "We have something in common, then. Shall we go inside?"

Wyatt's companion drone parked itself on the lintel of the doorway as they approached, but didn't follow them inside. Good riddance. The things always made Nova feel like she was being spied on. Which was ridiculous, because surely the entire factory was outfitted with security cameras much more sophisticated than what was in the drone. Plus, she lived in a mercenary barracks, which had cameras everywhere.

*Maybe it's the idea of* him *spying on you that's really making you squirm?*

She shut down that line of thinking almost as quickly as the thought had popped into her head. She was here to discuss a potentially serious problem, and perhaps have a casual fling to sate her inconvenient lust. Casual flings did not involve introspection or any squirming beyond the purely physical.

"Stairs are this way." Wyatt guided her to the left. "The guys should all be— Gah!"

He released Nova's arm and covered his head as half-a-dozen drones flew at him. Several had grasping arms or protrusions that looked to be for twisting or poking. One of the machines shoved between Wyatt and Nova, sending her stumbling into the wall.

Wyatt flailed, trying to shoo them. "Go away! I'm not in danger, dammit!"

He yanked at the buttons of his shirt, muttering more curses. When he got the collar open, he put a finger to his chest beneath his clavicle and tapped a few times. The drones stilled for a moment, then scuttled off to whatever work they were supposed to do here at the factory.

His hands dropped to his sides and he blew out a relieved breath. "Sorry about that. I completely forgot."

Nova straightened up and smoothed out her dress. "What happened?" She stared at the open collar of his shirt. A tiny white scar marked his skin at the place he'd touched.

If he noticed the focus of her attention, he didn't comment. "Um… that was my reminder to reconfigure my alarms. Maybe not my best idea ever, but it did serve its purpose. Now I only have to remember until I get upstairs."

He led her off the factory floor and up the stairs at a pace that would have put several of her fellow mercenaries to shame.

"Alarm, alarm, alarm," he mumbled, his voice almost sing-song in tone.

At the top of the stairs he unlocked a plain, unmarked door and waved her inside.

"Here's home." He switched on the light. "Please have a seat. Make yourself comfortable. I'm going to run into the office and fix the alarms. Be right back." He disappeared through the door on the opposite side of the room, leaving Nova to her own devices.

She didn't sit. Even a room as innocuous as a sitting room merited inspection before she would let her guard down. And in this case, her curiosity made as strong a case as her training for taking a careful look around.

The room was oddly bare. She'd expected colorful furniture, which the emerald green couch and crimson chair certainly were. A small table between the two was the only other thing in the room. No other furniture, no accessories, no books or other leisure items. The walls were a flat off-white, the carpet a medium gray. She might not have guessed it to be Wyatt's room at all, except for the animal perches hanging from the ceiling and the cage set into the wall where a window ought to have been.

Nova walked to the cage and peered inside. A single red light illuminated the interior enough for her to spy a fuzzy, winged creature hanging upside down. The bat was amusing itself with a plush toy that dangled nearby, spinning it, then hugging it, then spinning it again. Occasionally it let out a squeak or chirp, sounding pleased with itself.

"Ah. You've met Flurry."

Nova turned to smile at Wyatt. "I've never seen a real bat before. Only drawings in vampire books."

His grin turned wicked. "I'm afraid Flurry is a fruit bat, not a vampire bat. Which means the only one around here interested in biting your neck is me. Sorry to disappoint."

Nova took two steps toward him, emphasizing the sway of her hips. "Who says I'm disappointed?" Her third step brought her within inches, and he didn't back away. "My uniform has a high collar. Maybe I'd enjoy having a secret at work tomorrow."

"Hmm."

Wyatt trailed a finger lightly down her neck to where it met her shoulder. The touch was barely there, almost nonexistent, yet her skin burned. Tingles of sensation streaked down her arm and across her chest, and a hungry ache rose low in her belly.

"Hiding love bites," Wyatt murmured, his voice the same delicate caress as his finger. He shook his head in mock disapproval. "That sounds almost… illicit."

God, yes. She wanted illicit. Here. Now. With him. The rules could go hang. For once, she was going to do what she wanted rather than what other people wanted her to do.

A knock on the door stopped her from leaning in to kiss him.

Wyatt danced back a few steps. "That would be Leo."

Nova turned in time to see the door swing open. The Duke of Morland strode in, dressed in an immaculately tailored navy blue suit and a red ascot tie. A perfect queue held every strand of his long, mahogany-colored hair in place. Everything about him screamed tidy, respectable, and serious.

He was exactly the sort of man she ought to have been attracted to. One who could fit neatly into her carefully-ordered world. But for some reason, the word her brain conjured up was "boring."

The duke raised a single eyebrow as he looked at her. For a stoic man, his face was remarkably expressive. In that one tiny movement, Nova caught suspicion, curiosity, and even a tiny flicker of amusement.

"I see we have a guest," Morland murmured.

"Leo, this is Nova." Wyatt gestured between them. "Nova, Leo."

Despite the informality of the introduction, Nova couldn't suppress years of training and practice. She bobbed a curtsy. "Your Grace."

"What the fuck?" Lord Brandt stormed into the room, his dark brown eyes flashing almost black. "What is *she* doing here?"

"Rion, meet Nova," Wyatt replied calmly. "Nova, Rion."

Brandt glowered down at everyone in the room. He had to be nearly two meters tall, and he was burly as well, with thick, heavily muscled limbs and a bit of a gut. Another highly attractive man, especially if you liked the angry and protective type. Wyatt was right. She and Rion would either be mortal enemies or best friends.

"Sit down, Rion," the duke commanded. "I'm sure Wyatt has an explanation for us." He lowered himself gracefully onto the red armchair.

Rion huffed, but plopped down onto the couch. Wyatt took the place next to him, nudging him over until there was room for Nova on the opposite side.

Nova lowered herself onto the couch, squeezing in

between the padded armrest and Wyatt. The full length of her thigh pressed against his, and their shoulders bumped. It would be comfortable—cozy, even—if she slipped an arm around him, but in the presence of the other men she didn't dare. Mostly because she wanted both hands free in case something went horribly wrong.

"Is this everyone?" she asked Wyatt.

"Waiting on Aubrey."

Right. She'd seen Wyatt be friendly with Lord Wells at the ball, but she wasn't entirely certain how the marquess fit into this group of friends. He was younger than the others and spent most of his time in high society. Gossip called him either "idle and useless" or "a most eligible bachelor."

The man himself flew through the door moments later, dressed in red satin pajamas and fuzzy black slippers. Streaks of red so bright they almost glowed highlighted his short auburn hair. Up close, he looked like a younger, more casual version of the duke.

"Sorry," he babbled, "I was already in bed when I got the message. I have to get up early for an appointment with my tailor. Masquerade balls have become the hot new thing, and I need a different look for every one. I'm thinking… Oh!" His gaze landed on Nova. "Good evening, Ms. Pratt. A pleasure to see you. That's a lovely dress you're wearing."

He delivered this compliment with complete sincerity and not even a hint of flirtation, bringing a smile to Nova's lips. If he was a liar and a flatterer, he was damned good at it.

"Thank you. Please call me Nova."

He inclined his chin. "Aubrey. I suppose we ought to get started so I can get back to bed."

Aubrey didn't even bother to look for another chair, plopping himself easy-as-you-please onto the duke's lap.

Morland—she couldn't think of him as Leo—lost a bit of his austerity, smiling at his friend with brotherly affection.

"When I'm old and brittle-boned you're going to have to stop this, you know," the duke teased.

"But I love you, cousin." Aubrey widened his eyes in an impressive impersonation of an orphaned waif. "How will you get cuddles if I don't inflict them on you?"

An unusual twinge of jealousy pierced Nova's chest. These four men were deeply bonded, and free with both physical and verbal affection. She'd never considered herself friendless, but she'd never had anything like this. Like real family.

Wyatt launched into an explanation of his discovery, mercifully saving her from growing mawkish. She was too old for fantasy daydreams.

The other men listened attentively, occasionally asking for clarification or more detail. Their jolly camaraderie had transitioned to business without the slightest hitch. No matter who was talking, the others appeared to know when to interrupt, when to pause, and how to interpret non-verbal communication. Nova needed her full concentration to follow the conversation, but to everyone else it was easy.

This was what they did for a living. Working together. Strategizing and fixing problems. And it wasn't relegated to their behavior with each other. Wyatt clearly cared about the people in his restaurant and showed it openly. In a world that didn't really give a damn about anyone, a single "thank you" went a long way. Combine that with their laborer-focused policies and Earth-born, of-the-people image, and she could see why all of downtown adored the Lords of Dystopia.

It wasn't all a political ruse. These men actually did good work and were striving for real improvements.

Which made the issue of Wyatt's smuggling all the more

aggravating. Surely there had to be a better way to get books to schools. He had to understand the risks, and if he'd made the decision impulsively, Morland or one of the others ought to have talked him out of it.

"What if they're not the same ships?" the duke suggested.

"You mean one ship goes in the J checkpoint and another comes out the M checkpoint?" Rion asked.

Nova blinked, grateful for Brandt's clarification, as she'd nearly lost track of the conversation.

"Identical registration signals," Aubrey suggested.

They all looked to Wyatt, who nodded. "Technologically possible, yes."

Rion kicked absently at the carpet. "But they'd have to fly in and out of the splice area at some kinda…" He jabbed one hand in a diagonal motion.

"And that's dangerous, right?" Nova spoke up. All the men but Wyatt stared at her, as if they'd forgotten she was there. "It could lead to something like a collision that could destroy a smaller cargo transport."

Rion snorted. "It could lead to firing a missile to destroy a rival's pesky ship blocking your way."

"It has to be Deimos." The duke's authoritative baritone silenced the room. He cast Nova a sympathetic look. "I'm sorry, Ms. Pratt, to make such an accusation in front of you. But this could only be done by someone with a great many resources."

Nova responded with a polite nod. "No offense taken, Your Grace. I already suspect my father of nefarious affairs. But whether he's involved or not, the people behind this must believe they have something of great value. If this is too risky for a conventional smuggler to take on…"

She glanced at Wyatt. He was no conventional smuggler, but even he wouldn't put himself or his friends in unnecessary danger. He had a reason, even if it wasn't the typical lure of money and power.

"Go on," he prompted.

"The reward must be tremendous for my father or anyone else of similar means to do this," she said, continuing her train of thought aloud. "It risks destruction of ships and cargo, death of human pilots or bystanders—"

"As if they care about that," Rion scoffed.

"Loss of reputation," Nova continued, "financial ruin, expulsion from the Chamber, punishments up to and including banishment and death, and probably more that I'm missing. Messing with the splices isn't the sort of thing that can be 'overlooked' if you pay the right people or arrange the right marriage alliance. Whatever they're hiding must promise them… what? Unimaginable wealth? Control of the entire solar system?"

"Whatever it is, we're damned well going to find out." Morland nudged Aubrey off his lap and rose from his chair. "Everyone sleep on this, and we'll reconvene tomorrow. It's big, and we're going to need all our resources. I want a solid list from each of you of what you think you can bring to the investigation. No, Wyatt, you don't have to write it down."

"Thank God." Wyatt gave Nova an impish smile. "I doubt Leo expects a list from you, either, but if you really did want a chance to catch a smuggler…"

"Ha, ha," she retorted. "You're just trying to distract me from investigating you."

He clapped a hand over his heart. "You wound me. I am merely offering you the opportunity to do a good deed."

"I'm being *paid* to investigate you," she reminded him. "And while I believe pursuing justice is a noble goal in itself, I do also need to earn a living. I can't afford to investigate mysterious criminals for free."

"I'll pay you."

Nova's head snapped up to meet the duke's unwavering gaze. "I beg your pardon?"

"I will pay you to aid in the investigation of this matter," Morland restated. "Find me tomorrow with a list of skills and resources you can bring to the investigation. I'll have a contract prepared. If we're both satisfied, we'll sign."

Rion hopped up from the couch so he could glare down at the duke. "You can't be serious. She's the enemy. She wants to get Wyatt banished."

"I think we can trust her," Aubrey argued. "And so does Wyatt, or she wouldn't be here."

"Your opinions are irrelevant," Morland snapped, in the exact clipped tone Nova had heard from her usual aristocratic clients. "As a peer of the realm I am entitled to employ any member of the Royal Mercenary Corps as I see fit. Ms. Pratt, I will discuss the particulars with you tomorrow afternoon. Good night."

The duke spun away and strode out the door without looking back.

"Bloody fucking…" Rion grumbled, stomping out after Morland.

"And down comes the curtain." Aubrey executed a theatrical bow. "Excellent performance, everyone. Nova, do save me a dance next time you're working a ball. I'm always starved for agreeable partners. Good night!" He followed the others out the door with surprising elegance for a man in his pajamas.

The door swung closed with a *snick*.

Wyatt turned to face Nova, twisting mostly at the waist, so his knee remained in contact with hers. "Okay. Leo's giving you orders, Rion is still pretending to hate you, and

Aubrey is about to adopt you as his new best friend. I guess you're one of us now."

She chuckled. He was being silly. She was no more one of them than she was an aristo. But she appreciated their acceptance of her presence. And, sure, working for Morland clashed a bit with her investigation of Wyatt, but mercs took on conflicting contracts all the time. She could handle it, and she had receipts if Connington complained.

"I suppose I might be," she replied. "And what about you? How do you bid me welcome?"

Their gazes locked, and the distance between them seemed to shrink without either of them moving a muscle. Then Wyatt's hand was on her cheek, his thumb grazing her lower lip.

"I'm the shipping and delivery guy. I get people the things they want. So tell me, Nova Pratt." He leaned in until their foreheads touched and his breath mingled with hers. "What is it you want?"

# 11

*THANK THE BLOODY STARS.*

Wyatt had nearly expired from unfulfilled longing in the agonizing moments before Nova had lifted her chin to accept his kiss.

And then he'd tasted her, hot and sweet and eager, and he'd melted.

He threaded his fingers into her hair, dismantling the neat knot that had taunted him all throughout dinner. God, how he wanted to muss her, unsettle her. She clung to rules, laws, and order like a life preserver, when all he wanted was to see her swim. She would be so beautiful.

He might drown, though. Already, he could hardly come up for air. Nova kissed wildly, licking and sucking at his lips, sliding into his mouth as if she'd kissed him a thousand times before. As if he now belonged to her.

Which, to be fair, was consistent with his modus operandi. His first dates tended to end with either, "Nope, we don't suit," or, "Tie me to your bed and fuck me now."

Nova squirmed, awkwardly kissing the corner of his mouth as she tried to maneuver herself from her seated position into a reclined one. Wyatt twisted along with her, but only managed to clack their teeth together hard enough to send a jolt of pain through his skull. He jerked, lost his balance, and toppled from the couch, landing square on his backside.

For a second, they stared at one another, startled. Then Nova giggled. A true, bubbly, spontaneous little laugh that made Wyatt's heart flutter. Her eyes shone with delight, and her smile was so broad a tiny, perfect dimple had appeared in her right cheek. A slight shimmer coated her lips where his strawberry-flavored lip gloss had rubbed off on her.

She licked her lips. "Lisa Luna? My favorite brand too. Great for preventing chapped lips and gives a touch of sparkle."

"Yeah. The new Berry Blast."

Nova hiked up her skirt high enough to stretch one long leg out across the couch, while the other dangled off the edge. She patted the space between her knees. "Come give me another taste."

Wyatt scrambled to comply. He knelt between her legs and leaned down to kiss her, bracing himself with his hands on her hips. The silky fabric of her evening dress bunched beneath his fingers, sliding higher still when she wound her arms around his neck and pulled him down atop her.

Something hard jabbed his thigh, and he glanced down to see a knife in a slim sheath strapped high on her leg.

"Carrying weapons in the city?" He skated his lips across hers. "What a naughty girl you are."

"It's… perfectly… legal," she protested, managing to sound adorably irritable even while peppering him with kisses.

"Mmm." Wyatt pulled back far enough to look into her flashing dark eyes. "But you're not investigating tonight. Are you bending the rules?" He lowered his mouth to within a hair's breadth of hers and whispered, "Because that's sexy as hell."

"You're always under surveillance. Now shut up and kiss me."

He obeyed, though not in the frantic way he suspected she'd intended. Instead, he kissed her in languid, teasing drags, lingering in the taste and feel of her. With a single finger, he traced the outline of her weapon, creeping up the inside of her thigh until she began to wriggle beneath him. She gasped his name against his lips, clutching him tighter.

"Patience, sweet," he murmured. His finger continued around the knife, down her leg and away from the sensitive skin still hidden by her dress. "I'm exploring."

In response she yanked his shirt free from his trousers and shoved her hands beneath to splay against his back. Wyatt's skin prickled under her fingertips. His already stiffening cock grew harder yet, and he couldn't stop himself from thrusting against her leg.

"More," Nova insisted. "Faster."

"Patience," Wyatt repeated, as much to himself as to her. This was too good to rush. They were too hot together not to put in their best effort. And his best meant keeping her locked in a delicious battle of wills.

He nuzzled her neck, letting his teeth scrape her skin just enough to remind her of their discussion of love bites. She obligingly tilted her head to give him a better angle, even as she continued tugging at his clothes, hands greedily groping.

Wyatt stroked up her thigh again, sliding past the knife and nudging her hem a tiny bit higher before retreating. His whole body ached with desire. God, how he longed to sink his fingers into her wet heat and hear her moan. But every time he denied himself, the thrill ratcheted another notch higher.

Nova worked her hands down to his waistband and popped the buttons of his fly with shocking dexterity. Wyatt sucked in a harsh breath, his cock straining for her touch. He squeezed her leg and nipped at her neck, trying to distract her enough to maintain his sanity. When she answered with a pleasurable groan, he nipped harder, then soothed the spot with gentle strokes of his tongue.

*There's your love bite, darling. Remember me.*

She shoved his trousers past his hips. Cool air washed over his bare backside.

"I don't have all night," Nova rasped. "I have to work in the morning." She released him long enough to grab her skirt and pull it up past her waist.

She wasn't wearing any underwear.

Wyatt's gaze drifted over the expanse of tan skin, the thatch of black curls, and the hint of pink below. Nova spread her legs further apart, giving him a view of her sex, slick with arousal.

"Aw, fuck," he gasped. First victory to her. Hopefully he could try for best two out of three.

He fumbled for his trouser pocket, where he'd stashed a condom earlier. They'd both come prepared this evening. He sheathed himself and positioned himself between her legs.

"Yes?"

Her fingers clamped so hard on his ass he thought her nails might leave marks. "Hurry."

Wyatt thrust in slowly, letting them both adjust to the feel of one another. The moment he was fully in, she began to rock, setting the pace and taking him along for the ride. Wyatt followed her lead the way he had during their waltz, matching his strokes to the movement of her hips and letting her guide his finger to her clit and teach him exactly where and how she liked to be touched.

His heart thudded and his breaths grew quicker, more ragged. He pressed his face into her neck again, driving her harder, faster, harder, faster, until the couch was shaking beneath them. With each new thrust, her body clenched tighter around him, her moans growing louder and longer.

"Nova, I…" he panted, digging his nails into the cushions in desperation. "Christ, I can't…"

She spasmed beneath him, her back arching and her head lolling to the side as the orgasm rocked through her. Wyatt pumped into her, surrendering the last vestiges of control. He saw stars as the climax smashed into him, and he collapsed atop her, spent and breathless.

"Aren't you glad you listened to me?" Nova teased.

He made a muffled grunt of agreement. Talking was too hard. Moving was too hard. Maybe he could fall asleep on top of her and stay here forever. Her body was warm and firm beneath him, full of lush curves and powerful muscles. Like she'd been made for cuddling.

She nudged him. "I have to go."

"Right." Wyatt struggled to his feet. "Sorry."

They cleaned up quickly and adjusted their clothing until they were both some approximation of presentable. Nova's dress had survived the tussle surprisingly well, with only a few wrinkles visible. The knife had disappeared fully beneath her skirt, but Wyatt grinned as he gazed at the spot where it lay hidden.

"I'll enjoy finding that again next time we meet."

She folded her arms beneath her breasts. "What makes you think you're more than a one-night stand?"

He raised his eyebrows. "You've given up on the Viper hunt, then?"

God, what a scowl she gave him, the pout of her lips made all the more fine by the red bruising from their kisses. Her once-neat hair hung in strands framing her face, and his love bite stood out proudly at the junction of her neck and shoulder.

"I should go," she said gruffly.

"Busy day tomorrow?"

"I'm on diplomatic bodyguard duty. My father has a meeting with Noel Godfrey to discuss the mining treaty."

Wyatt cringed. Godfrey was the worst kind of capitalist scum, exploiting every part of the solar system he could get his hands on to secure his position as wealthiest man ever. He'd never murdered a rival—as far as anyone knew—but no one took chances when he or his minions were around.

"Leo will be at that meeting too," Wyatt said. "Helping Deimos and Phobos wrangle with the bastard. I think it might be the only thing all three of them agree on."

Nova nodded. "Security is top priority. Several of our best people will be on hand."

"Good. Please keep Leo safe."

A tiny smile softened Nova's features. "You really love him, don't you? You love all of them."

"They're my brothers. Stronger than any blood."

"I could see it when you were together tonight. There's something… special between you all. You seemed like a perfect team."

Wyatt laughed. "Hardly perfect, but I get what you mean. We're at our best together. Leo gives us all purpose. Rion brings the passion. Aubrey is the glue that holds us together."

Nova cocked her head and assessed him, the slight smile still on her lips. "And what are you?"

Wyatt shrugged. "The tech guy."

"No, that's a job. Not who you are." She walked to the door and opened it, but paused before stepping into the hall. "I think…" Her gaze locked on him, but her expression was distant, unreadable. "I think you're the sun rising in the morning. The rainbow after your Earth storms. You're their hope. Good night, Wyatt. I'll keep Morland safe. I promise."

She turned and left, closing the door gently behind her.

Wyatt sank down onto the couch, his legs still unsteady from the sex. Across the room, Flurry squeaked.

"Yeah. You're right, buddy. I'm so fucked."

# 12

NOVA RESTED A FINGER on the stun gun holstered at the small of her back and tried her best to fade into the wallpaper. Perhaps the Corps needed a uniform decorated with a profusion of pastel flowers to aid in situations such as this. Although then she'd be required to wear the hideous thing. And the paper itself was enough to make anyone scowl. It was almost as bad as the company.

"For the last time," Morland snarled, "the Planetary and Asteroidal Resources Agreement is *irrevocable*." He shifted forward in his seat, his fingers curling halfway into fists. His dark brown eyes were nearly black with fury. "I don't care if you've discovered a diamond as big as the moon or the goddamned Fountain of Youth."

Godfrey turned the full force of his icy smile on Morland. The pair of goons flanking him fidgeted—a purposeful show of their eagerness to pummel someone, Nova guessed. They would have done better to stand quietly, as she and her fellow mercenaries were doing. If this argument turned physical, she was ignoring the guards and going straight for Godfrey.

"TerraCorp had no say in your colonialist nonsense." Godfrey studied his nails and flicked away an insubstantial speck of debris. "On Earth, even a child can understand the concept of 'finders keepers.' The strong stayed behind, naturally. You Martians are the spawn of cowards and fools."

Morland wasn't as naturally pale as Wyatt, but apparently he could blush just as hard, because his cheeks flamed scarlet. "I am an Earthling, you fucking bastard. TerraCorp is only the latest name for the string of sadistic so-called companies that tore my homeland to pieces, and I will throttle you with my bare hands before I let you do that to the rest of the solar system!"

Damn. Leo had something of the lion in him after all. Nova gave him a slight nod of respect, though neither he nor anyone else was looking at her.

Phobos cleared his throat. "I believe what young Morland is trying to say is that all exo-terran settlements rely on resources from around the system. Earth, with its tiny population, has an abundance of unrestricted property for your businesses. You are welcome to continue asteroidal mining ventures as always, but cannot claim territory or obstruct our mining operations. Perhaps you would do better to focus on an underwater salvage operation to recycle the remnants of cities beneath your oceans."

Nova's father rose from his seat and walked over to extend a hand to Godfrey. "Let's be friends, Godfrey. There are plenty of valuable materials to go around. Share and share alike, I say." He flashed a smile and let his gaze sweep across the room, inviting everyone to join in his magnanimity.

Nova's jaw ticked. When Deimos employed that charming smile and smooth, easy voice, it never failed to spark an awful hope inside her. *Papa! Be my papa*, a long-ago child's voice whispered in her mind. Maybe he would care for her. Maybe he would be proud of her, if only he got to know her.

God, how she hated that voice.

"I disagree," Godfrey said coldly. "But I can see there is no reasoning with you." He stood and accepted Deimos's handshake, but let his distaste show on his face. "We will talk again in the future. Goodbye." He snapped his fingers at his guards and departed.

Nova kept her position by the wall. A different group would see that Godfrey and his people were escorted out of the building and then out of the city entirely. She and her fellow guards would remain with the dukes.

Phobos motioned to the mercenary nearest him. "Come. I have business to attend to. Do try to keep your temper next time, Morland. I have no desire to see our negotiations devolve into fisticuffs."

"'Negotiation' is not the word I would use for attempting to warn that blackguard off his plans of sabotage." Morland's tone had regained its customary calm, but rage still flickered in his eyes.

"I think Godfrey could be reasonable, given the correct motivation," Nova's father argued. "But we can speak on that another time. I, too, have other business. Ms. Vaughn, you may act as my escort."

The petite blond woman who had until this moment stood as still as Nova, bowed to the duke. "Yes, Your Grace."

"Ms. Pratt, keep an eye on Morland, would you?" Her father's dark eyes, so much like her own, fixed on her, and his smile turned sly. "Good day to you all."

Nova glowered at Deimos's departing back. She was never a daughter, only a useful tool. A convenient spy.

A prickle ran up her spine, and she spun to find Morland barely two steps away.

"Attempting to sneak up on me, Your Grace?"

"My apologies. I move quietly out of habit. I suppose I should be thankful you didn't pull a knife on me."

"Another step closer and I would have."

His lips quirked, but his expression remained hard. "Fair. I must also beg your pardon for my earlier outburst. I strive not to lose my temper, but now and then it gets the better of me."

She gave him a formal nod, as her training dictated. She quite liked this new Morland, who moved with stealth and shouted at his enemies, but he was still a duke. Propriety and authority clung to him like skin.

"I prepared my list for you, Your Grace." Nova slipped the paper from her pocket and presented it. Most of it had been taken directly from her RMC file, but she'd added a few additional skills and several relevant connections to her standard bio.

"I see you prefer a written list." This time Morland's smile did reach his eyes. "And it's well-organized."

"How else would it be?" But the moment she asked, she knew. She could envision Wyatt hastily scribbling on a scrap of paper before running to a meeting. Or rattling off each of his talents and abilities as they sprang to mind. "It's because of my military training," she added quickly. This was not the time for daydreams.

Morland made an indistinct noise of agreement, his focus on the list. His eyes tracked down the page, then widened abruptly.

"You can ride a motorbike?"

"I can. Not well enough for the races, but I can outdo any pretentious toff puttering around his estate in a fancy auto." Nova let her pride show in her voice. Most mercenaries did basic practice with automobiles or motorbikes, and occasionally one would be singled out for training as a racer. But few kept up with the skill the way she had. She loved to ride, with the wind in her hair and the landscape flying past.

Bike or motorbike, it didn't matter, as long as she could feel the freedom of the ride.

"Excellent." Morland returned to scanning the paper. "I think your abilities will nicely complement ours. But you did leave a key skill off your list."

Nova blinked. "I did?"

"Indeed. Possibly the most important skill. You're good at working with Wyatt."

"Wha—" Her jaw dropped. "I…"

Of course Morland would bring up Wyatt, after she'd spent her entire morning trying not to think about him. She'd had a job to do, and couldn't let her mind be consumed with the memory of last night and their frantic coupling.

Now it all came flooding back, unchecked—how arousing their back-and-forth had been, how good it had felt to touch him and taste him. The sense of peace and satisfaction afterward.

And then the way that peace had dissolved. The sex had eased some of her lust and curiosity, yet she was still left wanting. Leaving had felt wrong. She'd had to force herself not to linger in his arms. She needed another go 'round. One where she had time to go slow, explore, and learn what other kinds of fun he had to offer.

"Wyatt tends to be a loner," Morland explained. "It's always good to find a person he's compatible with."

Nova's body heated, as if the duke were speaking in euphemisms. God, she hoped he wasn't speaking in euphemisms.

"I am still under contract to investigate him." Best to keep that fact foremost in her mind at all times.

Leo chuckled. "We're not especially diligent about avoiding conflicts of interest when hiring, are we?"

Nova grinned. "I once had contracts with a husband and

wife at the same time, each wanting the other investigated for adultery."

"What did you discover?"

"They both were cheating." She shrugged. "They're aristocrats. It's a marriage of financial and political status, not of affection."

Morland grimaced. "Yes." He tucked Nova's list inside his jacket, and withdrew a different paper. "The contract. It's all standard, but please feel free to read it over before you sign."

Nova read the page quickly. She knew the mercenary contract backwards and forwards, and this one was exactly as expected. The assignment description was necessarily vague, stating only that she was to "aid in the investigation into transportation anomalies involving the J-M splice."

"Full scope of assignment TBD," she murmured. "Not surprising. Oh! Payment guaranteed, half up front. That's nice."

"I'm not going to deny you the ability to earn a living if we can't resolve this," Morland said gruffly.

"Thank you. I appreciate that. I'm happy to sign."

He presented her with a pen, and she scrawled her name at the bottom of the contract. Leo signed next, his letters large and swooping. Then he pocketed the pen, folded the paper, and tucked it back inside his jacket.

"Welcome to the team."

"Thank you. I hope we can do some real good."

The duke's mouth pinched into a tight line. He blew out a slow breath. "I hope so too. If you're available tonight, I have your first assignment."

"I can start as soon as I hear that Godfrey is away from the city. Until then, I'm sworn to see to your safety."

Truthfully, she didn't think Morland was in any danger. But she'd promised Wyatt, and she wouldn't break her word.

"Let's head for home, then," Leo suggested. "I can brief you and Wyatt when we get there."

Nova's belly lurched. She hadn't had time to work out what to say to Wyatt when she saw him next. Yes, she wanted to propose another tryst, but how could she do that when they were both meant to be working? And if he seemed uninterested after last night, she wasn't certain she could remain in close proximity for any period of time. Awkward at best, mortifying at worst.

"Are we… working together?"

Morland gave her a ducal frown. "Did you expect otherwise? I'm sending the both of you to bug the spaceport. Prepare yourself for a long night."

Nova squared her shoulders and called on a lifetime of training. "Yes, Your Grace."

# 13

Spaceports didn't have working hours. Beyond the tall fence, lights flashed, machines hummed, and business carried on with no regard for the clock. As far as Nova's circadian rhythm was concerned, it was the middle of the night. But drones didn't care. Nor did the human pilots who spent most of their hours away from Mars and its twenty-four hour day-night cycle. Or Earth and its slightly-shorter twenty-four hour cycle. Converting Mars days to Earth days was one of those super-annoying math problems all children were forced to do in school. It inevitably led to questions of why the calendar was still based on Earth years. (The answer: birthdays. People get mad if you try to change them.)

"When is your birthday?" Nova asked, hoping she sounded like a normal person attempting to have a normal conversation and not a person forced to work with the man she was supposed to be investigating but would prefer to be banging.

"The thirtieth of January," Wyatt replied without hesitation. "When's yours?"

"September four."

"Ah. A Virgo. That fits. Assuming the zodiac applies to someone born on Mars. I haven't studied inter-planetary astrology."

Wyatt pulled a small, round object from his pocket and tossed it in the air. His pet bat swooped from the sky to gobble it up. He circled Wyatt a few times, then flew off into the darkness.

"Is that really safe?" Nova asked.

"What? Inter-planetary astrology?"

She heaved a sigh. "The bat. Is it safe to have him out in public, flying around? Especially in a place full of ships and drones?"

"Flurry is an excellent navigator. He won't get lost and he'll always come home, even if we get separated. He imprinted on me as an infant, so I'm his family."

"You do seem prone to flitting around at night." Nova gestured at Wyatt's current outfit, a fitted black t-shirt, black trousers, and knee-high boots. He'd also repainted his nails in black, and accessorized with a string of black beads around his neck. He must have been to a hair stylist that morning, as his hair had been trimmed and the neon green tips were longer and brighter than they'd been only last night.

"I thought you might appreciate the vampire look." He gazed pointedly at her collar, and Nova felt an answering throb at the place where he'd marked her.

"I'm afraid we don't have time for that sort of appreciation. We have a job to do."

His expression tensed. "Right. Let's go." He strode off toward the entrance gate, looking as imperious as his friend Morland.

"May I help you, milord?" the guard on duty inquired.

"Lord Windborne requesting access for drone inspection," Wyatt commanded.

Nova gritted her teeth. She encountered enough haughty

aristocrats in her daily life without Wyatt adding to their numbers.

The guard unlocked the gate and held it open, smiling. "Enjoy your evening, milord."

Wyatt made a small bow. "Arigatou."

"What was that?" Nova whispered, when they were out of earshot.

"It was 'thank you' in the language of Nippon," Wyatt explained. "It's their Earth language."

"Oh."

Haughty aristocrats didn't thank the staff, and they absolutely didn't befriend them. Nor did they routinely perform mundane tasks like inspections. But here was Wyatt, showing up after midnight, with a bat circling around his head and greeting the night guard in a language from decades ago.

Once again, his downtown world defied expectations. Like at the restaurant. Or the factory.

"I need to start making a list," she grumbled.

Wyatt tossed another piece of fruit to his bat. "What was that?"

"Nothing."

He stepped into a deep shadow and paused. "I'm sorry if you didn't want to work with me toni—"

"It's not—"

"Leo does that duke thing where he forgets to ask people—"

Nova's hands balled into fists. "I didn't say—"

"Just because we had sex doesn't—"

"It's not you!"

Wyatt flinched. "Uh… sorry?"

Nova forced her shoulders down and rolled her neck. "I'm tired. That's all. I've been up since dawn."

The darkness concealed his expression, but he didn't scoff or argue. Good. He didn't need to know she'd been off-balance since the day they'd met. Or that her orderly life tilted a little bit more with every foray into his domain. Like any problem, this was a temporary aberration. She'd set it right soon enough.

"I've already mapped out all the best locations," Wyatt assured her. "We'll work fast."

He led the way toward the east end of the spaceport, where only cargo ships and other craft that didn't carry passengers were allowed. Stacks of crates and carts waiting to be loaded or emptied crowded the area. Large conveyor belts hummed as they moved containers through open sections of the glass dome into the airlocks beyond.

Drones buzzed by overhead, and a few people milled about, keeping watch over the cargo and the machinery. If any of them looked Nova's way, they wouldn't see much. Wyatt navigated the spaceport with practiced ease. He slipped from shadow to shadow with the same fluid grace he exhibited when dancing. In no time at all, they were up against the thick walls of the dome, directly between two of the whirring conveyor belts.

"Micro cameras first." Wyatt unlatched the pack slung around his waist and pulled out a fistful of tiny devices. "We'll have people monitor them for any cargo or activity going in or out that looks suspicious."

Nova held out a hand, and Wyatt dropped several of the bugs into her palm. All the bugs she'd used before had been reminiscent of their namesakes, with limbs for maneuverability. These were tiny discs, stuck together in a neat stack.

She pried one off the top. "Magnetic?"

"Yep. Watch this." Wyatt stepped out into the pool of

light surrounding the nearest conveyor belt. He ran a hand along the thick iron support separating them from the airlock. A wide groove in the beam allowed the window to slide open and closed, sealing the compartment any time a ship arrived or departed. "There's a little notch right… Aha!"

Keeping his gaze fixed on the spot, he took one of the cameras and popped it into place. Nova leaned in to look. The device fit perfectly into a small hole near the edge of the beam. It would be concealed and operational whether the window was open or closed.

"Take your devices and place them in the notches around all the cargo conveyors in that direction." Wyatt gestured. "I'll go the other way and do the same. You probably have a few extra bugs in that pile, so feel free to toss those through any open windows. It can't hurt to have a couple eyes in the airlocks too."

With one finger, Nova rolled the stack of bugs back and forth across her palm. "You knew these holes were here. And the dimensions."

Wyatt gave her the same gleefully wicked smile he used when he was flirting. "Most of the beams made in the last two decades have come from Leo's factory. The notches are for the installation of bars or gratings over a window, but they have other uses."

And the spaceport had undergone a major renovation only a few years ago. Honestly, she was a bit surprised the "Lords of Dystopia" hadn't provided beams with spy devices preinstalled. The way her father and his companions talked, Wyatt and his friends spent their days fomenting violent revolution. Which was utter nonsense. Their reputation for a lax attitude towards law and order, however…

Wyatt took a step away from Nova, his expression turning sober, sparking a sudden realization of how close they'd been standing. Until that moment, she'd thought nothing of it. His proximity had seemed normal, correct.

"We should get to work before we draw too much attention," Wyatt said.

"Yes." Nova hurried off, the magnetic bugs clutched in her hand. She had a job to do, and with luck a bit of separation from Wyatt would clear her head.

That hope proved futile. With every *click* of the magnets into place, she thought of him and the ingenuity and teamwork that permeated his life. He and his people got things done. They embraced and supported the people around them. They'd even lured her into their system. Enticed her with a common enemy.

*You are not part of the team. You're called mercenaries for a reason. Every person for themself. It's only a contract.*

No different than her contract to prove Wyatt was a smuggler. One night of intimacies didn't make them close, no matter how easy he was to like or how her body responded to his.

Nova slipped the last bug into its notch and turned to look for Wyatt. She'd hurried off without arranging for a rendezvous point, and now he was nowhere in sight.

She headed for the inspection building. No cargo went in or out of the city without passing inspection checks, and possible ways to sneak past were limited. Most required someone on the inside. If anyone knew what was arriving on the disappearing-reappearing transports, they likely worked in inspection.

The squeak of Wyatt's bat alerted her to Wyatt's presence a moment before he emerged from the shadows. The bat hung from the collar of his shirt, its big eyes peering plaintively up at him.

"I know you want more fruit, sweetie," Wyatt cooed.

"But we might need you to be a distraction." He scratched the bat's furry head and it let out a happy chirp.

Nova grunted. "I don't like this."

Wyatt shrugged one shoulder. "The inspection building is the most important place to watch."

"I understand." She huffed out a breath. "But I don't like that we have to break in. It feels wrong. My skin is crawling just thinking about it."

He gave her a sympathetic smile. "It's for a good cause. Security here is supposed to be entirely neutral. No one would let us wander in and tamper with the equipment. And Leo authorized this mission anyway. A-plus-plus. Duke-approved."

"*One* duke. He didn't run it by anyone else. Exactly like my father."

Wyatt winced. "Spare yourself and don't ever ask Leo and Aubrey about the constant political machinations. Some of that stuff would make you weep."

"Mercenaries don't weep."

"That's unfortunate. Crying is a natural and healthy response to strong emotions."

"Mercenaries don't have strong emotions. We're trained out of it."

"Hmm." One side of his mouth hitched up. "And how's that working out for you?"

If the bat hadn't been in the way, she would have poked him in the chest. She settled for leaning over him. "Am I strangling you right now? No. Therefore, it's working."

Nova braced for another sly retort, but Wyatt only shook his head and backed away.

"Follow me." He waved a hand as he turned from her. "I can get us through the employee entrance."

They closed the distance to the building in a circuitous

path, once more keeping to the shadows. When they did step out into the open, they didn't remain there long. Wyatt had a key in his hand. He slotted it into the lock, turned the knob, and the door swung open.

Nova darted inside. Wyatt closed the door as soundlessly as he'd opened it, then gently touched her arm to let her know where he was. For several seconds, the inside of the warehouse looked pitch black. Then tiny dots of light began to appear. Stacks of cargo and scanning equipment materialized out of the darkness, indistinct at first, then sharpening as her eyes adjusted.

She tilted her head toward Wyatt. "Did you steal that key?" she hissed.

"Of course not."

"Do you have it because you're a smuggler?"

"Also no. It's on loan, and I'm retur—"

*Be-beep! Be-beep! Be-beep!*

Nova spun automatically in a full circle seeking the source of the alarm. It was nearby. About where Wyatt…

"Shit!" He fumbled around as the beeping continued. "Shit, shit, shit!"

Light flooded the room.

# 14

WYATT SLAPPED AT HIS WATCH as Nova grabbed him by the back of the shirt and dragged him behind the nearest crate.

*Off. Off. Turn off, dammit!*

The beeping stopped, but now it seemed like his heart was pounding just as loud. Every breath echoed in his ears. He'd ruined everything. They'd be caught and arrested. Nova would hate him forever—which probably didn't matter because she didn't seem to want to sleep with him any more anyway, but, dammit, he *liked* her. And it didn't matter that he was a peer. The others would happily vote to convict a weirdo Earthling. They'd probably call it treason and have him executed by firing squad. Maybe they'd make Nova part of the firing squad just to make it extra awful. She wouldn't shoot him, though. She was too good a person. Better than he was, probably, even if some of her thinking was misguided. She at least didn't go so overboard setting alarms that she forgot about them until they went off at one o'clock in the morning. Meeting alarms. Late-for-meeting alarms. Remember to eat alarms. Let Flurry in and out alarms. Go to bed alarms. And the now notorious, "actually, seriously, go to bed" alarm.

Nova yanked on his shirt again, and he staggered. Flurry flapped his wings in annoyance, but didn't let go. Wyatt patted the bat with one hand, using his other hand to steady himself as he followed Nova deeper into the maze of cargo.

"I know someone's out there!" a furious soprano voice shouted. "Come out now or even more charges will be filed against you."

More than what? Trespassing, of course. Burglary, perhaps. Unlawful entry. Breaking and entering. Probably not firing squad worthy. Yet.

Around and around the thoughts buzzed in his brain. Nova, Flurry, alarms, crime, guns, smuggling. Wyatt couldn't stop it, couldn't focus. He had to move. He couldn't fix this without moving, but he was huddled behind a crate and Nova was holding him still.

"Slow." Nova's whisper caressed his earlobe, sending a shiver down his spine. "In, out. Nice and deep."

Wyatt tried to breathe easy, drumming patterns on his thigh to combat the twitching in his limbs. *Smack, tap, tap, tap. Smack, tap, tap, tap. Smack, tap, smack, tap, smack, tap, tap, tap.*

As he drummed, the bees in his brain settled enough that he could think. He had to summon the drones. It would give away their location, but if he worked fast enough maybe he could get at least some of the bugs planted. They'd never have time to move through the whole building before more security arrived.

Nova's hand clamped down on his, halting his drumming mid-pattern.

"Shh."

The whisper was harsh, angry, and Wyatt reflexively

jerked away, pulling his hands protectively up to his chest. Nova sprang back, her eyes widening in concern.

*Sorry,* she mouthed.

He blinked and shook his head. This wasn't Eton, where the schoolmasters had rapped his knuckles for fidgeting and daydreaming. Nova would understand, but he couldn't explain now. He tried to smile reassuringly.

"I know you're in there!"

Wyatt jumped. Crap. The guard was nearly on top of them.

Nova made a "follow me" motion and crept around another crate. Wyatt stayed close behind, making his footsteps as light and soundless as possible. He petted Flurry with one hand, digging into his pocket with the other to retrieve the bag with the last of the berries. When Nova glanced back, he held up the fruit.

She nodded, then pointed at him. She mimed throwing, then running.

*Exactly.*

Wyatt gently disengaged Flurry's claws from his collar. The bat flapped his wings and flew from Wyatt's grasp. Wyatt hurled the berries up into the air, over top of the stacks of crates they'd been slinking through.

Flurry let out a squeal of delight.

Wyatt didn't look to see if his pet managed to snag any of the fruits from the air. He broke into a sprint, racing at Nova's side toward the opposite end of the warehouse.

"What the— Aagh!" The guard's shriek echoed off the ceiling. "What *is* that? Security, hurry the fuck up! There's some kind of... of... *animal* here."

Wyatt kept his legs pumping, aiming for the massive x-ray scanner in the center of the room. He dove behind it and pressed a finger to his implant. The drones here weren't part of his army, but every one in the city had an identical transponder. They would come when he called.

Buzzing filled the air as the drones zipped to him from all corners of the warehouse. He snagged one out of the air and popped a hatch on the back. He wasn't as familiar with this model as he was with his usual toys, but a bit of prodding found him the control module he wanted. He yanked it out and replaced it with one from his pouch, then closed the drone back up. Wyatt couldn't begin to guess how long that had taken, but the next one would be faster.

He reached up for another drone, only to have Nova place one in his hands. She'd already opened the access panel.

Wyatt's heart jumped in delight and he fumbled to remove the correct control module. What could be better than a partner who caught on immediately and began helping without a word? She had another drone ready for him the instant he released the one in his hands. And when he spared a second to glance at her—God help him, but he couldn't resist—her body was crouched in a ready position, her eyes scanning for danger. Damn, her competence was sexy.

"I. Need. Backup!" The guard's furious footsteps joined the hum of the drones. "We have a probable intruder, there's some fuzzy bird creature flying around, and now the drones are acting weird!"

Wyatt shut out the noise and let himself fall into a rhythm. Old mod out, new mod in, close, release. His fingers flew faster. Out, in, out, in. He lost track of everything but the drones and the movements of his hands.

His focus snapped when Nova squeezed his shoulder.

"Time to move." She'd untucked her shirt and tugged it

up to make a cradle for all the discarded control mods. She pointed with her free hand. "Go. Finish later."

Wyatt ran. The unaltered drones followed him. Only a few remained. The others busily executed their new orders, returning to their usual stations as if nothing untoward had happened.

He slid to a stop behind a crate and immediately reached for a mod, expecting Nova to hand him a drone any second.

She wasn't there.

"Hey, you! Guard!"

The device slipped from Wyatt's hand and clattered to the floor. What was she doing? They could deal with missing a few of the drones. But Nova Pratt apparently didn't leave jobs half-finished.

"Yeah, you!" she shouted. "Try to catch me!"

Fucking hell.

Wyatt grabbed up the mod and snagged the nearest drone from the air. Nova had risked herself to let him finish the job, and he wasn't going to let her down. The process wasn't as efficient alone, and he couldn't tear his mind from the pounding of footsteps and angry shouts.

*Concentrate. Concentrate. Finish this.*

Wyatt snapped the access panel shut and sent the drone on its way.

*One.*

He started on the next, his mind jumping ahead to after. How to get out. How to avoid further security.

*Two.*

He grabbed the last drone.

"You are under arrest!"

"I'm authorized by a duke!" Nova's voice was distant and muffled. "He'll be very angry!"

*Three.*

Wyatt stuffed the discarded mods into his pack and hopped to his feet. All the running had put him back within ten or fifteen meters of the entrance. Perfect.

He steadied himself with a deep breath, then bolted for the door. An iron lever, much like a pump handle, jutted from the wall near the entrance. It was unlabeled, but the gleaming red paint gave away its purpose. Wyatt skidded to a halt in front of it, grabbed hold with both hands, and gave a mighty tug.

The fire alarm blared. Clouds of fire suppressant burst from pipes in the ceiling.

Wyatt flung the door open and ran outside. He positioned himself behind the open door, slotted the key into the lock, and waited.

*Come on, Nova. Run. You can do it.*

"Go, Flurry, get out!"

Wyatt's grip on the door tightened. She was looking out for Flurry. Goddammit, she was the most beautiful person in the solar system.

A furry streak shot through the open door.

"Good boy!" Wyatt applauded. He braced himself. "Run, Nova! I've got your back!"

His heart pounded against his ribcage as if it might shatter the bones. She had to get out. She had to. If she got caught saving his ass, he would never forgive himself.

*Come on, come on, come on.*

Nova burst through the doorway, both hands clinging to her shirt, where she still held the old control modules.

Wyatt slammed the door and locked it.

No time to waste. They darted into the shadows. Wyatt took the lead again, splitting the difference between the shortest path and the least visible one. When they reached the gate he flung it open, shouted his thanks to the—much friendlier—guard, and kept running until they reached the trolley station.

A trolley rolled in as they staggered to a halt, panting. A single passenger disembarked. Wyatt and Nova jumped aboard and made their way to the back of the empty vehicle, slumping low in their seats.

Wyatt's hands were shaking. He stared at the driver's back, willing him to close the doors and go.

"What about Flurry?" Nova whispered.

"He'll almost certainly beat us home… er, back to my place. Assuming we don't get—"

The trolley door closed with a hiss.

Wyatt's shoulders slumped in relief as they pulled away from the station. "Oh, thank God." He shoved a hand through his hair, finding it slick with perspiration. "I am so, so sorry. I fucked that up badly."

"It happens. We got the job done." Nova lowered the hem of her shirt and began moving all the old mods to Wyatt's pouch. "I figured you didn't want any of these getting left behind."

"Thanks. You were… You were…" Words wouldn't come. Maybe they didn't exist. He could only stare at her. Beads of sweat stood out on her brow, and wisps of hair had come free from her ponytail. Her cheeks were red, her shirt a wrinkled mess, and her trousers streaked with dirt. "You're just… so fucking hot," he breathed.

Her mouth started to pull upward. "Yeah?"

"And I get it if you're not interested, but if you still are, then, like, maybe—"

She shoved him down onto the seat and kissed him.

<h1 style="text-align:center">15</h1>

Nova loved the way Wyatt kissed. His lips were soft and supple, responsive to her every suck and lick. His mouth moved eagerly beneath hers, but he never demanded or tried to wrest control from her. Instead, he waited for her to ease off and let him take charge. There was no rhythm to the trading back and forth, no attempt at equal time or dominance. She led the way more often than not. Yet he still made her feel as if she was being kissed as much as kissing. As if he'd been yearning for this at least as much as she had.

Nova rocked her hips against him, and he made a desperate mewling noise. She broke the kiss, grinning. "You're adorable. Do that again."

Wyatt's brow furrowed. "Which part?"

"Where you make that noise like you're a helpless animal in need of rescue."

Nova rolled her pelvis in a slow circle against his thickening cock. Wyatt's eyes slid closed. His rosy lips parted on a half-groan, half-whimper.

"Yes." She lowered her head and nipped at the soft skin of his neck, causing him to make the noise again. "Keep doing that."

"Hey, back there!" The driver's irate voice startled Nova

from her haze of lust. "No playing hide the sausage on the trolley!"

"Don't have to hide it," Wyatt murmured. "I'm not picky. Lots of other options."

Nova had to stifle her laugh and make herself sit up. Getting arrested for public indecency with the man she was supposed to be investigating was not a smart career choice.

She patted Wyatt's thigh. "Another time."

He dragged himself upright. "There goes my chance to be ravished on a trolley."

"I'm sure you have many years ahead of you to look for another opportunity."

"Do I?" Wyatt adjusted his trousers and tried to settle himself more comfortably. "Here I thought you wanted to send me to prison for smuggling."

"No." The word spilled from her lips before her thoughts could catch up. When her brain finally processed the response, she had to pause before continuing. "No. I don't."

She didn't want him in prison. Or banished or harmed in any way. He didn't deserve that, whatever his crimes.

*Bollocks.*

For the first time in her life, she wouldn't be able to finish a job. Her father would be furious. Connington would be beside himself with glee. He'd see to it that she paid the maximum fine for breaking her contract.

"Well." Wyatt scooted backward, giving him ample space to look her up and down. "This is an exciting development. Am I to understand that you…" he paused, letting a sly smile play on his lips, "*like* me?"

Nova's skin warmed under the intensity of his heavy-lidded gaze and the slight flutter of his long, long lashes. Maybe he was a changeling or a fairy trickster. He'd bewitched her, for certain, because suddenly she didn't much care how her superiors would react.

"Yes, I like you. I'd hate to see you locked in a jail. And I'd like plenty of time to explore those 'other options' you spoke of." She took a long, deliberate look at the bulge in his trousers. It really was unfortunate that they didn't have a less-attentive trolley driver. She squared her shoulders and brought her gaze up to Wyatt's face. "But don't misunderstand me. I want you to stop smuggling. You can find better ways to accomplish your goals than circumventing the law."

"Darling, if the bastards who control this country would vote for anything other than their own self interest, I wouldn't need to circumvent the law."

Nova scowled. "But there must be some legal way—"

Wyatt cut her off with an abrupt wave of his hand. "We've been trying the legal way for twenty years. It's too slow. People need help *now*. That's why I started using my network for the Wealth Redistribution Operation. The Viper exists because somebody has to eat the rats before the whole city becomes their plague-infested garbage pit."

All traces of desire were gone from his eyes. His blue gaze had turned ice-hard and defiant.

"There. There's your confession. Go ahead and turn me in," he challenged. "While you're at it, why don't you tell everyone what I did tonight."

Nova slumped in her seat and let her head loll against the wall behind her. "You know I won't do that. It's not right. You're trying to do good."

"So you'll ignore the law."

She couldn't look at him. "I will accept the penalty for leaving the assignment unfulfilled. I'm sure they'll assign someone else, but you'll have time to reconsider before they come after you."

"Nova."

The gently murmured word pulled her gaze back to him. His expression was no less defiant, but his eyes had softened. He often sat or stood with his arms crossed, but now his posture was open, inviting.

Damn, she was tired. Her body itched with the desire to lay her head on his chest and rest there.

"You're not one of the rats, Nova." Wyatt grimaced and shook his head. "I need a better metaphor. Rats are cute and smart, and it's not their fault humans are filthy. They simply take advantage of it. And the fleas infected people with the Black Death. We spread it all over Earth via our trade routes. We really shouldn't blame the rats." He blinked. "What was I talking about?"

"I'm not one of them?" she prompted.

"Right. You're not. You're better than them. If you knew my world better, if you saw the way people are exploited, you'd understand. The smugglers and the spies are the real helpers. Let me show you. Let me take you around Dystopia so you can see for yourself."

*I can't. I can't live lawlessly.*

The words stuck in her throat. Nothing would come of rehashing the same argument. Facts were facts. She didn't belong in Wyatt's world any more than she belonged among the glittering ballrooms of the haut ton. Her place was and would always be in between, keeping the peace. Maintaining order.

She put a hand to her abdomen to quell a sudden discomfort. "I think it's been too long since I've eaten."

"Oh!" Wyatt scooted close and put an arm around her. "I should have thought of that. I always forget food. We're almost there. I can order out for sandwiches. What is your priority, food, sex, or sleep? I'm happy to provide all three in any order."

The pang in her stomach grew worse. "Food, I suppose. Much as I would enjoy ravishing you, it's probably best to ensure neither of us is feeling poorly."

"I will send for food and we can eat it naked in bed." He trailed a finger along the edge of her collar. "I'd like a good look at that love bite."

"And I want to see the tattoo on your upper arm and that little scar near your clavicle that you keep touching."

"A fair trade. I think the next stop is ours."

Nova peered out the window, but in the darkness the streets were indistinguishable from one another. Stone and brick buildings stood side-by-side-by-side, lit only by faint electric streetlamps. They could have been residential, commercial, or industrial. Her lack of familiarity with downtown left her struggling to orient herself. Perhaps she ought to let Wyatt give her a tour, simply to increase her knowledge.

The trolley traveled only a few more blocks before stopping. Wyatt offered Nova a hand, and she accepted, allowing him to lead her off the trolley and down the street until the facade of the Central Manufactory emerged from the darkness.

"Home sweet home," Wyatt pronounced cheerfully. "I can't wait to celebrate our success—messy though it was—with the time-honored traditions of feasting and nudity."

"The cornerstones of any good celebration, naturally. I would suggest we get drunk as well, but that would hamper our ability to take full advantage of the nudity."

"Heaven forfend!" He smacked the back of his hand against his forehead, as if about to swoon.

Nova bumped her shoulder into his. "No fainting until you've made me a sandwich."

He gasped in mock outrage. "I am an earl. Earls do not *make* sandwiches. We invent them."

Nova snorted. She yanked open the door and swept an arm out in a theatrical gesture. "After you, Mr. High-and-Mighty."

"That's Lord High-and-Mighty to you." He strode through the door. "Chet, do you have the name of that sandwich shop that's open all night?"

Nova stepped into the building, only to stop suddenly when Chet wheeled out to block her way.

"Beg pardon, your lordship," the night watchman said, "but your lady friend may wish to come back another evening. Morland's in a right temper and told me to send you to him the moment you arrived. Something about a fire at the spaceport, destruction of property, and an uncertified authorization."

"Aw, crap." Wyatt's shoulders slumped. "I'd better go apologize." He turned to look at Nova. "Would you like something to eat while I'm being castigated?"

She glanced toward the stairs, then back at Wyatt. "No." She heaved a sigh. "I ought to return to the barracks. It's late."

"Yeah. Another time, I guess."

"Yes." Ravishment would happen. She'd see to it. The desire between them was too strong not to explore thoroughly.

"Maybe another date?" Wyatt suggested. "I can give you that tour, or take you to a show or restaurant, or even take you out to my zoological gardens and let you see the animals. I will *not* feed you to a tiger, despite what my friends might say."

"I—" Nova choked on the word. His ideas sounded nice. Too nice. Maybe that was the secret of Dystopia. People were sucked in by things that sounded nice and before they knew it they were breaking laws and living in anarchy. "I will think about it," she finished.

He inclined his head. "Goodnight, Nova."

"Goodnight. Send word when I'm needed again." She raised a hand in farewell and departed.

As she walked to where her bicycle was parked, she rolled her shoulders, trying to shake off the sensation of wrongness. Leaving was the right decision. She'd only be in the way if she joined Wyatt and Morland's discussion. The mood had already been spoiled and they would have other opportunities for sex. Yes. This was right. Everything was as it should be.

Her unruly stomach gave another lurch.

She really needed that sandwich.

# 16

WYATT DOWNED HALF A MUG of tea in a single gulp. As usual, he'd forgotten about it until it had gone cold. He'd also severely oversteeped it, so it tasted like he imagined burnt motor oil might taste: revolting, but hopefully strong enough to wake him up.

*Clack. … Clack.*

His fingers were slow on the keyboard this morning, his limbs stiff from a short, uncomfortable night of sleep. Even on a good day, he wasn't up and about at seven a.m. Leo had mastered the art of elegantly devastating retribution.

"Report?" Leo loomed over Wyatt's desk, as tidy and clear-eyed as always. He lifted a dainty porcelain cup to his lips and took a dignified sip of his coffee.

"Three drones destroyed by the fire suppressant. Two others damaged and undergoing repairs. Fortunately, I did get our modules into all of them, so six remain functional. That should give us acceptable coverage throughout the facility. Human security has been temporarily increased, new hires provided by the RMC. I don't have names yet, but when I get them I'll ask Nova for details on their reliability."

"Any additional fallout from last night?"

"There was a fabulous article in the paper this morning," Aubrey cut in. He still wore his pajamas and held a tall glass of murky green liquid. "Quite sensational. Apparently, there has been a rash of exotic pets being let loose and causing mischief. They get into buildings, set off alarms, attack unsuspecting people. The paper warned readers to keep their eyes open and report any sightings to the Center for Zoological Conservation."

Rion, who leaned against the wall with his eyes half-closed, gave a massive yawn. "You're welcome."

Wyatt made a quick scan of his list of drones and called up video from Drone 23. It hovered above a sugar beet field, recording a harvester robot rolling lethargically down a row of greenery. The massive machine lumbered along, churning up dirt as it scooped the beets into its belly.

There weren't even any human overseers in the area. He rarely checked the drones in the Ag sectors unless someone reported a problem. Ag Sector 3 lay a stone's throw from the mercenary compound. It wouldn't hurt anything if he sent 23 on a quick detour. Just to check that Nova hadn't been put on kitchen duty for his mistakes, or anything.

His index finger twitched above the keyboard.

"As humorous as your distraction is…"

Leo's chilly tone startled Wyatt so badly that his finger slipped and hit a random key. "*Error: invalid parameter*" flashed on the screen.

"It solves only a portion of our problem," the duke continued. "The public will accept wild tales of escaped animals. Our enemies will not. And now they know we are investigating."

"I'm sorry, okay!" Wyatt kept his gaze locked on the screen. Drone 23 continued broadcasting its view of Ag

Sector 3, as happy as if it were a sophisticated spy drone. "I'm not a trained covert operative. You should have sent Aubrey."

"I'm not trained, either," Aubrey replied. "I simply have more practice."

"And you remember everything." Wyatt picked up his mug. "I can't even remember my tea."

Rion thumped his head against the wall. "Do we have to do this? We all fuck up sometimes, even though His Grace of Dukeville likes to pretend he's perfect. Surveillance is in place, but they know we're watching. So what's the next step? That's all that matters."

Wyatt downed the last of his cold tea before spinning his chair around and speaking. "I think we need to wait and watch. Monitor the surveillance cameras, look for abnormal activity. Search old records for the registration numbers of the ships involved. That's all me."

"Good." Leo sounded satisfied for the first time that morning. "Aubrey, I want you to get the word out that you're looking for a new investment. Imply that profit takes priority over legality. We can fake some gaming debts for you to make it plausible."

Aubrey swirled his vegetable drink. "Investments. You think there's more than one player at work here?"

"Let's just say I find it suspicious that we made this discovery around the same time Godfrey showed up with his latest demand for territory. I didn't think about it at the time, but he capitulated quickly and departed without incident. Looking back, he may have deliberately enraged me to divert my attention. I'll look into his mining ventures."

"I do love a good conspiracy." Aubrey lifted his glass in salute and took a long drink.

Rion straightened up and stretched. "And my assignment, fearless leader?"

"Forge a series of gaming debts for Aubrey, going back many months," Leo replied. "Make sure they're from the seedier establishments no one will admit to frequenting. Then find a journalist to do an exposé on aristocrats going slumming. No names."

"I'll pay a prompt visit to the widow Buxley. She pens the best exposés."

"And always wants to shag in semi-public locations," Wyatt added.

Rion smirked. "I'm a giver."

Leo cleared his throat. "I will ask Ms. Pratt to report on the mercenaries assigned to spaceport security. Feel free to use your usual networks, but don't tell anyone more than what they strictly need to know. I want a daily progress meeting, starting tonight at eight p.m."

Wyatt swiveled back to his workstation and set an alarm. The harvester robot continued plodding across the screen.

Leo's coffee cup made a gentle *clink* as it landed on the saucer. "Good luck, gentlemen. I will see you all tonight. Do try to be on time and awake. And watch your backs. I suspect our foe will be displeased with our endeavors. Good day." He strode out the door.

"Our foe?" Rion echoed, once Leo had vanished. "Seriously, what the hell is wrong with that man?"

"He was literally born a duke," Aubrey pointed out. "We're probably the only people in his entire life who talk to him like a normal person."

Rion sighed. "I figured he'd get better over the years, but I think he's only gotten worse." He yawned again. "See you all later. I'm going for a nap."

"And I'm going to go lounge on a couch in my pajamas and read a freshly-ironed newspaper like a proper aristocrat."

Aubrey waved his drink. "If anyone asks, this isn't a kale smoothie, it's a single-malt Scotch, neat."

Wyatt gave his friends a wave as they departed. Despite a heap of potential problems and his lack of sleep, he couldn't help but smile. He loved those three weirdos, and never doubted that they loved him back, oddities and all. Whatever else happened in his life, he was damned lucky to have them.

Which meant he needed to get to work and fix his screw-up before someone decided to harm them. He had plenty to do.

*And none of it with Nova.*

He shut off the feed from Drone 23. He was stuck here in the office for the foreseeable future. If he wanted to see her, he'd have to arrange a date. Which meant convincing her to come downtown for nothing but her own pleasure. And from what he'd seen of her, doing things for her own pleasure fell low on her priority list.

Maybe this was it. Maybe their affair was over, and this was the time to move on.

No, that was silly. He'd seen her less than six hours ago. She was probably asleep, or freshly awakened and well-rested. Unless someone had discovered her late-night escapade.

Wyatt punched out a series of commands, and her contact information appeared on the screen. He selected her direct address, checked that he was using his best encrypted channel, and typed out a message.

**WyHart: Hey. How are you? Hope my fuck-up last night didn't cause you any trouble?**

She probably wouldn't even see it, since she was always busy with work. The mercenaries might not even have personal vidscreens. She'd have to answer him in a common room where anyone around could see.

His fingers hovered over the keys. *To delete or not to delete?*

Text flashed on the screen.

Pratt-Nova-RMC: Hello. I haven't heard any talk, but I haven't gone out to breakfast yet. Did Morland give you a tongue-lashing?

WyHart: More a stern lecture and an "I am disappointed in you" look. I spent the whole time thinking about sex and sandwiches.

WyHart: With you, not with Leo.

Pratt-Nova-RMC: I knew what you meant. I'm not interested in sex and sandwiches with him, either.

WyHart: But you still are with me, I hope. When is good for you? Do you want me to take you out or just take you to bed?

Pratt-Nova-RMC: Bed seems safer. We might get arrested if we try to eat sandwiches naked in a restaurant.

WyHart: It's unsanitary. The restaurant could be shut down, people would be out of a job, mass hysteria.

Pratt-Nova-RMC: Aha! You CAN see things my way!

WyHart: When your way is right, I can. So, bed? Tonight? Did Leo ask you to join the meeting at 8?

Pratt-Nova-RMC: What do you mean when my way is right? Are you telling me I'm usually wrong? Maybe I don't want sex and sandwiches with you.

WyHart: Was that a joke? Please tell me it was a joke. I thought I was flirting.

Pratt-Nova-RMC: I know. I will see you tonight. Make sure the sand … Shit.

Pratt-Nova-RMC: … ??? …

WyHart: Nova? Are you still there?

Pratt-Nova-RMC: ??? … ???

Dammit. She was probably dictating and the device couldn't pick up her words. It continued spewing question marks at a steady pace. Was her vidscreen low on power? Had she dropped it?

WyHart: Nova, I'm not getting any response. Is your microphone dead? You might need to type back to me.

Pratt-Nova-RMC: ??? … now … ??? … yes … ???

The messages stopped. Wyatt typed out a reply, but deleted it before sending. He tried again. And again.

Fuck. He couldn't come up with anything to say that he hadn't already said. Sending panicked messages wouldn't help anything. Chances were it was an equipment problem. And if it wasn't…

He typed and deleted one more message. No. Panicking wouldn't help in that case, either. This needed a rational approach. He closed the conversation.

"Hey, 23." Wyatt's fingers flew over the keys. "I know you like farms, buddy, but I've got another job for you now."

# 17

"Care to explain?" Connington's smile was all teeth, like he was a predator baring his fangs. Nova couldn't say for certain what animal he resembled, but Wyatt would know.

She kept her posture rock-still, though inside she fumed.

*Yes, I do care to explain. I'd like to explain to Wyatt why I ran off in the middle of a conversation. He's probably freaking out, thinking I've been arrested.*

"I'm afraid I don't know what this is about," she said aloud.

Connington jabbed a finger at a piece of paper on his desk. "You contracted with Morland."

Her eyebrows rose in surprise. Not "Where were you last night?" or "You were observed at the spaceport." Perhaps she could get through this meeting without evading any questions.

"Yes," she replied. "A standard contract. The paperwork was all in order when I filed it."

"Hmm." He folded his hands and rested them atop the desk. "And you did not consider that this might be inadvisable?"

"Not at all. He reviewed my skills, offered me a job, and I accepted. It was no different from any other contract I've undertaken."

The commander's head tilted slightly to one side as he looked up at her, and a small furrow formed in his brow. When he spoke, the words were slow and deliberate, as if he were explaining to a confused child. "Except that you were already under contract to investigate Morland."

"I was investigating Lord Windborne," Nova corrected.

"And you honestly believe they're not conspiring together?" He huffed. "I didn't think you were that naive."

Nova held her posture and kept her tone even. "I state the facts as I see them, sir. If my father is unhappy with my performance on the Viper contract, he may terminate it and I will not dispute. I do not believe I will be able to gather any more information he would find useful."

"Is that so?"

"It is. My suggestion is to let the matter drop. Any harm done by the smuggling is negligible compared to the time and resources it would take to prevent it. I can write a report stating as much and have it on your desk by the end of the day."

"No."

Nova blinked. "I beg your pardon?"

"You cannot abandon the contract. You will continue until Lord Windborne and his confederates are behind bars."

"I have nothing more to contribute." Nova put her hands on her hips and glared down at Connington. Let him reprimand her for unbecoming conduct. She didn't care any more. Scrubbing pots and pans was better than putting up with his condescension. "If you want to waste time on a hopeless assignment, do it yourself."

His brows shot up and his mouth opened and closed. Good. He deserved to have his composure rattled now and then.

Nova gazed out the window past his shoulder. The view

was nothing special, only the glass forms of farm sectors spreading out into the distance. But it was less tedious than Connington.

A drone glided past the window, and she almost flinched. *Wyatt?*

Drones were ubiquitous downtown, but here they were rare, usually remote-controlled by a construction or cleaning crew. This drone paused, hovered for a moment, then slowly approached the window. It was a small camera drone, a rounded metal box held aloft by four little rotors—the exact type that usually trailed in Wyatt's wake.

*Definitely him.* If she were alone she would have smiled and waved to reassure him of her wellbeing. *Sorry for leaving you hanging. I'm fine.*

"I suppose you think you're tough, don't you?" Connington's snarled words pulled Nova's attention away from the drone. "Hiding your failings beneath insubordination? And after all I've done for you."

Nova barked a laugh. "All *you've* done?"

Connington rose from his seat. Even in her thick-soled boots he had a few inches on her, and he straightened fully until he could look down his nose at her.

She rolled her eyes. The taller boys had been trying to intimidate the tall girl since she was in primary school. Some people never learned.

"I gave you that contract as a favor to your father." Connington flattened his hands on the desk and leaned over it. "I could have left you with nothing but routine security jobs for the rest of your life. But he wanted *you* to hunt the Viper. So I let you have it. I let you add 'investigator' to your bio and increase your pay rate. And you repay that by going fishing for money from the likes of Morland and abandoning the assignment I gave you."

Nova folded her arms across her chest. "They're contracts, not assignments. You can advise all you want, but we choose what we do and do not do. I don't give a flying fuck what kind of arrangement you have with my father. I have every right to take any contracts offered to me, and I have every right to terminate one that is no longer worth my time. Good day. Sir."

She spun and strode from the office.

"Traitorous, ungrateful bitch," he shouted.

The slamming door cut off any further insults or threats he hurled at her. That was the last time she would ever report to him. So what if he reprimanded her in front of everyone and deleted everything from her bio but junior security skills? The money she'd already gotten from Morland would more than cover any fine she owed. Maybe she'd receive fewer offers now, but the ones she did get would be from Morland and his allies, and would likely pay better. They wouldn't care if she disregarded protocol.

Nova's shoulders tensed as she hurried toward the mess hall. Disregarding protocol. What the hell was she doing?

"The right thing," she declared. Connington's job was to advise and support the members of the RMC and handle disputes if a contract was illegal or exploitative. Not to bully people for his own gain.

Truth. Unfortunately, her perfectly rational argument did nothing to convince her body to relax. She'd taken a step into the unknown and she didn't like it. Not even a little bit. Sometimes doing the right thing sucked.

She ducked into the mess only long enough to grab a muffin and two bananas. Technically, bananas were limited to one per person, since they didn't grow well on Mars and had to be imported from the few banana farms on Earth. But they were her favorite, and she wasn't going to chance missing out tomorrow if she got called for server duty. Servers never got anything but scattered leftovers.

Another step into the world of disobedience. Maybe this was how Wyatt had ended up a smuggler. First you yell at some privileged asshole, and the next thing you know, you're stealing bananas. Wyatt probably smuggled bananas so the people of Dystopia could buy them at a reasonable cost.

Nova jogged toward her room. She could pop back on the vidscreen and ask him. *Sorry I disappeared. I was summoned to a "conversation" with a giant prick. Speaking of which, do you smuggle bananas?*

He'd laugh at that.

A bit of tension leached from her body. Sure, life was one big snafu, but she could make Wyatt smile. And yes, maybe that was more due to his sunny nature than her admittedly paltry ability to spread happiness, but it eased her heart nonetheless.

She had slid her key only halfway into the lock when the *clip-clop* of high-heeled shoes against the synthetic floorboards made her head snap up.

"Nova!" Dr. Irene Castelbury jogged down the hall, her long locs bouncing around her shoulders. She wore bright pink scrubs today, with matching eyeshadow to frame her amber eyes. A slight copper flush tinted her warm brown cheeks. She skittered to a halt at Nova's side, then glanced behind her, as if afraid someone might have followed. "Do you have a minute?"

Nova opened the door and waved her friend inside. "What's the trouble?"

Nova took a seat on the bed, beside her abandoned vidscreen. The blank screen taunted her, but she shoved it aside to make room for Irene.

The doctor shook her head and fidgeted with the

stethoscope hanging around her neck. "I need to be getting back to work ASAP. But I couldn't not tell you what popped up in the appointment requests. Your name was flagged as urgent for a mandatory psychiatric evaluation."

"What?" Nova fumbled her breakfast, and the muffin slipped from her grasp and rolled across the floor.

Irene scooped it up and checked that the paper wrapping hadn't come loose. "No harm done." She handed it back to Nova. "Eat. You'll want to keep your strength up."

Nova snorted. "Why? You know as well as I that psych evals are nothing more than an excuse to kick someone out. So that's it." She shrugged. "I'm done. Out of a job."

Nova could remember only two instances when anyone in the Corps had been sent for a mandatory eval. Both had been dismissed within a day, and no one knew the real reasons. There had been plenty of whispers, though.

"I could try to take the assignment. I'd have to swap things around and come up with a reason to move you from psych staff to med staff…"

Nova held up a hand. "Not necessary."

Irene gave her a skeptical look. The doctor was a natural helper, always the first to offer assistance in a crisis. In the years Nova had known her, she'd completely overhauled the reproductive health system, making sure the often under-represented members of the Corps had sufficient access to menstrual products and contraception. She never hesitated to offer medical advice, and was unwaveringly dedicated to the health and wellbeing of her patients.

"I should pack up and leave," Nova continued. "Better to leave on my own terms than be thrown out. Maybe I'll go freelance." She tried to smile, but could only manage a bit of a grimace. They both knew freelancing was illegal.

"Are you sure you don't want help? You know you don't deserve this."

Nova bit her lower lip and took a few seconds to mull things over. "Yes." She blew out a slow breath. "Yes, I'll go. This place isn't right for me anymore. Maybe it's not right for anyone. I don't really know. But I… I don't belong here."

She didn't belong anywhere. Fuck, that hurt. But for now she still had Morland's contract. She wasn't giving that up.

Irene nodded. "I'll miss you. And I won't be the only one. A lot of the younger women look up to you."

"Good to know." This time Nova did manage a smile. "I could use friends on the inside. I have a feeling that secrets are going to start spilling sooner rather than later. And I'm sure C is in deep. It might take work from both in and out to put things to rights."

Irene's fingers stilled on her stethoscope. "I'm not sure things were ever as right as you think they were. The system has flaws. Most systems do. And eventually, they crack." She sighed. "I need to return to the clinic. Good luck."

"Thank you. I'll be in touch."

Nova waited until the door had fully latched behind Irene, then opened her locker and began stuffing all her possessions into her duffel. Each drop in the bag compounded the sense of how small her world had been. Basic health and hygiene items. A few uniforms. Some casual clothes, mostly black and gray, all military style. Two dresses: the one she'd worn on her date with Wyatt and the ballgown.

She spread the dresses out on the bed. When she left, she'd sling them over her arm to hide the duffel, and if anyone asked, she'd say she was taking the dresses to a professional cleaner.

And that was it. Her life, in a single bag. The only things

left were her breakfast and the vidscreen—which as far as she knew wouldn't work outside the RMC network.

She tapped the screen. The conversation with Wyatt had closed, but she called it up and tapped a quick message.

**Pratt-Nova-RMC: Got a spare room?**

# 18

"This thing has been following me."

Wyatt grinned. He'd missed that lovely scowl more than he'd realized. Running around with Nova in the dark hadn't allowed him to see it at its full force, and talking over the network left him with nothing but his imagination. This was much better. He swung the door wide to allow Nova and Drone 23 into his sitting room.

Nova strode in and deposited a plain canvas duffel and two beautiful dresses onto his sofa. The moment her hands were free, they went right to her hips.

"I appreciate you checking on me when I vanished without explanation," she huffed. "But don't you think this is unnecessary? You know perfectly well I have no need for an escort."

"Of course not." Wyatt held out a hand, palm up, and the drone landed there. He gave it a pat. "Good boy. Nova, this is Drone 23. He monitors Ag Sector 3 and was close enough to call on for this mission. I'll be reviewing his camera footage to see who took notice of your departure and who, if anyone, followed. Another set of eyes would be appreciated, especially since you might recognize people I don't."

"Oh, fine." She glanced up at the ceiling and heaved an exasperated sigh. "Send your pets after me. But don't expect me to make repairs when they interfere with me and get whacked or stepped on."

"She won't step on you," Wyatt told the drone. "She only pretends to be mean." He walked into his office and ended the temporary assignment. The drone zipped out the open door, headed back to his usual work.

"Better?" he asked, returning to Nova.

"Yes. I don't understand how you're never bothered by machines hovering around you."

He shrugged one shoulder. "I know they're there to protect me. You know how to stab and shoot and fight. I don't. All I can do is scream and run."

Her scowl faded, and she folded her arms in a casual stance. "An underrated talent. You ran well at the spaceport."

"Thanks. So…" He gestured at her belongings. "You need a place to stay? Is that my fault?"

"Indirectly, yes. Connington lost his shit because I took the job for Morland and terminated the contract to investigate you."

Wyatt's heart did a funny little skip. "You did? Officially?"

"I cursed at Connington and stormed out of his office."

*Good for you.* Wyatt swallowed the words, fearing she might interpret them as patronizing, when they were anything but. He had nothing but pride and admiration for her and what she'd done today. It was damned hard to walk away from everything you knew. Twenty years later, he still smarted from it, still couldn't bring himself to claim this space as anything but a temporary home. The bare walls testified to that well enough.

Nova continued, saving him from the need to reply. "I could hardly do anything else. He's done nothing to earn my loyalty. And how could I throw you in jail? You smuggle textbooks for kids who can't afford them. I'd figured you were a selfish bastard, like most toffs, and a criminal to boot. But you turned out to be a decent person."

She sounded almost annoyed, which somehow made it one of the best compliments he'd ever been given.

"I humbly apologize for my inconvenient integrity." He gave her his best smirk.

She gave him the finger.

Wyatt laughed. God, she was magnificent. He wanted to hug her and dance with her and take her to bed.

Bed. Shit. She didn't have a bed anymore.

"I suppose we've gotten off topic," he said soberly. "You need a place to stay."

"I do."

*Stay here. With me.*

Again Wyatt quashed the impulse to speak the first words that popped into his mind. Too presumptuous. Much too presumptuous. Her desire to get him naked didn't equal a desire to live with him.

"Unfortunately we don't have any guest rooms," he admitted. "But I'm sure we can make a place for you, if you'd like."

"That won't be necessary." Her expression was impassive, showing neither pleasure nor disappointment. "If I can leave my things here, I'll go out in search of a room for rent."

"You and your things are welcome here for as long as you need. Please don't rush out on my account."

Of course she already had a plan. She hadn't come here for his help. She wanted a temporary base of operations while she executed her mission, and she'd come here to inform him of the situation. Silly to think otherwise. With all that had happened, it was a wonder she hadn't decided he wasn't worth the bother.

His watch began to beep, and he slapped at it to silence the alarm. He hadn't eaten breakfast. Oops. The thought triggered a tremendous growl in his stomach. Or was that her stomach? Crap, had she eaten this morning?

"Did you get breakfast before you left?" he blurted.

"I have some food in my duffel." Another growl, definitely hers this time.

Wyatt motioned for her to follow him. "Let me give you the tour and make you some breakfast. I could use something to eat myself."

This, he could do for her. If she walked out never to be seen again, at least she would have a full belly.

"Here's the tuppence tour," he announced as they stepped into the hall. "You've seen my suite. Next door down is Rion's. Identical to mine: sitting room, office, bedroom with attached bath. And through that open arch to the right is the shared kitchen and dining area."

Wyatt flicked on the light as they stepped inside. Nova stopped in her tracks. The kitchen was, frankly, enormous, easily large enough to hold all the cooks and servers needed for the rare occasions when Leo hosted a formal dinner. Wyatt hadn't even opened more than a fraction of the cabinets, and still wasn't sure what some of the equipment was for. The only area he cared about was the small space with a simple stove and sink where they could cook for themselves.

"Ignore all that. Have a seat." He waved a hand at the row of barstools along a high marble counter. "Do you like eggs? Toast?"

"Both," Nova replied. She pulled out a stool and sat.

"Excellent. I'm no professional, but I'm highly competent with eggs and toast. How about to drink? Coffee? Tea? Milk?"

"Just water, please."

Wyatt filled a glass with cool water from the tap, then began gathering everything he needed for eggs and toast. "Scrambled okay?"

"Mm-hmm." Nova picked up a newspaper—probably left behind yesterday—and began leafing through it.

Wyatt cracked eggs and popped toast into the toaster, humming the song that had been stuck in his head since he'd woken up. Behind him, Nova remained quiet except for the occasional clink of her glass or the rustle of the newspaper. He let his hips sway to the music in his head, in case she was watching him work. Maybe he could entice her into a mid-morning tryst.

His imagination ran wild with the idea as he pushed the eggs around the pan. Him on top on his couch. Her on top on his bed. Up against the bedroom wall. Taking turns kneeling by his office chair with their hands tied so lips and tongues had to do all the work. God, he was hornier for her than he'd been for anyone in years.

He plopped a scoop of eggs atop a piece of toast and added twice his usual amount of hot sauce. Today was a day for spice.

He arranged Nova's food separately so she could eat it however she liked, then turned from the stove to place both plates on the bar counter. "Do you want anything to put on your eggs or toast?" Next time he'd know how she liked things. Maybe he could even surprise her with food already prepared.

Nova glanced up from her paper. It lay open to a page of advertisements, and her finger rested halfway down the page, beneath bolded text reading, "room for rent."

*She is leaving. Don't get used to this. There probably won't be a "next time."*

"Plain is fine."

"Are you sure? We have cheese, onions, jam or butter for the toast?"

"Butter would be nice, thanks. Only salt for the eggs."

"That I can do." Wyatt fetched her both, then took a seat beside her. "Find anything promising?" He was going to be helpful, and not a creep who insisted she stay with him. He took a large bite of his eggs and toast, hoping the burn of the hot sauce would distract him from his lust.

"I don't know," Nova admitted. "I don't know all the street and sector names. I don't know if these prices are reasonable. Or whether 'with view' means it looks over something nice or only has one small window."

"Probably the latter. The best way to find a room is to know someone."

"Figures." She sighed and shoved the paper aside, then dug into her food. "The eggs are good, thanks."

"You're welcome. I'm happy to whip some up any time. Or take you out. I like feeding people."

She nodded around another mouthful before swallowing and saying, "The way you like feeding your animals."

"Um…" He'd never thought about it like that, but maybe she was right. He liked providing for the animals in his life, making sure they were safe and healthy. And he wanted the same thing for his friends: a comfortable home, good food, companionship. He liked making them happy.

Huh. Maybe that was the reason he wanted Nova to stay here. He was naturally inclined to be a provider.

"Do you smuggle bananas?" she asked.

His fork stabbed into the eggs and stayed there. "What?"

"Do you smuggle bananas? You said you like to feed people, and the import tax makes bananas expensive."

"Ah. Yes, I've smuggled a number of food items. Bananas, chocolate, tea, coffee, sugar, alcohol. If it's taxed, I've probably smuggled it. Are you bugged? Is a group of goons about to swoop in now and haul me away? You know, since I failed the secret passphrase."

Nova cocked her head and frowned at him. "What secret passphrase?"

"The banana thing. It sounded like a secret code. You say, 'Do you smuggle bananas?' and then I'm supposed to reply, 'No, but I once swallowed an aubergine.'"

Nova choked on a bite of toast. "That…" she half-coughed, half-laughed, "is not a passphrase. It's the world's worst innuendo."

Wyatt grinned at her. "Why not both?"

She pointed her fork at his chest. "You are a force of chaos."

"An emissary of entropy," he agreed.

"You're lucky you're cute. You can smile and wiggle your tight little ass and everyone forgets that you're an hour late, you've replaced their coffee pot with an automaton, and there are fifteen different animals trailing in your wake."

Wyatt fluttered his lashes. "I sound sexy as hell."

"Nah," a deep voice said from the hall. "You sound the same as always. But you cooked breakfast, and that's pretty fucking sexy." Rion strode into the kitchen, making a beeline for the stove. "You two seem cozy. Breakfast date?" He grabbed a plate and dumped all the remaining eggs onto it.

"Nova's on the hunt for a flat," Wyatt said quickly. "I was just feeding her."

"Ah." Rion took a seat on Nova's other side. "He's trying to lure you into bed by way of your stomach? A decent start.

He doesn't know how to cook much, but have him bake you the triple chocolate cookies. I'd do him every which way for those cookies."

Wyatt snorted. "You'd do me every which way if I crooked my little finger. You are notorious, Brandt."

"Look, Aubrey's ace and Leo's an old maid. They don't get around much and the team needs someone who's gonna score."

"You should have been born a bastard," Nova murmured dryly. "The RMC has a betting book for who will sleep with the most fellow mercs. Guess I'm out of the running now."

Rion's smile faded as his eyebrows rose. "Did they kick you out, or what? Why *are* you looking for a flat?"

"You could say I resigned."

"Congrats!" Rion held up a hand for a high-five, but Nova only eyed him doubtfully. He shrugged and put his hand down, then grabbed the newspaper and tossed it aside. "You don't want any of those hovels. I know a place."

"Do you? Great! Would I be able to look at it today?"

"I'll take you after breakfast. It's on the way to my office."

Wyatt peered around Nova to frown at Rion. His "office" could mean anything from one of his newspaper buildings to the brewery that made his favorite beer.

Rion gazed studiously at his plate, shoveling eggs into his mouth.

Wyatt leaned back with a sigh and finished his own breakfast. It didn't matter whether Nova ended up at Rion's mysterious place or halfway to Jupiter. She wasn't staying with *him*. And it was ridiculous to fret over it.

He swallowed the last of his eggs, relishing the burn of the spicy sauce. Their affair was like this—still hot on his lips and tongue. They'd been flirting when Rion had interrupted.

The heat hadn't faded, and they had time yet to savor it. At her place or his. His bed was no different than any other.

His imagination, however, continued to conjure her in that single location, her black hair a sharp contrast against neon-green satin, her soft exhalations punctuated by the squeaks of a bat and the hum of factory machines below.

Brains were weird.

# 19

"Good evening, Ms. Pratt."

Nova turned her head to see Aubrey only a few paces behind her. He was dressed to the nines in a black tailcoat, snow-white cravat, and red brocade waistcoat. His polished boots made hardly a sound on the cobblestone street. Stealthy.

"Lord Wells." She paused for him to catch up and they entered the factory together. "Going somewhere tonight?"

"Always. A ball or the club or a dinner party. Endless entertainment."

His tone had a sarcastic edge she'd never heard from him before, and she gave him a quizzical look. "Boring?"

"Exceedingly dull," he confirmed. "I have to spend this evening losing at cards. I might pretend to be drunk to spice things up."

"My brother Jaime despises parties, but he's my father's heir so he has to attend."

"Lucky for him, he won't be at this particular party. Let me show you up to the meeting room."

They ascended the stairs to the apartment level and walked past Wyatt's rooms, Rion's rooms, and the kitchen before turning down another hall.

"This door is the conference room." Aubrey reached for

the handle. "Next door down is the official Chamber room, and everything beyond is Leo's."

"You don't have rooms here?"

He held the door open for her. "I like my house in the country. It's only fifteen minutes by trolley."

Nova stepped into the conference room to discover that she and Aubrey were the last to arrive. Even Wyatt was already seated in one of the leather chairs that ringed the heavy, oval-shaped table. The room itself was sparse, with beige walls and no extraneous furniture or decor. Simple recessed lighting illuminated the tabletop. She'd sat in a number of nearly-identical rooms on the RMC campus.

"Welcome," Morland greeted everyone, when Nova and Aubrey had taken their seats. "Thanks to your collective promptness we are able to begin five minutes early tonight." The staid duke wore a boyish smile, as if he'd been given a special gift.

Rion and Wyatt high-fived.

"Alarms for the win!" Wyatt declared. "Oh. Better shut off my late-for-meeting alarm."

Nova smiled as he fiddled with his watch. She shifted in her seat until she felt comfortable and folded her hands atop the table, ready for the meeting to formally begin. No one had a notebook or paper to take notes, so she glanced around the room for the camera that would be recording them. She found none. Odd.

"Aubrey is officially a wastrel," Rion stated, without any call-to-order or by-your-leave.

Nova swallowed her instinctive response to question the protocol. None of the others appeared in the least perturbed. In the RMC, meetings adhered to a strict code and documentation. No one would dare start their report until given leave to do so.

"He's a spendthrift and a gambler, and has racked up thousands of pounds of debt. When the matchmaking mamas find out, they'll be snatching their children away faster than a racer at the hippodrome." Rion withdrew a slip of paper from his pocket. "Here's Fanny's quick draft of an article about slumming. If you all like it, she'll clean it up and we'll run it tomorrow."

"I'm sure it's fine, but I can look it over when we're done here," Leo replied. "Anything else to report?"

Rion flashed a devilish smile. "Not that you want to hear about. Oh, but I did help Nova find a flat."

Leo's brows rose. "You're not living in the barracks anymore?" he asked her.

"I quit."

"She told Connington to eat shit and die," Wyatt added proudly.

Her cheeks warmed and she felt a funny twinge in her belly. "Not in those words."

"But you told him off all the same." He beamed at her, and the power of that smile penetrated down to her bones.

Oh, God, she was blushing. Blushing and desperate to kiss him senseless. Had she been so starved for praise that a single compliment brought her to her knees?

*Fuuuuck.* Now she was envisioning things she might do while down in that position.

She quickly turned her head. If he kept grinning at her like she'd been awarded the damned Victoria Cross, she was going to do something foolish.

"Yes, I quit," she repeated, staring at Leo's perfectly knotted, entirely unthreatening, blue silk tie. "I'm still honoring our contract, of course, and I am open to continuing to take contracts from you or others in the future. The rooms Lord Brandt recommended are not far from here, and suit my needs. I don't expect any disruption because of the change in circumstances. I also have contacts in the RMC in the event we need information from that quarter."

Leo rubbed his chin. "That is an unexpected development, but one we can adapt to. At present, the contract was entered into legally and therefore remains valid. You can consider yourself still under my employ. I did get a list of the crew taking over security at the spaceport. Mercs, not DPST, thank God. The team is headed by a Michael Pratt and a Trevor Pratt. I assume you know them."

"My brothers," Nova replied. "They're assholes. But both exceptional at what they do. Probably the best security people in the nation. And you don't need to worry that they're Connington's lap-dogs. They're too ambitious for that. They're aiming to be his replacement someday. Or maybe to take over my father's dukedom. If you wanted someone to pressure him to support a change in inheritance law, they'd gladly help."

Aubrey let out a low, feral growling noise. "If he wants to name one of them heir, I'm voting no for real. James will be a good duke—a far sight better than some power-hungry twat."

"Oh, absolutely," Nova agreed. Jamie was the only one of her siblings who didn't take after their father. Her other brothers were selfish jerks, and the youngest of the bunch, her only sister, was possibly actually evil.

"When do we get to abolish all dukes?" Rion asked. "Down with dukes! And not in a fun way."

Morland appeared unfazed by this declaration and similarly unconcerned that they'd wandered off-topic. He merely steepled his fingers and rested them against his chin, his expression pensive. No rules, no note-taking, no hierarchy of command; this had to be the strangest meeting she'd ever participated in.

"Back to security?" Wyatt prompted. "The drones are doing great. Everything has been normal on the security feed. Did a scan for the anomalies with the ships going through the splices. They only go back a few weeks and the number increased recently. Only one more instance since we discovered it, though, and that came at a low-traffic time. It was a little harder to spot because the whole thing happened before any other ships passed through. I tweaked the program to mark any more like that. They're probably trying to be more circumspect now that they know we know. Not much more to do on my end except continue to watch and wait."

"I hate waiting. I want results, goddammit!"

All eyes turned to Leo. From the utter silence, Nova surmised that the others were as surprised by the outburst as she was.

"Sorry," the duke amended. "None of this is your fault. I'm just..." He steeled himself with a deep breath. "We've been making such incremental progress, and now there's a probable conspiracy threatening to upend the status quo, and I'm afraid we're going to have to start all over again. I don't know if I have another twenty years in me."

Aubrey scooted his chair over and took his cousin's hand. "You're doing great, Leo. None of us would have gotten this far without you."

Yeah, this was one hundred percent the strangest meeting she'd ever attended. In her world, every interaction involved jockeying for position. Alliances were common, but far from permanent, and in a situation like this no one paused to comfort another. It was all who could get the most contracts, who could make the most money, who could earn the favor of the highest-ranking aristocrat. Nothing else mattered.

Fuck that world. This world was uncharted territory to her, but at least people here cared about each other. From now on, she was a Dystopian.

God, that was terrifying.

Her apprehension must have shown on her face, because Wyatt looked at her and mouthed, *You okay?*

She nodded. There was work to be done. The world was a mess, and someone had to fix it.

Aubrey gave Leo's hand a squeeze before releasing it. "I do have a lead, so that should make you feel better. I spent the afternoon at the club with the gamesters—I hope you all appreciate that I'm ruining my reputation for you—and was subjected to exhaustive detail about all their 'tiresome' creditors and the number of clubs and gambling dens they've been kicked out of. The only man there not feigning happiness was Lord Eberwhite."

Leo grimaced. "That man has never once voted with an ounce of forethought. I think he would happily lick Deimos's boots if asked. The worst sort of sycophant, but a loyal one."

"He let slip that he's expecting his fortunes to improve," Aubrey explained. "He wasn't supposed to mention it, obviously, but he was in his cups. When he realized, he panicked and made some vague comments about an investment, followed by a bald-faced lie about hydrogen mining. That's all I learned, but I think he's worth pursuing. I'll keep an ear open when I'm out tonight as well."

"We could interrogate him at the races," Rion suggested. "The first race of the Imperial Cup is in two days, and Eberwhite's box is next to ours. He'll be there to place bets, and we go often enough that it won't look strange."

"Excellent!" Leo's face brightened. "In two days, we'll

gather at the hippodrome. Be dressed in your best. We'll need everyone's support to protect my cousin from his terrible gambling habit."

"I hate this job," Aubrey muttered.

"Am I to accompany you on this outing?" Nova wondered.

Surprise flashed across the duke's face. "Of course. You're part of the team."

"I'd wager Wyatt wouldn't go without you anyway," Rion added.

*Part of the team.* Nova liked hearing it. The words rolled around nicely in her head. They also made her a bit queasy. Once again she had the sensation of being given an award she hadn't earned.

"Anyone who wants can bring a date," Leo suggested. "We want it to appear that we are solely there for fun. That's all for tonight. Be here at the same time tomorrow for a quick update in case anyone learns anything new."

Rion slapped a palm down on the table and pushed himself to his feet. "Drivers, start your engines! Night, all."

One-by-one, they filed out of the room. Wyatt brushed up behind Nova, placing a gentle touch to her arm.

"Are we still on for tonight?" he murmured.

In all the ups and downs of the day, she'd forgotten about their scheduled tryst, but the husky tone of his voice brought back a flood of lurid thoughts. A healthy romp sounded just the thing to end a wild twenty-four hours, and mark the beginning of her new life.

She pressed her body against his in an unmistakable answer and whispered in his ear, "Do you smuggle bananas?"

# 20

NOVA PAUSED IN THE MIDDLE of Wyatt's office. The room had the same bare walls and neutral carpet as his sitting room, but here the contrast between those and Wyatt's personal belongings was even more dramatic. Three large screens stood atop his desk, along with a gleaming brass and copper keyboard. Mechanical parts she couldn't identify, bottles of nail polish, and small puzzle toys in various stages of completion covered the remainder of the available space. A pair of large bookshelves flanked the desk, books and papers haphazardly mixed with knickknacks and framed photographs of his friends and pets. Colorful stickers plastered the sides of both shelves and the desk, mostly rainbows, flowers, and cartoon animals.

"Yeah, it's a mess," Wyatt said. "Every six months or so I'll go on a cleaning spree and make it all look nice, but it never lasts long."

Nova's gaze shifted to Wyatt's face. Oddly enough, the thought of tidying the room hadn't occurred to her until he'd mentioned it. If it had been her workspace, she would have thrown everything out and started over. But this was his place, and it was so *him*. Chaotic, yes, but also vibrant, joyful, and fascinating.

Yet still strangely impermanent.

"No need to apologize on my account," she assured him. "I prefer the insight into your character to a pristine, sterile room."

His brows rose. "Do you? I must be corrupting you." His smile turned wicked. "Shall I go down on my knees and beg your forgiveness?"

"Hmmm."

She followed him into the bedroom, where a massive wardrobe and a comfortably large bed dominated the otherwise empty space. The unmade bed gave her a momentary twinge of discomfort—she couldn't remember a day in her life when she'd not straightened her sheets with perfect military precision. The gleaming neon green of the bedding, though, made her smile.

"Your favorite color, I'd wager?"

Wyatt ran his fingers through his spiky hair. "How did you guess?"

"I've been investigating you, remember?" She took a seat on the corner of the bed. "And now it's time for you to remove those clothes, as they are obstructing my surveillance."

He whipped off his t-shirt and tossed it aside. He was leaner than any of her previous lovers, his muscles less defined, and his skin was a pearlescent, almost translucent white where the sun had never touched it. In the RMC, he would have been called a pampered debutante and relentlessly mocked. As if raw strength and pent-up aggression were prerequisites for manhood.

Thank God she was out of that place.

"You are so damned pretty," Nova said, as he worked the button of his jeans.

Wyatt blushed, the color starting in his cheeks and rapidly spreading down his neck past his collarbones.

Nova's gaze snagged on the small white scar, now

highlighted by the surrounding pink flush. Even as he continued to undress, that scar held her attention. He habitually touched the spot when talking to his drones, and she wanted to know the reason, in exhaustive detail. The curiosity gnawed at her, warring with her sense of propriety. Scars could be badges of pride or of trauma, and asking without permission was a hard no.

Wyatt twisted and bent to pull off one leg of his snug jeans. The change of position gave Nova her first good look at the tattoo adorning his upper arm. It was a bird feather, about four inches long. The tip of the feather was a mottled tan, fading to nearly white at the bottom. Wide horizontal bands of a darker brown punctuated the background at regular intervals.

"That's a beautiful tattoo."

Wyatt wriggled his other leg free from his pants. "Thanks. It's a tawny owl feather."

"It looks quite true to life." Nova almost cringed at her own words. She had no idea what a tawny owl looked like, much less its individual feathers. "Owls are night birds, right?" she continued rambling. "That's why people who stay up late are night owls?"

This was absurd. He was standing nearly naked in front of her, his cock a hard bulge beneath his underwear. And she was making inane comments about owls because she couldn't suppress her burning need to know things about him.

"Correct," he replied, as if her questions were entirely normal. "They're incredible birds. Silent hunters gliding through the darkness, using their large eyes and finely tuned ears to catch tiny prey a mere human could never even hope to find." He took a step toward her, holding his arm out. "If you take a good look at the feather, you can see that the edge is fringed. It's one of the special adaptations that allows for noiseless flight. Would you like to see it up close?"

The flutter of his lashes was flirtatious, but his tone of voice reminded her of an excited child showing off a toy. Her curiosity pleased him.

A new wave of desire swept over her body and she made a sharp gesture at the bed. "Lie down."

Wyatt obeyed without hesitation. He stretched out atop the sheets, displaying his body for her perusal.

Nova removed her boots and jacket, then settled beside him. The rest could wait.

"You offered me 'other options' that night on the trolley," she said. "What do you like?"

He laughed. "Better to ask what I don't like. Don't use your teeth on my cock, and if I end up not liking something else, I'll tell you. Fair?"

"Fair." She allowed herself a moment to take him in, noting the pale hairs scattered across his torso and the small freckle near his navel. She circled his tattoo with a finger. It was the only one he had, unless something lay hidden beneath the tight briefs he still wore.

*Tell me the meaning behind this. Tell me about your scar. Tell me all your secrets.*

Nova had no right to such private information. But she did—for the moment, at least—have the right to look at him. To study him.

"Touch yourself," she commanded.

Wyatt squirmed free of his underwear, tossed it aside, and wrapped a hand around his erection. The bright blue of his fingernails screamed, "Look here!" and Nova was happy to oblige. He pleasured himself with slow, steady strokes, as though content to allow her to watch him all night.

She sat up and began methodically removing the remainder

of her clothing. Her intent was purely practical: get herself naked. But when she glanced at Wyatt's face, she found his eyes glazed with lust, his lips parted in eager anticipation.

"Don't stop," he urged. "I like this show."

Show. Nova didn't know whether to laugh or wince. Not once had she even imagined herself performing a strip tease for a lover. It seemed ridiculously unnecessary when both parties already knew they were going to fuck. Why not just get on with it?

Wyatt's grip on his cock tightened, and the flush of pink continued to deepen and spread across his body. Then again, perhaps the idea did have merit. If her ordinary undressing turned him on, what could she do with something more deliberate?

Nova slid off the bed and stood where he would have a clear view of her. Holding his gaze, she undid the buttons of her fly one-by-one, then let the trousers slither to the floor.

"You like this?"

"Yes," he breathed.

"Good." She kicked the trousers away and pulled off her stockings. "Don't expect any singing or dancing."

Wyatt let out a choked laugh. "I won't." He licked his lips. "But I can do that for you sometime, if you like."

Hell yes, she would like. She could watch him all day and still not get her fill of his teasing smiles and boundless enthusiasm.

Nova pulled down one strap of her plain black brassiere. "You also don't get frilly undergarments. I don't own any."

Everything she had was made for practicality and comfort. Even the corset she wore with her ballgown had been designed for flexibility and support rather than fashion.

"I like what you have." Wyatt waved with his free hand. "It's very you." His eyes slid briefly closed and he slowed the pace of his self-pleasure. "If you don't want me to get off just looking at you, you'd better say so."

Nova discarded her bra, then folded her arms beneath her bare breasts and scowled down at him. His breath hitched, and she felt an answering throb between her legs.

"Are you telling me to tell you what to do?" she demanded.

"Yep." His smile was sultry and unrepentant. "I like to challenge authority."

Nova stepped out of her panties and climbed back onto the bed, kneeling beside Wyatt. "But you *are* the authority, Lord Windborne. In your little realm of Dystopia, with your army of mechanical minions."

She bit her lip. For God's sake, couldn't she keep her mind on what she was doing for more than one damn minute? She was here for sex, not to slip back into interrogation mode for a contract she'd walked away from.

"I have a 'mechanical minion' in the nightstand behind you, if you'd like it," Wyatt offered. He arched his eyebrows and increased the pace of his masturbation while his gaze traveled up and down her naked body.

"Not so fast. I'm not done with you."

He held up both hands. "Yes, ma'am."

Nova turned to open the nightstand drawer. A gleaming vibrator, a strap-on with two different-sized attachments, lube, condoms, a pair of fuzzy handcuffs, and several silk scarves were inside. So many possibilities. So many things she could do to him or he could do to her.

She selected the vibrator. Enough woolgathering. It was time to get down to business.

She clicked the vibrator up to a moderate speed and slid it between her legs. A sigh escaped her lips as she rubbed the toy against her clit. Yes. That was what she needed.

"Get up here and kiss me."

Wyatt scrambled to his knees and caught her up in an embrace. He kissed her hard, thrusting his tongue into her mouth with desperate hunger and little finesse. Nova threaded the fingers of her left hand into his hair, holding him where she wanted him, answering the kiss with equal fervor.

Her breasts flattened against his chest, and their hips rocked together, his cock making contact with her hand and the vibrator. She pressed the toy against his rigid length and he moaned into her mouth. She clicked the speed up a couple notches.

"Nova," he gasped against her lips. "Fuck."

Nova positioned the tip of the dildo precisely where she liked it best, sending pleasure spiraling through her. "Stroke yourself again," she commanded.

Wyatt wrapped his hand around both his cock and the vibrator, fingers clenching tight beneath hers. He set a frantic pace, stroking and thrusting, his breaths coming faster and faster.

"Fuck, yes." His head tipped back and his eyes closed. "Nova... Shit... I..."

Nova grabbed the headboard for support. She whimpered and ground against the toy, adding pressure to the merciless vibrations.

*Yes, oh, yes, oh, yes.*

Wyatt made a strangled noise, and it was all the encouragement she needed. She gasped and bucked as pleasure exploded inside her. Ripples of ecstasy trembled down her limbs to the very tips of her fingers and toes. If her hand hadn't been clenched on the headboard, she surely would have toppled off the bed. Some distant part of her brain noticed Wyatt's own shuddering climax and the wet, sticky feel of his spend where her fingers clutched the still-buzzing vibrator.

They sagged against one another, chests heaving, bodies limp. Wyatt's skin was soft and warm, and he smelled of sex and herbal shampoo. Drowsiness fell heavily on Nova, and she imagined crumpling onto the sheets and falling asleep in his arms.

"I, um, guess we ought to clean up," Wyatt said, voice raspy.

Nova jerked, awareness of her surroundings flooding back in. "Oh. Yes." She struggled to her feet, her legs unsteady in the aftermath of orgasm. "I should be getting home."

Or whatever passed for home. Home wasn't the barracks anymore, but it wasn't an empty, unfamiliar apartment, either. And it certainly wasn't here in Wyatt's room.

"Yeah. Bathroom's there if you want to go first." Wyatt indicated the open door.

"Thanks."

Nova made quick use of the facilities, then gathered up her scattered clothing and dressed while Wyatt cleaned himself. By the time he emerged—naked except for a towel wrapped around his waist—she was presentable enough not to attract the notice of anyone on the street.

"Thanks for a nice evening," she said. "I'll see you tomorrow at the meeting, if not before."

He nodded. "Tomorrow. Goodnight."

"Night." She turned and let herself out.

When she stepped out onto the street a minute later, the squeak of an animal stopped her in her tracks. She looked up in time to see Flurry flying away from the factory in search of excitement or fun or whatever bats did. She'd have to ask Wyatt.

Adorable, captivating, sexy-as-hell Wyatt.

Fuck. She should have kissed him goodnight.

# 21

"No BAGS, NO DRONES, no outside food or drink," the bored event staffer called out over the crowd shuffling through Gate A of the Victoria Regina National Hippodrome for the evening's big race. "Have your tickets ready as you enter. No bags, no drones, no outside food or drink."

Wyatt tucked another drone into one of Leo's pockets.

"No bags, no drones—"

"For the love of God, Wyatt," Leo grumbled. "Do I look like a walking suitcase?"

"I can't fit them in my own pockets," Wyatt whispered.

"It's not my fault you'd rather show off your ass than carry anything useful."

Nova patted said ass appreciatively. They'd barely spoken since she'd fled his room like it was on fire, leaving Wyatt disappointed and extremely confused. Today, however, she touched him possessively, taking his arm or placing a hand on his hip or shoulder. He hadn't even realized he'd been on edge the past two days, until the first brush of her fingers had caused his entire body to unclench in relief.

Well, every part of his body except his too-eager cock and his poor, bewildered brain.

"Can't you stride up to the entrance surrounded by weaponized machines and say, 'I am Lord Windborne. Let me pass'?" Nova wondered.

Wyatt wrinkled his nose. "That would be awfully rude."

"Whereas breaking the rules is perfectly polite."

"Leo is breaking the rules. Not me."

This earned him a glare from Leo, but the duke didn't remove a single drone from his pockets as he strode up to the VIP ticket-taker and displayed his pass.

"Good evening, Your Grace." The ticket taker—a middle-aged white man in a worn uniform—bowed. "How many tonight?"

"Seven," Leo replied.

"Excellent." The man tapped the vidscreen in his hands. "Refreshments will be sent to your box shortly. Enjoy the race." He bowed again and waved the group in.

The walkway to the box was all but empty, most of the VIPs having arrived well ahead of the race to begin their drinking and gambling. A few men lingered outside the box entrances, talking odds and predictions, but most people had already settled themselves.

Wyatt glanced at his watch. Twenty minutes to race time, which meant the fanfares were about to begin.

Aubrey pushed impatiently past him and yanked the door to the box open. His red shirt emblazoned with the blue wave of Team Aqua and his matching plaid cap proclaimed his unwavering allegiance. He'd been scowling when Wyatt had arrived half an hour late to their meet-up, and hadn't stopped since.

"I'm sorry," Wyatt said for probably the tenth time.

"It's fine. We made it in time," Aubrey grumbled, but he disappeared into the box without looking back.

"I think it all works out perfectly." Nova took Wyatt's arm to lead him inside. "Aubrey shows up grumpy at the last minute and everyone thinks we deliberately kept him away to prevent him from gambling." She looked Wyatt up and down. "But maybe you shouldn't have worn green."

Wyatt sighed. He couldn't care less about team allegiances. He liked the technology. He routinely scoured the newspapers for articles on new formulas for tire rubber, or the latest designs in light-weight steam engines. He knew the names of the techs in the pit crews and the team engineers. But he didn't give a damn who won, as long as he had machines to ogle.

"I'll wear blue next time," he murmured, taking a seat in the front row of the box beside Aubrey.

Aubrey gave him a small smile as the band struck up the opening fanfare. "We're good. I'm just nervous. We have a real chance this year, but our qualifying placement put us next to the Comets, and they're notorious for rough driving. If we take damage at the start, it could fuck up the whole season. Plus I'm the only one who didn't bring a date today, and it feels kinda weird."

"Well, Leo's date isn't really a date."

Wyatt glanced over his shoulder, to where Leo had taken a place beside Harriet. The spymaster wore a red beaded dress that gleamed against her ebony skin and flowed over her long, lean body. She looked absolutely gorgeous, but she was dressed up for herself, not for Leo. Though maybe the outfit was aimed partially at Lady Buxley. Fanny wore a similar dress to Harriet's, but in a dusky rose shade. She had her hand on Rion's thigh, but was leaning toward Harriet and giggling.

Wyatt left them all to their flirting and turned to Nova. "Do you come to the races often?"

"No. I worked security years ago, and it's so mind-numbingly boring that hauling rocks seems like a better career choice. Assuming by-blows had a choice."

"Okay. Well, I like the cars and sometimes I babble about them. Aubrey and Rion can fill you in on all the sporty details. The box beside you belongs to some Vaughn, I forget who, but it looks like Ladies' Day today."

Nova took a brief look across the rail at the cluster of debutantes in pastel gowns and hats covered in feathers Wyatt desperately hoped were artificial.

"Two of Phobos' daughters," Nova whispered. "I think the rest are their cousins. All irrelevant to our interests, as far as I know. The Vaughns espouse 'ladylike' education."

Wyatt looked again at the young women. They appeared happy enough, but he couldn't help but wonder if any of them were seething inside and wishing to be anything other than decorative.

"The box on our left is the one we'll want to pay attention to," he said, determined to keep his focus on work.

Nova nodded. "Eberwhite and his gambling friends."

"Yep. They're usually drunk and rowdy." He twisted in his chair again. "Leo?"

Leo patted an empty pocket. "Already under your seat."

"Oh, great. Thanks."

Wyatt gathered the mini-drones and started them up one-by-one. Under the pretext of searching for the seat with the best view, he moved around the box, placing the drones at intervals along the left-side rail. The recorders would pick up some conversation from there, and he could send any or all of them closer with a command from his watch.

With the task complete, he squirmed his way past the

still-flirting ladies back to the seat beside Nova. "I suppose this will have to do." The words came out too loud and stilted, and he slumped quickly into the seat, hoping no one was looking. "Sorry," he muttered. "I'm a horrible actor. And I think I made it sound like I don't want to sit by you."

Nova made a vague sound of agreement, her gaze fixed on the track. "Bad at acting. Likes cars. Can't stop smuggling, even at the races. Got it."

Wyatt shifted closer until their knees almost touched. "Are you memorizing facts about me?"

She blinked out of whatever fog she'd been in. "Oh. Is that not a normal part of getting to know someone? Dating isn't common in the RMC, so I don't have a lot of experience."

A jolt of excitement shot through Wyatt's veins. "We're dating?"

Nova's brow furrowed. "Yes?"

"Yes!" He had to grab the seat of his chair to prevent himself from throwing himself at her. "I mean, yes, if you want. I just didn't want to assume, after you left so quickly the other night, and—"

A cacophony of trumpets mercifully cut off the awkward conversation. The cars were in position and the race was set to begin.

Wyatt slid back to an appropriate distance from Nova, in case anyone was looking. She claimed a lack of dating skill, but it seemed he wasn't any better, because he kept misreading her. His typical understanding of dating was: he liked someone, they had sex, eventually they were satisfied and moved on. Sometimes they stayed friends, like with Marcus. Sometimes they drifted apart.

Now it was like the rules had changed and he was staring at a hand of cards with no idea which one to play. One choice might make Nova hop into his bed. Another might make her withdraw. Maybe they were both throwing cards at random.

And maybe that wasn't a bad thing, because right now what he wanted most was for the game to keep going.

Below them, gleaming cars with brightly-colored logos flew around the oval. Eberwhite and his buddies groaned and cheered as they won or lost wagers ranging from "leader after lap one" to "first lady to lose her hat when the cars speed past."

Wyatt tried his best to pay attention, but neither his brain nor his body was in the mood to cooperate. The damned stadium chair was fixed in place, which meant he couldn't get comfortable, no matter how he slouched or straightened or crossed his legs. He jiggled his foot restlessly and tapped out patterns on his thigh, all while Nova sat still and silent beside him.

"I can't fathom what it's like to be a person who doesn't fidget," he mused aloud.

Nova glanced at his drumming fingers and gave a small shrug. "That's okay. I can't understand what it's like to be you, either. You don't find it exhausting to be always in motion?"

"Nope. I find it exhausting to hold still."

"Whereas I find it peaceful."

Wyatt shifted—again—to look her in the eye. "*You* should have the nickname Viper. Lie quietly in wait and then, *bam!* You strike your prey."

"And you're…" She pursed her lips in thought. "A queen bee, I think. You buzz around your hive, receiving cryptic messages from your workers and making sure there's so much honey that people can come and collect it."

"Don't forget the part where I get to mate with the sexy, sexy drones."

Nova leaned in until he could feel her breath on his neck. "I've seen how you enjoy buzzing things."

Searing desire flashed across Wyatt's skin. Damn. There went any hope of paying attention to anything but Nova.

A waiter arrived with appetizers and champagne, and Wyatt gulped down a whole glass of the chilled wine. It didn't cool his body, but it did make him slightly tipsy. He'd forgotten to eat, hadn't he? Blast.

After a second glass of champagne and a plate full of little meats and pastries, he no longer cared that he wasn't working. The gamblers had gotten drunk enough to shout, so the drones would catch anything important. He could sit and flirt and relax and pretend this was a normal date.

He rambled on about the race cars and which ones were using which technologies. Nova probably didn't care about boiler configuration and pressure regulation, but she listened to him talk and even asked an occasional question. Maybe she was slightly drunk too.

"Aubrey's Aquas like to balance speed and power. They have a strong engine, but it's not the lightest, so they counter that with a small, sleek body design. But it makes them vulnerable to the heavier, rougher cars, like those Comets he hates. I don't know the rules about how you can and can't ram into the other cars, but you can see for yourself how many have already been damaged. I think if the races were more regulated we could really see the influence—"

The screech of twisting metal made Wyatt jump so suddenly he sloshed champagne down his shirt. Directly in front of them, the loser of the collision spun off the track, steam billowing from its crumpled body. The driver leapt out of the broken vehicle. His shouts were inaudible above the noise of the racers and the crowd, but he was almost certainly cursing out his opponent.

Nova pulled a handkerchief from her jacket pocket and began blotting Wyatt's shirt.

"Thanks. Did you see how that car had all the required safety tech? The driver wasn't crushed or trapped inside and the boiler had a pressure relief system to prevent an explosion."

"Yes. I'm glad of that." Nova continued to pat at Wyatt's clothing. "I think you're going to be a sticky mess no matter what."

He arched an eyebrow. "Oh, am I?"

Nova adopted a serious expression, but at this close range she couldn't disguise the sparkle in her dark eyes or the tic at the corner of her mouth. "I suppose you could try removing your shirt."

"Hmm. Considering how I ended up the last time I was unclothed in your presence…"

"Now you see why I said, 'no matter what.'"

"Maybe I should go home and change. How much longer is this race?"

Wyatt glanced over at Lord Eberwhite, who was leaning precariously over the edge of his box.

"Place another bet, boys!" he slurred.

One of his so-called friends smacked him upside the head. "You're outta coin, you cad!"

"I got shares! Investment shares. Worth more than you lot all together."

Wyatt tapped his watch to send the drones a bit higher. Of course the conversation would become relevant right when he was considering skipping out.

He nudged Aubrey, but the other man's attention remained riveted on the race.

Wyatt tried again. "Hey, Aub."

"What the…" Aubrey didn't take his eyes off the cars. "That line is all wrong. Why would—"

If Aubrey kept talking, Wyatt didn't hear it. His brain thrived on patterns. When something didn't fit, it was like an alarm bell going off in his head. The anomaly blazed in his vision as if it were as brightly colored as the green of his hair.

The otherwise unobtrusive racer had deviated enough from the usual course that it had fallen behind the majority of its competitors. Now it accelerated hard, slashing diagonally across the track like a torpedo locked on a target.

Words tore from Wyatt's throat, maybe a curse, maybe a warning. He flung himself at Nova, tackling her to the floor an instant before the car slammed into the wall beneath their box and detonated.

# 22

SCREAMS OF HORROR WHISPERED like ghostly sighs through the ringing in Nova's ears. The concrete wall beside her left arm heaved and cracked, and a foot-long section crumbled into the wreckage below. Heat and smoke from the burning race car flowed through the hole, thickening the air with dark, acrid fumes. She tried to turn her head and push herself up, but Wyatt's body still pinned her down.

*Oh, fuck. Was he…*

"Wyatt!"

"I'm okay, I'm okay."

He scrambled off her and took her arm as she staggered to her feet. Nova scanned him for injuries. No blood, nothing obviously broken. Five mini drones hovered protectively around him.

He turned his back on the rising smoke, wincing. His shirt was torn on the left side, near his shoulder blade. The exposed skin glowed an angry red.

"Wyatt." She curled her fingers to stop herself from touching the injury.

"A little bruised, maybe," he admitted, fanning smoke away from his face. "We should probably get out of here."

Nova's security training kicked in. One, two, three, four, five, six clients, all alive and standing. Exit door clear.

"Go," she commanded. "Out the door. Regroup in the concourse. Now!"

She made a check of the box full of debutantes, but they were already rushing out under the direction of Lady Phoebe. Good. Despite their foolish families, the girls had some sense. The box full of drunk men on the other side could be a problem, though.

Nova spun to assess their situation, but smacked into Wyatt, who had completely ignored her instructions and bent over to pick something up.

"So that's what hit me." He straightened. A broken drone lay cradled in his palms, a jagged shard of metal jutting from its body. "Poor little guy. I'll make sure I save as much of your data as I can."

A knot formed in Nova's gut. Fuck, that piece of metal could have been buried several inches deep in Wyatt's back. She tore her gaze away, only to have it land on the deformed remains of Wyatt's seat, now the resting place of a twisted chunk of steel.

Her stomach heaved.

"Go!" She pushed Wyatt hard enough to emphasize her point.

Wyatt kept hold of the broken drone, but he nudged Aubrey, who was bellowing down toward the track.

"For God's sake, call the race! People are injured up here!"

"Enough, Aubrey!" Nova snapped. "This whole box could collapse at any moment."

Aubrey took a few reluctant steps backward as he continued his rant. "Stop it before anyone else gets hurt!"

Nova squeezed past Wyatt, grabbed both men by the arm, and hauled them out the door. The air in the corridor was cool and clean. She took a deep breath and blinked away the stinging tears the smoke had caused.

Nervous chatter hummed through the concourse. People poured from the nearby boxes, then froze in uncertainty. Waiters gulped drinks they'd been meant to serve, and junior mercenaries wandered aimlessly, unable to act without specific orders.

"You!" Nova barked at the nearest one. "Go into that box and drag all those drunkards to safety. Check people for injuries and make them sit down and shut up!"

"Yes, sir!" The boy ran for Eberwhite's box.

Nova made another count of her group. Six, all alive. Injuries, at least three. Lady Buxley had gone deathly pale. Her dress was torn, and she cradled one arm to her chest. Rion and Harriet stood to either side of her, holding her steady.

"Fanny, you should sit," Harriet urged. "We'll fetch a doctor."

Rion dropped to his hands and knees. "Here. Use me for a chair."

Harriet helped her friend sit. "I'll go find a medic."

"No," Leo cut in. Blood ran down the right side of his face, but he wiped at it with the back of his hand, as if it were no more than a minor nuisance. "Stay with Lady Buxley. I'll go."

"Oh, but, Your Grace, you can't!" Lady Phoebe raced over, one hand holding her skirts off the ground, the other clutching a handkerchief. "You're wounded."

"I am fine." Leo's voice rang with ducal authority.

Wyatt started walking, drones at his back. "Stay here, Leo. I'm going."

Nova jogged to catch him. What the devil was wrong with all these men? "You're hurt and you're not going anywhere.

Harriet's already on her way. Morland, put pressure on that gash this instant!"

"It's a superficial head wound," the duke groused. "They bleed profusely. It is inconsequential."

Nova glared at him.

He glared back, even as he wiped more blood out of his eye.

Lady Phoebe took advantage of the distraction and pressed her handkerchief to Leo's temple.

"Ow!"

The young woman smiled smugly up at him. "Maud?" she called to one of her cousins. "His Grace is in pain. Could you fetch him some brandy?"

"Ladies." Leo took hold of the handkerchief and stepped away. "I appreciate the concern, but I must respectfully decline any offer of assistance." He used his free hand to dig a clean handkerchief out of his own pocket and offered it to Lady Phoebe. "Please see to your own wellbeing. There are matters I must attend to."

"Yes. Your health." Nova pointed at the ground. "Sit. You, too, Wyatt. That bruise looks bad and you're still grimacing."

Both men babbled on as if they hadn't heard her.

"Of course I'm grimacing! Drone m447 gave his life for me!"

"Does anyone know if this stadium has a secure location where we can meet?"

Nova rubbed her temple.

Wyatt cast a sorrowful look at the drone in his hand. "I don't even know if I'll be able to retrieve any of his data."

Leo had begun to pace. "We may have to adjourn to Aubrey's trolley car. Wyatt, can you send one of those things to find Harriet? She and the doctor can meet us at the station. Aubrey—" He looked around in confusion. "Where did Aubrey go?"

Nova made a quick count. Shit. The sneaky bastard. Now she had three injured clients and one missing. "I hate you all," she moaned.

Rion's voice rose from the floor. "That makes two of us. Try being a piece of furniture. It's more comfortable."

He was probably right. At least Lady Buxley no longer looked on the verge of passing out, thanks to his assistance.

"Sir!" The junior mercenary pushed his way between a pair of inebriated lordlings to address Nova. "I got them all out, sir. Numerous cuts and bruises. One serious injury."

Nova craned her neck for a look. Lord Eberwhite lay on the ground, face twisted in pain. His companions stood around him in a circle, arguing.

Nova grabbed Wyatt's wrist and pulled him close. "Don't let the duke wander off," she whispered. "I'm going to get us some information."

Wyatt's brow furrowed, but he nodded.

His acquiescence caused a burst of pleasure to bloom in her chest. Finally, something had gone right. Two things, if you counted her decision to wear her normal uniform today.

A grim smile touched her lips. Connington would be furious if he knew what she was doing.

She shouldered her way to Eberwhite's side, the junior merc close behind her. "I'll tend to him," she told the kid. "You corral the others and see if you can get them to sit down. A doctor has already been sent for. Do you have a med kit on you?"

"Yup." The young man detached a small pouch from his belt and offered it to her.

The med kits were mostly intended for self-administration, to deal with pain or minor injuries on the job. She'd rarely bothered carrying one herself. No bloody way would she dose herself with laudanum while on a mission. Nor would she sell the opiate to a fellow merc looking to get high, like many others had.

She cracked open the kit and pushed aside an assortment of sticking plasters. A small glass vial rested at the bottom, untouched.

*Yes.* The kid did things by the book. She was going to find out his name and send in an anonymous commendation.

Nova plucked the drug from the pouch and knelt beside Eberwhite. "I'm here to help you, my lord. I have something to ease the pain."

"Give ith to me," he slurred. "Bloody hurts."

Nova uncorked the vial and tipped the liquid into his mouth. It was probably double the dose he needed, but she didn't want him to remember the conversation they were about to have. Or anything about her at all.

She made him comfortable as she waited for the laudanum to take effect. Most of his cuts only needed the blood wiped away and a small bandage, but his right leg looked badly broken. She had to commandeer suit coats and ties from several others to get the limb elevated and temporarily immobilized. As she worked, a drone hovered at her shoulder, its gentle hum curiously soothing.

"How are you feeling?" she asked when she'd finished.

"Nice." Eberwhite blinked dreamily up at her. "So nice."

"I'm glad." Nova lowered her voice to a low purr. "I hear you've made excellent investments of late."

"Investment," he mumbled. "One. Best one."

"How lovely. Can you tell me about it?"

He attempted to shake his head, but only managed a slight wobble. "Nope. Secret. Very secret."

"Mmm. Orders from Deimos?"

"Yes. I'm loyal. Loyalest."

"You must be for him to trust you with something so valuable." Nova made a show of adjusting the jacket she'd used to cushion Eberwhite's head.

A bit of his dreamy smile faded. "No trust. Doesn't trust."

"He should. You deserve it."

Nova put a hand to her abdomen. Lying to a drunk, drugged man to pump him for information was the sort of thing her father would do. Fuck, she was going to be sick. She didn't want to be like him. Not in any way. But they needed answers.

Eberwhite smiled again. "I do!" he declared. "I'm the loyalest."

"He should tell you about his… discovery?"

The wounded lord grunted assent.

"He found something valuable? If he appreciated you he'd share it."

"Mmm-hmm. Wants to use my ships, but won't tell me why."

Nova glanced around. She'd run out of ways to assist Eberwhite, and if she didn't get up soon someone would start to wonder. Time to go all in.

"Where do the ships go? If you tell me what you know, I'll tell His Grace how very loyal you are to him."

Eberwhite's eyes couldn't seem to focus on her anymore. "You're a nice person. Do you want to buy some ships too? Deimos bought the identical ones. All the same. Stealthy. Good for smuggling." He giggled. "Did you know he hired some bitch to stop Morland's pretty-boy from smuggling? Doesn't like the competition. Hates it. Wants to do away with Godfrey, too. Lure him to the secret moon. Stab him in the back. I'm not supposed to know that." He giggled again, but the laughter quickly trailed off. His eyelids had begun to droop. "Tired."

Nova pushed herself up onto one knee, preparing to stand. "Sleep. The doctor will take care of you."

When he didn't reply, Nova left him and returned to Wyatt, who leaned against the wall beside Leo. Not quite as good as sitting down, but she'd take it. She crossed her arms and gave them both a stern look.

"You two should get cleared by a doctor, but then we can have that meeting you wanted, Morland."

Leo arched a single eyebrow in a manner that managed to clearly inquire, *Learn something interesting?*

Nova nodded in acknowledgement. "Lord Eberwhite is resting comfortably. He thinks I'm a bitch and Wyatt is a pretty-boy."

Wyatt grinned and straightened his spine. "He thinks I'm pretty? How sweet. And we all know you make bitchy sexy as hell."

"You give the most peculiar compliments." She kissed his cheek. "I'm not sure why I like that."

"I can't imagine," Leo said dryly.

Nova ignored him. What she and Wyatt did in private was their own business, and she wasn't going to waste time deciphering the duke's cryptic comments on their affair. She didn't require his approval.

She gestured at the drone hovering by her side. "Did this one record me while I tended to Lord Eberwhite?"

Wyatt waved a rainbow-manicured hand. "Naturally."

"Good." Nova snatched the drone out of the air. It trembled in her grasp, its rotors spinning faster. "Could you turn it off, please?"

Wyatt tapped his watch a few times and the drone shut down. "She can't protect you if she's off."

Nova tucked the drone inside her jacket. "But I can protect her. And starting right now, I'll also be protecting you." She turned her head to include Leo in the conversation. "All of you. I want a codicil for our contract, Morland. Full bodyguard authorization for all of Chamber Three. Because someone," she tossed a significant look at the door to the damaged box, "thinks we already know too much."

# 23

Wyatt drummed his fingers on the keyboard as he replayed the recording from drone m381. By now he could recite the conversation word-for-word. The cajoling murmur of Nova's voice and Eberwhite's groggy replies echoed in his head.

Unfortunately those voices were accompanied by a hive of brain-bees, all of which were currently screaming.

*Investigate the identical ships!*

*Re-check the splice logs!*

*Look into Godfrey. Is there footage from his recent visit?*

*What secret moon? Remember to get a Jovian moon map.*

*Did I eat breakfast? Shit, what time is it?*

*I wish Nova had stayed here last night.*

Plus m447 sat on the desk looking pitiful, he hadn't bothered to put in his contact lenses or brush his hair, he had half-a-dozen messages to read regarding his zoological gardens, and someone had probably tried to kill him last night.

Wyatt shoved his chair away from the desk. He couldn't

stay here like this, too overwhelmed to do anything. He needed to get up. Get out. Go… somewhere.

He rushed out of his apartment and started for the stairs, only to pause when he heard voices emanating from the kitchen. Voices including a no-nonsense alto with a bit of an exasperated edge. Grinning, he danced down the hall to join the conversation.

Nova, Rion, and Leo sat together at the bar, eating from a shared bowl of popcorn. Leo had a pained expression on his face and a white-knuckled grip on what appeared to be a glass of brandy.

"Day drinking?" Wyatt blurted. "You okay, Leo?"

"No. My head hurts and *they* are making it worse." He gestured with his glass at Rion and Nova before downing half the contents.

Nova used her foot to hook an empty stool and drag it clear of the bar for Wyatt to sit on. "My friend Irene is a doctor. I invited her to come here, and His Grace believes I have overstepped my authority."

Leo gulped more brandy. "No. His Grace believes he does not need a doctor, especially when the bloody world is falling apart all around him."

Wyatt sat and grabbed the bowl of popcorn. "Mmm," he replied, shoveling food into his mouth.

Rion slung an arm around Wyatt's shoulder. "Have I mentioned that I love you? Because I really love you and I will love you forever for banging someone who will barge in here and boss Leo around. Please keep her, because I love her too. Don't tell anyone I said that. I have a reputation to maintain."

Wyatt slid out from under Rion's arm, partly because he wasn't in a cuddly mood, but mostly because his bruised back throbbed with pain at the slightest touch. If Nova noticed him wincing, she'd yell at him too.

"I'm glad she's looking out for your stubborn asses." He scooped up another handful of popcorn, then hopped off the barstool. "Have fun chatting with Nova's doctor friend. I'm going to pop by the zoological gardens."

Nova leapt from her seat. "Oh, no, you're not."

Leo smirked at Wyatt before draining the last of his drink.

Wyatt ignored them both and started for the door. "I'll say hi to the animals for you."

"You're not going anywhere." Nova caught up to him in two quick strides. "Not without protection."

"Hmm." Wyatt paused and rubbed his chin. "The veterinarian who works with the reptiles is quite the looker. I think he's in a committed relationship, but I could bring a condom, just in case. Good idea."

"You ass." Her lips quivered as she fought not to smile.

"Or you could come with me and we could make it a date," he offered.

Wyatt nibbled on his popcorn as he waited for an answer. Nova cast a look back at Rion and Leo. She opened her mouth, hesitated, then closed it again.

Wyatt shifted his weight from one foot to the other. *Please say yes.*

A date was exactly what he needed. Time alone with her where he could simply exist, without the burden of the rest of the world. Time to enjoy the beauty of life and share a piece of his passion with an agreeable partner.

"Go." Rion made a shooing motion. "Wander around hand-in-hand and make calf-eyes at each other, or whatever infatuated couples do. In the unlikely event an enemy gets past our security alive, I'll snap their neck and hurl them down the stairs before Morland can say, 'Let's call a meeting.'"

Nova dipped her chin in a sharp, militaristic nod. "If Aubrey ever shows up, keep an eye on him too."

Rion made an exaggerated salute.

Wyatt took Nova's hand before she could change her mind. "Let's go."

They reached the street in time to see a trolley approaching and jogged to catch it. Once again, they took a seat in the far back, but this time the driver had no need to scold them for indelicate behavior. Nova sat straight-backed, in full bodyguard mode, silently eyeing each and every passenger. Wyatt hugged himself and tapped patterns.

Stepping off the trolley felt like gulping in a huge breath of air after being underwater. Wyatt didn't uncross his arms, but his hunched shoulders dropped, and his chest expanded. They were alone and safe.

"I'm sorry for making you worry about me." Wyatt walked toward the iron entry gate of what he hoped would someday be his masterpiece. "I understand it. But I needed to get away from…" He waved a hand. "Everything."

The implant in his chest vibrated, and the gate swung ponderously open. Nova followed him through, but remained silent.

"It's okay if you're mad at me," he went on. "I probably would be mad too if I was a bodyguard and my person was like, 'Hey, I'm going out in public alone when someone wants me dead. Bye!'"

When the gate closed behind them, Nova finally spoke. "Yes, I'm a little bit angry. And a lot worried. But I understand your side, too. You don't function well under strict parameters."

The last of the tension eased from Wyatt's body. He

grinned. "Agent of chaos, right? Come on, let me give you a tour and then we can pet the squirrels."

Nova's eyes widened, then quickly narrowed. "Um…"

"I can pet the squirrels and you can watch."

"Okay." She extended a hand. "Rion said we're supposed to wander around hand-in-hand."

Wyatt accepted the offer, lacing their fingers together. "It's a time-honored Earthling courtship ritual. Second only to challenging your rival to mortal combat."

Nova lifted her nose in the air. "A Martian would never engage in mortal combat on a first date. Anything before the third date is considered gauche. Since I'm not sure being nearly exploded at the races counts as a real date, best to wait until next time."

"Then petting squirrels it is. But first, come meet Flurry's relatives."

He led her past the empty buildings that would eventually house restrooms and a gift shop to a low concrete and stone structure built to resemble a cave.

"This is our first fully complete habitat. We started here because we had so many bats. You know how most younger children of aristocrats study law or medicine or some other similar profession?"

"Yes." Nova walked up to the window to peer in at the bats, most of which were hanging upside-down, asleep at this time of day.

"Well, Lord Pinckford's third son decided he didn't like any of those options and thought it would be a great idea to instead raise a whole colony of bats and sell the guano for fertilizer."

Nova almost choked on a laugh. "Bat poop fertilizer?"

"Yeah. It's a great source of nutrients, and does have monetary value. But he knew absolutely nothing about bats and how to take care of them. We found dozens of bats living in a storage shed. Sick bats, injured bats, orphaned babies. It was a mess. We had to hand-feed some of the little ones, like Flurry. The others were all happy to stay with their bat buddies, but he wouldn't leave me, so that's how I ended up with a pet bat."

"I'm glad you rescued them. They're not the prettiest of animals, but they're rather interesting."

"What?" Wyatt dropped Nova's hand and took a step back. "They're adorable! They're fuzzy and they fly and like to cuddle."

Nova turned away from the bats to face Wyatt. "I don't think I will ever love animals the way you do. I like to look at them, but I don't want to touch them. I think it's wonderful that you do, though. It's endearing."

Wyatt's cheeks warmed at the praise. "Okay. That's fair. It's probably weird that I think even leeches are cute."

"But the good kind of weird." She took his hand again. "Show me more."

Wyatt walked Nova through all fifty acres of his zoo, on the most comprehensive tour he'd ever given. He talked about the latest updates on the areas under construction and expounded on his issues acquiring and growing plants to simulate native habitats. He led her through the rescue and rehabilitation building, where he cooed over abandoned exotic pets from salamanders to wild turkey. They spent nearly half an hour watching the tiger eye them suspiciously while Wyatt detailed his hopes for releasing her into the wild.

By the time they looped around to the petting and feeding enclosures, he'd been talking so much and for so long that his throat had gotten scratchy and his voice had gone slightly hoarse. He wasn't stopping, though. Not as long as Nova continued to hold his hand and smile at him like he was the most precious baby snake, squirming and flicking its little tongue.

He stopped in front of the mesh screen of a large avian habitat. "Would you like to feed my conspiracy?"

Nova frowned. "I'm sorry, your what?"

"My ravens. A group of ravens is a conspiracy. It's a small conspiracy, though, because I only have three of them. I usually go inside the cage and play with them, but visitors can take a few treats from the dispenser there and toss them inside."

When Nova hesitated, Wyatt stepped in front of the glass and iron container full of small food pellets. He turned the crank once and a pellet dropped into his hand. He threw it through a narrow slit in the screen, and a big, black bird swooped down to peck at it.

"Like that."

Nova gaped at the raven, then eagerly tossed in more food. The other ravens joined the first.

"These are the birds from the fairy stories I read as a child! The ones that collect shiny things!"

Nova's voice rang with such pure wonder that Wyatt reeled as if the enviro-generators had all malfunctioned at once, robbing Dystopia of its breathable air and enhanced gravity.

He clutched the railing to steady himself. Stern, organized Nova already made his blood boil. Unabashedly delighted Nova turned night to day and winter to summer. The mere second-hand experience of her joy filled his heart near to bursting. All he wanted was to give her more. More ravens. More discoveries. More pieces of the universe she'd never been allowed to see in her strictly prearranged life.

"Corvids are highly intelligent," Wyatt explained. He

couldn't guess at what else might excite her, but he could certainly tell her about the birds. "They can recognize human faces. They will befriend people and chase off enemies. I've heard stories of crows, ravens, and magpies gifting pretty rocks or trinkets to people in exchange for food, or returning a jewel to someone who lost it.

"These three are named Edgar, Allan, and Poe, by the way. A book lover bought them as babies and then didn't want them when they grew. Poe is on the left. He loves the treat pellets. Edgar is the slightly smaller one, and she prefers blueberries. Allan is very sensitive and sometimes he'll eat nothing you put in front of him and other times he'll eat absolutely anything. He'll let me pet him only when he's in the mood for it."

"They're so beautiful." Nova tipped her head from side to side. "The way their feathers shine and change in the light—not just black, but blues and greens and purples."

"Like your hair."

She froze, then slowly lifted a hand to brush the purple streak behind her left ear. "You think I'm a raven now?"

Wyatt leaned toward her. "You're smart and beautiful. You're wary of people, but loyal and protective of those who earn your trust. You have a strong sense of fairness. If I feed you, I bet you'll give me something shiny in return."

She settled her hands on his waist and dragged him to her. Her lips hovered a breath away when she whispered, "*You* are the shiniest thing I know."

And then her mouth was on his, soft as a feather and sweet as fruit.

Wyatt drifted away into the kiss, rising and falling in the currents of Nova's gentle breeze. Their previous kisses had been deep and lusty. This one was delicate. Fragile. As if it might fracture or dissolve if they moved too much.

She lifted her hands to cup his face, holding him to her as she moved incrementally from one corner of his mouth to the other. Each tiny sip shot sparks of longing through his body. A languid sweep of her tongue made him gasp like he'd been burned. She had hit his resonant frequency and now even the slightest vibration undulated through him like an earthquake.

He grabbed hold of her jacket to keep himself anchored. Their lips parted and their tongues danced, dipping in and out of each other in light, worshipful strokes. Wyatt treasured every taste of her, every breath they shared. He would let her kiss him like this until the stars winked out of existence.

Minutes passed, or maybe years, or eons. He'd never been good with time, so what did it matter? Any time between an instant and forever in the perfection of Nova's warm, intoxicating kiss was worthy of celebration.

Eventually, Nova broke the kiss, easing away from him not with an ending, but a promise of yet-to-come. Her chest rose and fell in rapid breaths. A pink glow tinted her cheeks. As Wyatt came slowly back into himself, he felt the swiftness of his own pulse, his heavy breathing, the heat of his skin. The spell he'd been under was over, but its effect on his body and heart lingered.

"Shit. Nova." He released her, stumbling a little. "That was… magical."

She stared as if looking through him into the distance, a slight crinkle forming in her brow. "Yes. It was lovely."

"So, um…" The connection between Wyatt's brain and his mouth short-circuited. He had completely forgotten how to talk to another human. Especially a human who had rocked his world in a non-orgasmic sort of way. He wanted to babble about how fabulous she was and how he wanted to take her on dozens more dates until he knew every secret part of her. But another part of his brain said that was weird and too much too soon, and there was nothing—nothing—he could say that would make any sense right now.

"Uh, yeah." Nova twisted the end of her ponytail around her finger. "Maybe…"

"I guess…"

The irritated *cack* of a raven interrupted the string of useless syllables they had substituted for conversation.

Wyatt and Nova both looked up. Allan had flown into a tree branch, where he peered censoriously down at the peculiar primates who were bungling a simple mating ritual.

*Cack!*

"Sorry, I didn't introduce Nova to you, did I?" The words coming out of Wyatt's mouth probably still didn't make sense, but at least they were forming now. "Allan, Poe, Edgar, this is Nova Pratt. My… my girlfriend."

The word felt oddly formal on his tongue, like he should have been in a tailcoat and cravat, announcing, "My betrothed."

"Hello," Nova said to the birds. "You are all very beautiful and interesting, and I'm glad Wyatt brought me to meet you. Maybe next time I'll bring you some shiny trinkets and we can become friends." She looked at Wyatt and whispered, "Do they understand English?"

He shrugged. "Probably some of it, yeah."

She pursed her lips in thought. "And they understand that we're, um, together?"

"Likely. Ravens form strong pair bonds. I'm sure they can tell we are friends and not enemies. But speaking of together, is 'girlfriend' okay with you? Not too juvenile? Too gendered? Too serious? Too not-serious? I don't know what I'm saying, don't mind me."

"It's fine. Though the tradition among mercenaries in a relationship is to call one another 'comrade.'" Nova delivered this pronouncement with a dry tone and an entirely straight face.

For a moment, Wyatt's jaw wouldn't close. "Please let that be a joke."

"Of course it's a joke. I told you, mercs don't date."

"Right. Sorry." He folded his arms tightly across his chest. "It startled me, is all. I had a horrible vision of Rion deciding to call me 'comrade' for the rest of my life. Then I'd have to feed him to the tiger."

Wyatt expected at least a smile from Nova, but instead her whole body tensed.

"What time is it?" She shoved up the sleeve of her jacket to get at her watch. "We've been here too long. We have to go. I should have checked on the others lightyears ago." She took off toward the exit at a near-run, muttering curses as she went.

"Nova, they're fine." Wyatt jogged after her. "They've lots of practice taking care of one another."

"They're my responsibility." She kept her gaze trained dead ahead. "You're all my responsibility. I've been selfish. I can't keep doing that."

"Hey. It's okay." He touched her arm, but she flinched away, so he tried for levity instead. "I'm sure Leo will be excited to spend the rest of the day having meetings."

Nova marched on without reply, a soldier on a mission.

Wyatt trudged after her. He hadn't even gotten to pet the squirrels.

# 24

NOVA PACED THE CONFERENCE ROOM, following the perfectly symmetrical pattern of the carpet. The tabletop gleamed, every chair had been properly pushed in, and she was ten minutes early for the evening meeting. None of this soothed her. Nor did the fact that all her clients were whole and healthy.

*We have to break up. I have to end things.*

The door opened. Morland strode in.

"Nova. Thank you for your punctuality."

She executed the small bow she'd had drilled into her from the moment she could stand. "Your Grace. How is your head?"

"Fine, fine. Your friend Dr. Castelbury gave me something for the pain." He grimaced. "I am to 'take things slow' for the next week."

For a man who probably never stopped working except to sleep—and then, only reluctantly—this advice must have gone down about as well as a spoonful of hot chili powder. Fortunately, Irene was accustomed to ornery mercenaries. A grouchy duke would be nothing she couldn't handle.

Morland swiftly changed the subject. "How was your date?"

*Beautiful. Peaceful. Perfect. We have to break up.*

Nova didn't move a muscle. "Wyatt's zoo is impressive. I hope he's proud of his work. I think the public will be thrilled when it opens."

"Ah." Leo gestured at the conference table. "Please, have a seat."

Nova would have preferred to continue pacing, but one did not disobey a duke, even when his request was politely phrased. She sat. She had a duty, to both her clients and to the people of her homeland. And if clinging to protocol helped keep her focus where it belonged, she'd grab hold like one of Wyatt's "cute" leeches.

*Duty, duty, duty.*

Damn Wyatt Fucking Hartford and his ravens and tigers and magical kisses. Why did he have to be so adorable? He was a menace to society. Or at least to Nova's sanity.

Wyatt was, predictably, the last to arrive. He waltzed into the room, carrying a vidscreen and blowing on his fingernails to dry a fresh coat of green polish.

"Found all the purchase records for Eberwhite's identical ships," he announced. "And wouldn't you know, several of the registration codes match those of the ships disappearing and reappearing around the splices. All are owned by H2Freight, Inc., which is owned by the Duke of Deimos. But not operated by him, since that would be working in trade, and we all know how disgustingly plebeian that is."

He passed the vidscreen around the table so everyone could take a look at his data. Nova spared it only a cursory glance. She'd already known her father was involved up to his eyeballs. What mattered now was how to stop him.

Leo had come prepared. He smoothly steered the meeting into a focused discussion on ways to apply political pressure. The idea had merit, since they couldn't take a duke to court unless he'd been caught piloting a ship of smuggled cargo, and maybe not even then.

Unease coiled in Nova's gut, growing and spreading as the men brainstormed. Many of the tactics tossed around sounded borderline illegal. Or perhaps wholly illegal—she couldn't be sure her moral compass pointed true north anymore.

Seditious pamphlets. Mocking cartoons. Whispers in the ears of certain people. Tax audits. Leaked documents. Bribery.

Aubrey sighed in frustration. "If we were the bad guys, we could simply assassinate him and be done with it."

Nova flinched. Stopping assassinations was literally her job. She'd spent the majority of her adult life working to maintain peace and prevent violence. And despite everything, Deimos was still her father. Even if—as if she needed further complications—he'd attempted to orchestrate an assassination himself.

Wyatt's fingers brushed her arm. "Hey. If you don't want to listen to this, we can go. I'm no help with this side of things either."

"I'm so sorry," Aubrey babbled. "That was absolutely inappropriate. I'm used to this being my safe space to run my mouth, and I didn't... I should've... Fuck. I'm not planning to kill your father or anyone. Promise. And I won't joke about it again."

Nova nodded in his direction. "Thank you. It's the word 'assassin.' We're trained to react."

"I will avoid it except for emergency situations." Aubrey blushed, transforming his features from what Nova considered generically handsome to almost as pretty as Wyatt. "And I apologize again for my macabre sense of humor."

"Apology accepted." She rose from her seat. The men immediately stood as well, as if she were a Lady-with-a-capital-L. "But I think Wyatt is right. I won't be a help in this discussion. I should leave so I can focus on protecting all of *you* from assassins. Maybe we can outline a security plan."

Leo's eyes lit up at the word "plan." "Good thinking. Come back in an hour and we can all update one another on our conclusions. Is that enough time for you?"

She nodded. "Thank you, Your Grace. I will return in an hour."

Nova strode from the room, her pace brisk but not rushed. The assignment of a suitable task had restored her equilibrium. No more wandering through a dust storm without instruments to guide her.

Wyatt fell into step beside her. "Are you okay?"

"Yes. Fine."

"Because you've seemed upset since the zoo. You've been quiet and stiff and formal. More than you usually get, I mean. You're bowing and using Leo's title. And I think maybe that was my fault?"

Nova veered toward the kitchen. "You haven't done anything wrong." She headed straight for the fridge, where she selected a can of soda water.

Wyatt grabbed a bottle of something called Nebul-Ade, which was fluorescent purple and full of sugar. Nova could only hope it wasn't radioactive.

She slid onto one of the barstools and opened her drink. Wyatt took the place beside her.

"I must have done something, because you freaked out at the end of our date," he said. "Do you need more structure? A specific time limit? Because I could program one of the drones to beep at appropriate intervals—"

An unexpected laugh rose in Nova's throat, and she

choked on a mouthful of soda water. She coughed so hard her eyes began to water and Wyatt had to pat her on the back.

"S-sor—" *Cough.* "Sorry." She wiped at her eyes. "You caught me off guard. I really don't think you need more mechanical noisemakers in your life."

"You're probably right. I was starting to tune out the alarms, so I deleted a bunch of them." He took a small sip of his soda. "Is there something else I can do? Because I don't want you to get upset on our next date. And you were very thoughtful when you said you understood that I needed to not have strict boundaries or what have you. But you need organization or rules or something similar, right? I thought we could do both. Like if I randomly decide to go out because I can't stand being inside anymore and you want to come with me, we could say, 'It will only be for this many hours and here's what we'll do about lunch.'"

Nova felt a sudden pricking at the corners of her eyes. Her body steeled itself automatically. Mercenaries didn't have strong emotions. Nova had long accepted this as fact, at least in her case. She'd never been an emotionally demonstrative person.

Wyatt's words must have hit a particular sensitive spot inside her, however, because she could barely prevent herself from flinging her arms around him in the biggest hug imaginable. He cared about her. Truly cared about her comfort and happiness, in a way precious few people ever had.

*We have to break up.*

It was an imperative. Already she'd been too distracted by his kisses and his kindness to people and animals. It was all too easy to let the world fade away while he rambled on about the things he loved. She could never be quite certain she could maintain control around him. And now, if he started putting her needs ahead of his own…

Her vision blurred. He was too much temptation. Too sweet beneath his shiny. Protecting people had to be her priority. No more dates, no more sex, no more flirtation.

"Nova?"

She blinked and refocused on his face.

"If it's a terrible idea, you can just tell me," he said. "I won't be angry. Or you can propose a different idea. I'd like us to have dates we can both fully enjoy."

*I did enjoy our date. I enjoyed it too much. That's the goddamned problem!*

She tried to find words, to tell him they couldn't be together, that as lovely as he was, they didn't fit. But the words wouldn't come. She couldn't formulate a complete sentence, much less speak it aloud. Anything she might say would hurt him, and she didn't have the ability to convey how impossible the two of them were.

"We should discuss our security plan," she blurted.

Wyatt's eyebrows rose. "Oh. Yeah. You said something about an outline? Pretty sure that made my brain temporarily shut down. But you can tell me your ideas if you want. We can talk about other stuff later."

No. They wouldn't talk later. But she could show him. Her actions would speak better than she ever could. He would see that her round peg would never fit the square hole of his life. She could never be carefree and idealistic.

She cleared her throat. "Security and safety. We'll want to establish an easy-to-follow protocol, including transparency and frequent communication."

# 25

ONE DAY OF NEW SECURITY PROTOCOL was one day too much.

Wyatt tapped the repaired and upgraded shell of drone m447 with a random piece of a wooden cube puzzle. "I dub thee Sir New Wyatt."

The little drone would now send a ping every two hours with the message "Wyatt has checked in." Technically, when he was at home, he was supposed to get up and literally make a checkmark on a bloody slate board, but that wasn't happening.

He'd already tried bribing Rion with cookies to do it for him, but Rion had decided to draw penises instead of checkmarks. Which might have been funny if it hadn't told the entire household who was checking in for Wyatt.

Leo loved the check-in board. He'd practically swooned when Nova had proposed it. It wasn't quite a map that displayed exactly where all his loved ones were at any given moment, but it was close.

Wyatt turned on m447's rotors and let it fly from the room. If anyone really wanted to find out where he was, all they needed to do was hack into one of his drones, gain access to the transponder, and use it to send a request for response to the implant in his chest. And then keep doing that until they found a drone in close enough range to him. Without any of the drones recognizing unauthorized access and sending an emergency alert or attacking. Simple.

The words "Check Cookies" flashed across his screen in giant red letters.

Wyatt popped up from his seat and dismissed the alert. Much better than a noisy alarm. It wouldn't work for his watch, but maybe he could get a new watch made that contained a small vibrator… Ooh, wrong word. He really didn't need to be thinking about vibrators right now. Because that made him reminisce about the way he and Nova had used one together. And how he'd used it on himself last night, imagining her beside him instead of sleeping alone in her flat.

Uh… what was he doing?

Wyatt followed his train of thought backward. Nova, vibrators, watch… Oh! Cookies.

He jogged to the kitchen and retrieved the last batch of cookies from the oven. The rich smell of molten chocolate filled the air, and he drew in a deep breath. Perfect. He ate one warm, gooey cookie to check that the taste was also perfect, licking every last drop of chocolate from his fingers.

He was about to eat another one when Aubrey walked in.

Wyatt flung his arms out to shield the cookies. "You can't have these. They're for Nova."

Aubrey grinned. "You two are so cute. If you get married, can I be your flower boy? I want to wear a fluffy red dress and fling white rose petals everywhere."

Wyatt stared at his friend for several seconds. "I… guess?

But we've been on two and a half dates, so maybe, uh, get back to me on that?"

"Will do. And I won't steal your cookies. I came to make a smoothie."

Wyatt stepped to one side to clear a path to the refrigerator. "Be my guest."

While Aubrey tossed assorted vegetables into a blender, Wyatt packed an insulated bag for his scheduled outing. Four cans of soda water went into the bottom of the bag, then a pair of sandwiches he'd ordered from his restaurant, two bananas he had definitely not paid taxes on, and finally a tin full of his fresh-baked triple chocolate cookies. The last batch was still warm, so he wrapped them in parchment paper and laid them atop the rest.

The bag barely zipped and was heavier than he preferred, but they would have an excellent lunch. They could even eat it exactly at noon, if Nova liked. Wyatt had also armed himself with a drone full of music and a book of fairytales. He would cheer her up, whatever it took.

With provisions packed, Wyatt left Aubrey and his questionable beverage choices and headed back to his room to dress.

His goal: maximum cuteness. His tightest white crop top was an obvious choice, and he paired it with black leggings and sturdy red combat boots. A denim jacket with "Dystopian Pride" emblazoned on the back in rainbow letters completed the look. Wyatt styled his hair carefully, touched up the green paint on his nails, and lined his eyes with kohl for extra emphasis. His usual gold earrings were sufficient. As a finishing touch, he added a pendant in the shape of a corvid. It wasn't detailed enough to declare it a particular species, but it was pretty, and Nova would like it. Satisfied with his efforts, Wyatt took his bag of goodies and his chosen drone companion, and set off for the appointed meeting place at the top of the stairs next to the stupid check-in board. Early.

Too early, as it turned out. He got bored, and by the time Nova arrived, he was thoroughly occupied adding extra detail to Rion's dickmarks.

"It's nice to see that our country's leaders are so responsible and mature."

Wyatt spun around, responding to Nova's sardonic drawl with a brilliant smile. "I came to this godforsaken planet when I was thirteen and wasted several of my best juvenile humor years learning how to be a damned earl. I deserve some indulgence. Also, I'm merely improving Rion's shoddy attempt at art."

He set the chalk onto the chalk ledge and dusted his hands clean on his pants.

Nova's gaze dropped to his thighs, where smears of white now decorated the black fabric. Oops. Her mouth curved upward in a slow, appreciative smile.

His cock stirred in response.

No, no, no. He couldn't go outside sporting a massive cockstand that would be obvious to the world.

*Think of something cold. A cold shower. Ice cold. Buckets of ice water pouring down over your head, one after another. Ice cubes piling up around your feet, making your toes go numb.*

He shivered. Thank God.

"We should go. Out." He waved a hand feebly at the stairs. "Do the… thing."

Nova's attention was on his face now, but her smile had disappeared. "Yes. It would be a pity to waste your efforts on just me." She turned away from him and started down the stairs.

"It wouldn't be a waste," he whispered, before picking up his bag and following. Not a waste at all. He'd dressed up for her, not for anyone else.

Aubrey's private trolley car awaited them at the nearest trolley stop. It was holding up normal traffic, resulting in a crowd of angry passengers who were probably going to be late for something. Wyatt stared down at his feet as he slunk aboard. He was an ass, disrupting people's lives for his own convenience. But part of New Security Protocol [TM] was avoiding public transportation and other crowded places.

"I hate this," he declared, throwing himself down onto a couch. He'd forgotten there was a carefully packed bag slung over his arm, and missed crushing it by mere inches.

"It's necessary." Nova perched on the edge of a chair in her bodyguard posture, despite the fact that they were alone on the trolley save for the driver who'd been loyally shuttling Aubrey around for more than a decade.

Wyatt responded with a less-than-effective grunt. He'd let her have her grouchy guard time. He could spend the ride to the hippodrome preparing himself for the upcoming investigation.

They hadn't wasted any time yesterday getting started on their propaganda campaign. Speculation surrounding the crash and explosion at the races had filled the newspapers, including some strong insinuations about possible perpetrators. The underground publications that always seemed to find their way into the hands of every person in Dystopia didn't bother with circumspection. One had so blatantly accused Deimos of colluding with Noel Godfrey that Wyatt wondered if Chet the night watchman had penned it.

Gossip was also supposedly spreading throughout the ranks of the aristocracy, though Wyatt hadn't witnessed any of that in person. What he had witnessed were Leo's long-winded Parliamentary speeches about mining oversight and the need for strict enforcement of the Planetary and Asteroidal Resources Agreement. Deimos, naturally, had shown no reaction other than disinterested acceptance.

Today it was Wyatt's turn to further the cause. Leo had given him an official appointment to study the "potentiality of the Incident to have been triggered via outside influence." There was a whole document full of phrases like "hereinafter defined" and "apropos of" that he'd signed without reading.

Nova had read it twice.

She didn't slip from her professional mode for a second during the trolley ride, even after Wyatt's drone began playing some of his peppiest music. She hardly looked at him and didn't ask about the bag of provisions he'd brought along. The cheering her up business might be even harder than he thought.

When they finally arrived at the employee entrance to the hippodrome—after what felt like about twenty years—they found a pair of stern-faced guards barring the way.

"No visitors," one said.

Wyatt faced them down. "Lord Windborne on official Chamber business."

Neither guard appeared impressed. "You got papers?"

"I have—" Nova started, but Wyatt held up a hand to stop her. He didn't need papers or authorization or anything. These people knew who he was, and after all the recent talk, likely knew exactly why he was here.

"Perhaps you didn't hear me," Wyatt said, in his best be-like-Leo tone. "I am Lord Windborne, and I am here on official business for the Third Chamber."

One of the guards looked him up and down and sniffed in disdain. The other didn't react.

Very well. Wyatt conjured up the sliver of blue-blooded contempt that lurked somewhere in his DNA and channeled every bit of it into his voice. "Get out of my way *immediately* or I shall have my bodyguard physically remove you from my presence." He waved one hand lazily. "And I don't think she's in a very good mood today, so I wouldn't recommend that course of action."

Maybe he shouldn't have added that last part. It was definitely more Wyatt than Leo. The guards got the point, though, and stepped aside with a unison, not-quite-sarcastic, "My lord."

Wyatt gave them a winning smile and strode past.

He had to lord his way past three more guards en route to the crew areas, aided each time by Nova's increasingly rigid scowl. He'd never seen her so tense. Or maybe he had, but simply hadn't noticed before. By now, though, he knew her face well enough to catch the subtle shifts around her eyes and mouth. He could see the tiny hitch in her usually-fluid movements.

He fiddled with the strap of his cooler bag. He wanted to reach out and give her arm a comforting squeeze. He wanted to offer bananas and cookies. He wanted to ask her what the problem was and how he could help. Maybe returning to the scene of the attack had ratcheted up her worry. She definitely had that knight errant protector thing going. But they couldn't stop and have a picnic and talk about their feelings right now. They had work to do.

Wyatt pushed through a door into a mechanic's hanger. A lone mechanic lay on their back, only their coverall-clad legs peeking out from beneath the car they were working on.

"That you, Rosy?" they called.

"It's Lord Windborne. I have a few questions for you."

The mechanic slid out from under the car and stood.

They were a bit shorter than Wyatt and much stockier, with medium-brown skin, pink hair, and adorable dimples.

"Jace. Team Aqua. What can I do for you, my lord?"

Wyatt beckoned to his drone. "Are you willing to be recorded in your professional capacity as a trained and licensed automotive technician?"

Jace's eyebrows rose. "Yes, if the questions pertain to cars."

"They do."

Wyatt started the recording and launched into his rehearsed set of questions. He'd gone over the list in his head at least half a dozen times, starting with the basics for ease of understanding, then delving deeper. It took only a few questions for Jace to grasp the purpose of the discussion and begin freely elaborating without waiting for Wyatt.

"...resulting in superheated steam under extreme pressure. All that energy has to go somewhere. So, boom." Jace made a hand gesture mimicking an explosion. "But these cars aren't like old steam trains. All you have to do is glance at the dashboard to see how well the systems are monitored."

"Could you list these devices and explain the function and purpose of each?" Wyatt prompted.

Jace was doing a brilliant job. With each new piece of information they gave, Nova nodded along, following the explanation without needing clarification. If she could understand without prior knowledge of steam engine tech, others could too.

The proof piled up as Jace continued. Only egregious negligence—which no racing team would ever allow—or deliberate sabotage could cause catastrophic boiler failure, and only on certain models. This evidence would hold up in a court.

Wyatt had just steered the conversation to the topic of fuel explosion and fireball size, when the door to the hangar flew open. He, Nova, and Jace all spun around at once.

A tall blond man dressed in the exact same mercenary garb as Nova stalked into the room. His blue eyes gleamed with malice and his smile was all teeth. He carried a wild-west style revolver in one hand. Another gun rested in a holster at his hip.

"Nova Pratt." He pointed his weapon at Nova, then at Wyatt. "And Wyatt Hartford. You are both under arrest on suspicion of high treason."

# 26

THE SON OF A BITCH hadn't even used Wyatt's title. Nova hated that this was her breaking point. She didn't like to think of Wyatt as an aristocrat. And she absolutely despised it when he started acting arrogant and giving orders. He wasn't an asshole like her father, and he shouldn't have to act like one to get people to take him seriously.

But here she was, ready to plant her fist in a man's face for disrespecting His Lordship.

She took one step forward, letting the fingers of her right hand brush the hilt of her knife. "Have you forgotten how to address your betters, Zeller?"

*Say something nasty. Give me a reason. I want to hit something.*

Zeller's toothy smile widened. "Betters?" he scoffed. "A traitor forfeits all right to rank and title, as well you know. And I believe you meant to say, 'Captain Zeller.'"

"No. I really didn't."

Nova took another step. The only reason she hadn't already jumped the man was his blasted gun. She glanced at Wyatt out of the corner of her eye. He stood with his arms crossed over his chest, a drone hovering protectively in front of him. If Zeller made any kind of threatening move toward Wyatt or the innocent mechanic, she would attack and damn the consequences.

"You. Mechanic." Zeller gestured at Jace. "Get lost."

Jace took a hesitant step forward, eyes wide with fear.

"Go," Wyatt urged. "Thank you for your assistance."

"M-my lord." They gave a shaky bow, then dashed out the door.

"Huh. No witnesses," Nova scoffed. "How very honorable of you. But what else could we expect from one of Connington's little lap-dogs?"

Zeller snarled. "You want to do this the hard way?" He aimed the revolver at her chest.

Nova curled her hand around her knife. As long as Zeller's attention remained on her and not—

Wyatt's drone shot past like a cannonball and slammed into Zeller's hand, sending the gun flying across the room. Nova lunged, cutting off Zeller's cry of pain with a solid blow to his midsection. They crashed to the floor together. His body took the brunt of the fall, but her elbow came down hard on the concrete, sending a jolt of agony up her arm.

Nova roared, half in pain, half in fury. She slammed her fist into Zeller's nose, feeling the crunch as the bone gave way beneath her knuckles. She wrestled his backup revolver from the holster and scrambled to her feet.

"Come after Lord Windborne again and I'll break more than your fucking nose." She tucked the gun into her belt—it was hers now, and she wasn't going unarmed until this mess was over—and snapped her fingers at Wyatt. "Let's go."

Wyatt raced out the door, clutching the strap of the bag he wore slung across his chest. The drone followed him, and Nova followed it.

A choked laugh echoed behind them. "My men..." Zeller rasped, "will... flay you."

He probably deserved to be punched again, but Nova had more important duties at present. She matched Wyatt stride-for-stride as he ran for the exit.

"Best bodyguard ever." He glanced over long enough to bestow a dazzling smile on her.

"Thanks for the drone assist."

"You're welcome. In the movie version the drone will be playing dramatic music and I— Shit!"

They both staggered to a halt as three armed guards came barreling around the bend toward them. Wyatt's drone slewed to avoid a collision. Nova dodged too, but not fast enough to prevent one of the whirring rotors from slicing into her arm. Her left arm, right above the elbow she'd smacked moments ago.

"Fuuuuck," she moaned.

Her legs, fortunately, seemed oblivious to the pain. She pivoted and sprinted back the way they'd come, putting herself directly behind Wyatt in case any of the guards opened fire.

Wyatt fumbled with his bag, pulling it up to cradle it with two hands like a baby or a small animal. Crap. Did he have an animal in there? That would explain why he hadn't simply dropped the thing.

"Faster." She placed a hand on his back and gave him a nudge.

He obeyed, his smooth rhythm making his lengthening strides appear almost effortless. He really was good at running.

They careened around a bend, temporarily out of sight of the men chasing them. Now, however, they were on one of the long sides of the oval-shaped building. The corridor stretched out ahead like a never-ending nightmare hallway. The race track was a mile-long loop, the path through the stadium even longer. She was no distance runner. She'd never be able to maintain this pace all the way back to where they'd started. And if enemies came at them from the other direction, they were screwed.

As if her negative thoughts had summoned them, a group of people stepped out of a doorway about halfway down the hall. Their black and gray clothing could indicate mechanic as easily as mercenary, but she couldn't risk waiting to find out.

"Take the next door," she panted.

Wyatt turned, and this time Nova gave his drone more room to maneuver. The stinging in her arm had turned to burning, but she didn't dare look at the injury.

Nova didn't know the hippodrome well, but the moment she followed Wyatt through the doorway she knew they'd made a serious error. Rugged, knobby tires lay propped against the walls. Streaks of reddish dirt coated the floor. This was the storage and prep area for the Terrain Races, contests that took place outside the safety of the gravity and climate-controlled enclosures. This area jutted out from the rest of the stadium, joining with the glass and iron dome around it to allow the vehicles in and out.

She cursed. Any other crew area would at least have had an exit to the race track. Why had she not told Wyatt to take the first door *on the right*?

The crack of a gun made her stumble. A cloud of plaster sprayed from the wall where the bullet had impacted. Too close. She grabbed Wyatt's arm and hauled him around the nearest corner.

The room was small and dark, filled with shapes and shadows that could trip them up or bar their way through. Light trickled in from whatever lay beyond. Nova used it like a beacon, keeping her gaze locked on that narrow sliver as she pushed through the tangle of equipment. She kept her grip tight on Wyatt's arm, putting him behind every crate or rack or whatever other goddamned things bashed her shins and caught on her clothing.

Another gunshot pinged off something metal.

"Almost there." The words were as much to herself as to Wyatt. They'd gotten close enough that the sliver of light appeared to be a crack between a set of double doors. A few seconds' sprint and they could be through. If the doors were unlocked. "Ready. Set. Go!"

Nova lowered her shoulder and ran, only to nearly fall on her face when the doors turned out to be a pair of curtains. She flailed, arms windmilling as she fought for balance. This time, Wyatt caught *her* arm and steadied her.

"I got you."

Nova looked up. They'd stumbled into an enormous chamber, at least fifty meters wide with a ceiling two stories high. At the far end of the room, sunlight slanted through a wall of glass, illuminating an array of vehicles kitted out for the rocky Martian terrain. The main hangar.

"This way!" She waved Wyatt toward a row of bulky cars, lined up and waiting for someone to open the doors and let them free.

Nova crouched low as she ran, expecting more gunfire from the guards chasing them. None came. She didn't even hear footsteps. Had they changed tactics? If she and Wyatt could get into one of those cars, it wouldn't matter if anyone snuck up on them. She'd been given an override code as part of her motorcar and motorbike training. In theory, she'd be able to start up any vehicle and simply run over anyone who attacked.

A hissing that reminded her of a hydraulic lift broke the silence. A second later, the clang of metal-on-metal shook the ground beneath her. Alarms blared and yellow lights all around the room began to flash.

Wyatt froze, like he'd been turned to stone.

Nova looked over her shoulder. A wall of steel sealed off the section of the room where they'd entered. A quick glance around showed her that what must have been a second entrance was similarly blocked.

They were trapped inside the airlock. Shit, shit, shit.

"Wyatt."

He didn't move.

"Wyatt!" Nova put a hand on his shoulder and shook him. "We have to run!"

He trembled beneath her hand, but remained rooted to the spot. His face had gone completely white, his blue eyes huge with terror.

"I d-don't…" His voice was a mere whisper. "I d-d-don't want to d-die."

"You are *not* dying. Not while I'm on duty. Come on."

She tugged on his jacket, but he still seemed unable to move, his whole being fixated on the wall of glass and the thin, unbreathable air beyond. All around them, the lights continued to pulse in time to wail of the siren.

More hydraulic hissing filled the spaces between the alarm's shrieks, but this sound came from in front of them.

Fuck! If that door opened, it was all over. They'd never make it into one of the cars.

Nova seized Wyatt with both hands and dragged him to the nearest vehicle—a four-wheeled motorbike meant for stunt riding.

"Get on."

He did, thank God, swinging a leg over the seat in a stiff, almost robotic fashion. He clutched the strap of his bag with his left hand, reaching for his drone with his right.

Nova leapt onto the bike in front of him, jabbing at the control panel to punch in the override code.

"Two, two, four, three, nine, five, seven," she sang, thankful for the first time in her life for the brain-meltingly irritating tune her teacher had set the numbers to. "Six, five, eight, three, and eleven."

The bike vibrated to life. Nova slammed her hand down on the shield button, and the glass bubble lowered over them, clamping into place under her feet with a hiss that matched her exhale of relief. Ahead of her, past the line of cars, the massive doors began to open.

"Hold on," she cautioned.

Wyatt's only answer was a sob.

Nova kept her right hand on the controls and reached back with her left—aw, fuck, that hurt—until she found Wyatt's hand. She dragged his arm around her waist.

"Hold me. It's going to be bumpy."

"I can't." He pressed his face into her back.

Nova set the bike into motion. Wyatt's fingers dug into her hip.

"That's it. Hold tight. I won't let anything happen to you."

They couldn't go back. They couldn't stay here. This was the only way. Nova adjusted her position, gripped the handlebars, and for the first time in her life left the safety of the enclosures.

# 27

Wyatt couldn't stop crying. He wanted to. God, how he wanted to, but the tears kept flowing and the sobs kept coming, bigger and faster and bigger and faster until his chest ached and he was gasping for air.

He was wasting oxygen with his crying. The glass bubble surrounding the motorbike only held so much air. He was using it all up, one heaving breath at a time, and he couldn't make it stop. He was going to die. He was going to die all alone on this horrible, empty, *lifeless* planet.

His brothers would be heartbroken. He hadn't said goodbye to Flurry. He hadn't even gotten to pet the squirrels.

"Wyatt!"

That sharp, commanding voice. He wasn't alone, was he? Nova would die out here with him, and that was worse. The world would be so much colder and lonelier without her in it.

"Wyatt, you need to breathe," she said, sternly but not angrily. "You are hyperventilating. I want you to breathe with me."

Yes. Nova was right. He was hyperventilating. He needed to breathe. Nova was good at being right.

"In and out," she instructed. "You can do it." She said this last as if it were a simple statement of fact. Wyatt liked that. He liked the straightforward way she said things and the orderly way she solved problems. She made sense to his brain, the way his machines did.

"With me. In, two, three, four. Out, two, three, four. In, two, three, four. Out, two, three, four."

He drew in a shaky breath and expelled it in time to her counting. *In, two, three, four. Out, two, three, four.* It took a few tries before he settled into the pattern. The tears continued to flow, but the tightness in his chest began to ebb.

*In, two, three, four.* He tapped the fingers of his left hand in time with the breathing. *Out, two, three, four.* He tapped with his right hand.

In, out. Left, right. Wyatt sank into the comfort of the rhythm. Four beats in, his fingers brushing the sturdy canvas of Nova's tactical pants. Four beats out, the cool metal of the drone. His chest, rising and falling against the solid warmth of Nova's body.

The bike hit a particularly large bump, and for an instant they seemed to float, weightless, adrift in the nothingness. Wyatt's breath hitched, the cadence forgotten.

Then the tires hit the ground again, and he slammed back down onto the seat so hard it might literally have crushed his balls.

New tears pooled in his eyes—sharp, stinging tears of pain. If his mind had disconnected from his body for a time, it was now back with a vengeance. He was one hundred percent alive, one hundred percent real, and one million percent in agony.

He pressed his face harder into Nova's back. "Fuck, fuck, fuck." His voice rose higher with each syllable. "Fucking, fucking, fucking fuck!"

"I'm sorry, I'm so sorry!" Nova's voice also sounded a bit shrill, or maybe it was only a distortion caused by his pain. "I've never driven in low gravity before, and I'm trying to keep us on rocky ground so we won't leave obvious tracks."

Wyatt continued swearing. Swearing was supposed to help ease pain. It *really* didn't feel like it was helping, but if he could form words, at least he was still breathing.

"More bumps ahead," Nova warned. "Hold on."

Wyatt clamped his thighs to the sides of the bike as tightly as he could. The bike bounced and rocked, but he stayed mostly in his seat. The drone he cradled in the crook of his arm jabbed into his ribs each time they lurched to the right. That was good. He could feel pain somewhere other than between his legs now.

For the first time since Nova had started the bike, he lifted his head and opened his eyes. Hell and damnation. No wonder it was so bumpy. Nova had driven them into the hills, cutting a winding path between boulders on her way up the slope. In the distance, sunlight sparkled off the angled facets of aristocratic estates. Everything else was rock, some jagged and broken, some worn smooth by eons of windstorms. So many shades of red and brown.

Wyatt's pulse leapt. His breathing grew ragged.

*Tap, tap, tap, tap. In. Out.*

His body understood the assignment now. He kept breathing, kept counting, and kept his eyes open.

"Where are we going?" he asked. She must have a destination in mind. No one was chasing them that he could see, and Nova wasn't the sort to drive into the mountains on a whim with a limited air supply and no backup. "You're taking us somewhere."

"I know where we can get back in. An emergency shelter of sorts. How are you doing? Okay?"

"If hoping this is all a nightmare and I'm going to wake up soon counts as okay, then yes."

"It does not. But you're making jokes instead of crying or swearing. Let's try to keep doing that. Why don't you turn on some music?"

Brilliant! Wyatt switched on the drone's speaker and started up one of his favorite playlists. Why hadn't he thought of this earlier?

A sudden jolt reminded him that he was in the Martian wilderness and still rather sensitive in certain areas.

*Right. Panic attack plus seat to the balls. Let's not do that again.*

"You like it, don't you?" crooned the music, the singer's voice husky against the eerie harmonies of the keyboard. "When I'm a little bit naughty?"

Wyatt's hands started to move. Then his feet. Soon, he was singing along. It was a million times better than before. Like the rhythmic breathing, the music kept his body in motion and his lungs functioning. He wasn't enjoying the ride—as evidenced by the painful tightness of his shoulders and the roiling in his stomach—but he was tolerating it.

The drive felt endless. At one point, Nova had to navigate around a ridiculously enormous estate while Wyatt squeezed his eyes shut. If he saw anything green and living on the opposite side of the glass, he was going to panic again, even with the music playing.

*Beep!*

Wyatt sang louder, because for some illogical reason it helped more.

*Beep!*

That wasn't part of the song. He craned his neck, trying to look over Nova's shoulder. "What was that?"

She swiped at the control panel. "Nothing."

The beeping didn't stop.

Wyatt's throat grew tight. "Nova, I'm starting to feel not okay again. Could you please tell me?"

"It's the oxygen sensor. It's not an emergency yet, and we're almost there."

"The… oxygen sensor." The words squeaked out of him. "Fine."

"Sing, Wyatt," she commanded. "I'm not going to let you die, so turn up the volume and sing."

The muscles of her back were rock-hard against his chest. A bead of perspiration trickled down her neck.

He sang. For her.

Because he needed her to be okay, even if he wasn't. Even if his legs were trembling and his voice was cracking on the high notes. He sang for her because someone had to. Because she was so bloody-mindedly determined to help other people and so was he, and neither of them was going to fail right now.

So he sang, through the beeps and the jolts and the fear, on and on, until she pulled the bike to a stop in front of a wall of stone and let out a breathless, "We're here."

Wyatt broke off in the middle of the chorus. "We are?"

Nova began fiddling with the controls. "I just have to give the passphrase. How do I…" She flipped a switch and pressed several keys, then slammed her fist down. "Dammit, can't this thing send an access request?"

The oxygen sensor was beeping triple time now. Wyatt swayed, suddenly lightheaded. His chest was constricting again, his pulse racing.

"My drone," he gasped. "My drone can do it." He shoved the sleeve of his jacket up to expose his watch and sent a command.

The music stopped playing. A sensor light flashed.

"Please state the passphrase," a soothing feminine voice requested.

"Quocunque modo," Nova blurted.

The wall of rock parted. The moment it was wide enough, Nova shot through the gap. Lights winked on, illuminating bare concrete floor and walls and a single, steel exit door. A bunker? Or a dungeon? They both had air, so Wyatt's vote was for dungeon, because that would probably have rats or centipedes, and he desperately wanted to see something alive right now.

The rock door sealed closed behind them. A short time later, a green light turned on above the exit. Nova's hands flew over the controls, and the bike's protective dome popped open.

Wyatt sucked in a deep breath. Air. Normal, breathable air, all around him, and not a fucking red rock in sight. His body went so slack with relief, he nearly toppled off the bike.

"Whoa." He steadied himself before dismounting slowly, giving his legs a moment to adjust to standing on solid ground. He shut off the speaker on the drone and turned the rotors on so it could hover again. Then he lifted the strap of his cooler bag over his head and set the bag on the floor. They were safe. They could fortify themselves with a picnic before heading for home. His hands might be shaking, but he was alive and more-or-less in control of his body.

He turned to Nova, who for some reason had dismounted slower than he had. "You are fucking amazing, you know that? You deserve a goddamned medal. I think I can do that. Give people medals, I mean. Like, 'I, Lord Windborne, hereby—'"

Nova staggered and Wyatt reached out to help her catch her balance. He took her elbow, only to recoil when his hand met wet, sticky cloth. Streaks of red crossed his palm where he'd touched her. Blood. Her blood.

"Shit, Nova, you're hurt!"

"I'm fine." She tried to wave him off, but her hand barely lifted. "It's only a scr… a scr—" Her eyes rolled upward and she pitched forward into his arms.

# 28

Nova's eyelids cracked open. The blurry world around her began to coalesce into something almost recognizable. She lay on her back. Someone—Wyatt—knelt over her. And he was… shirtless?

"Am I dreaming?" she mumbled. That probably wasn't the sort of question she would ask during a dream. Unless it meant she was about to wake up.

"Lay still, sweetheart." Wyatt adjusted something soft beneath her head. "You're going to be okay, but I need you to stay where you are while I finish the bandage. Can you do that for me?"

"Yes." She could hardly do otherwise. His voice was so soothing, almost hypnotic. She wanted to float away wherever it would take her.

"Good girl."

Her stomach fluttered. Usually that phrase came as an insult. *Be a good girl and let the boys handle it. That job's too dirty for a good girl like you. Good girl Nova does everything by the book.*

But Wyatt said it like it was something to be proud of. Like she pleased him.

A surge of pain obliterated that satisfying line of thought.

For an instant, the world went black, trying to pull her under once more.

"Sorry."

Nova clung to the sound of Wyatt's voice, willing him back into focus.

"The worst is done," he promised. "When you're ready to sit up, I'll see about fashioning some kind of sling to keep your arm still, but for now you should rest. I'm going to get you some food and drink."

Food and drink. He'd also mentioned a sling and bandages. This wasn't home, and it wasn't a hospital. Where… Oh, shit.

Everything came flooding back. The chase through the hippodrome, the mad escape on the bike, Wyatt's panic. And the pain in her arm that she'd shoved aside while she'd done her duty driving them to safety.

"Are you remembering what happened?" Wyatt asked. "You were incredible, but also very foolish. I'll give you the benefit of the doubt and assume you didn't realize how much blood you were losing with all the adrenaline pumping through your veins."

He disappeared from sight. Nova levered herself up with her good elbow. The movement caused a wave of dizziness, but she held still until it passed. Wyatt had turned away from her and was now pulling an assortment of things from the bag he'd been carrying all day.

"You have cookies?"

His head whipped around. "Hey! Didn't I tell you no sitting up?"

"No, you told me you'd make me a sling when I was ready to sit. I'm ready." She pushed hard with her right hand and managed to get her torso mostly upright. Colored lights danced in front of her eyes, and she breathed slow and deep until they cleared. "See?"

Wyatt's blue eyes blazed like fire, and an angry flush turned his cheeks pink. "Fine," he growled. Growled! Like he had fangs and claws and wanted to tear something apart. Of all possible reactions, that was not one she'd ever expected.

Wyatt stomped over to the bike and rolled it behind Nova so she could lean against it. It wasn't the most comfortable back rest, but if she was honest, she couldn't hold herself up forever, and this was far better than lying on the floor. With her left arm folded across her chest, the pain was bearable. Wyatt had cut away her sleeve entirely, leaving her a clear view of his handiwork. The bandages he'd crafted from his shirt were tidy and effective: an admirable job of administering first aid with few supplies.

His jacket had apparently been serving as her pillow. Now that she was no longer using it, he pulled it back on. Fuck, he was gorgeous. The bare chest with the jacket was even hotter than complete lack of a shirt. Even with his hair in disarray and his eye makeup smeared across his cheeks he possessed the beauty of an ancient god. If she weren't hurt she'd be climbing all over him.

He sat down beside her and pulled the food closer.

"Look." He heaved a sigh. "I'm angry at you, I'm angry at me, and I am absolutely livid at the people who put us in this position. I don't like feeling like this, and I don't want to yell at you, so can you rest now and let me feed you?"

Despite everything, she laughed. "Yes. I suppose fair's fair."

"It is." He opened a can of soda water and handed it to her. "You saved me, I get to save you. Not that I'm a general proponent of lex talionis, but in this situation it's apt."

"What is lex tali-whatsit? I don't know Latin."

"You don't? Lex talionis means 'law of retaliation.' Like 'an eye for an eye' kind of thing." Wyatt unwrapped a sandwich and laid it in Nova's lap. "I thought you said something in Latin to get us in here."

"Mm." Nova took several sips of water before replying. "I said, 'quocunque modo.' It's the Pratt family motto. I think it means something like, 'whatever it takes'?"

"By any means," Wyatt corrected. "It shows up in a well-known passage from one of the Odes of Horace. 'Rem facias, rem si possis, recte, si non, quocumque modo, rem.' Which approximately translates to, 'Make money, honest money if possible, if not, money by any means.'"

Nova almost spit out a mouthful of soda water. She swallowed hard and coughed. "Because of course my family motto is about making money any way possible."

"It certainly suits your father. Though, to be fair—to Horace, at least—the entire ode is like: Should you really be listening to people who say things like this? Are those front-row theater tickets worth your soul? Yeah? Really? Although I don't think my tutors at Eton actually told me that the correct answer is, 'No, money is not better than doing right.' I don't think they were supposed to instill that kind of plebian sentiment in an aristocrat."

Nova snort-laughed. Her arm still throbbed, but their conversation had her feeling like herself again. She raised her drink in salute. "Thank you. Apparently all I needed was a bit of hydration and some snarky comments about classical education and now I'm fine."

"No." A flash of fury again lit Wyatt's eyes, then quickly faded. "It's still my turn. Drink your water and eat your sandwich. If you do that without complaining or trying to get up, I have bananas and cookies."

"Bananas and cookies? I thought you had an animal in

that bag, you seemed so reluctant to let go of it." Nova took a bite of her sandwich. Aged cheese and crisp lettuce perfectly complemented the thinly-sliced meat. A spicy sauce added a nice kick without detracting from the flavor. "Mmm," she murmured appreciatively around the mouthful.

"No animals, just lunch," Wyatt explained. "And a book of fairy tales. I was hoping to have a picnic to cheer you up. I guess this sort of counts as a picnic, but I suspect I'm mostly failing on cheering you up, since you've got a badly bruised arm and enough blood loss that you probably shouldn't attempt anything more than a slow walk and we're hiding out in some kind of dungeon that doesn't even appear to be infested with vermin—"

"No vermin is a *good* thing!" Nova interrupted. "And it's not a dungeon. It's a hidden emergency tunnel that runs beneath my father's estate."

Wyatt fumbled his sandwich. "His estate? Super. Not a dungeon, just a secret hideout beneath the enemy's lair. I need a cookie." He picked up two cookies, holding one out to Nova. "Have one. It is my completely non-professional medical opinion that they are an excellent aid in healing wounded arms."

Nova set her sandwich down and accepted the cookie. The texture was soft without being gooey, the chocolate rich and decadent on her tongue. She didn't know whether to gobble the whole thing down and demand another or to nibble at it and savor each delicious bite. What she did know for certain was that she wanted to kiss Wyatt after he'd eaten one and taste the bittersweet chocolate on his lips.

The cookie turned to ash in her mouth. Dammit, it was happening again. He was distracting her from the things that mattered. She'd failed so comprehensively in her attempt to behave in a distant and professional manner that he'd baked her cookies, for fuck's sake! He was feeding her, soothing her, and protecting her, not to mention seducing her with his alluring smile and revealing clothing.

She was going to have to tell him after all. She would have to make her mouth form the words and then offer him an explanation for why they couldn't keep dating. And it had to be better than, "We just can't."

Wyatt's brow furrowed. "You're frowning. Is your arm hurting, or is it the cookie? Did I use too much baking soda? I may have lost track of how many teaspoons I put in."

"The cookie is delicious. But I… we…" How the hell was she supposed to do this? "I think we need to—"

Wyatt scooted closer, until they sat shoulder-to-shoulder. He pressed a quick kiss to her cheek. "Is anyone likely to realize that we're here?"

"No."

"Then *you* need to not worry right now. Be kind to yourself and your body. You deserve it."

Nova's shoulders sagged. "I'm so tired," she admitted.

"I know. You can lean on me if you need to. How about I read you fairy tales while you eat your lunch, and then you can nap as long as you want." Wyatt pulled a book from his bag and opened it to a marked page. "The Raven," he read. "Once there was a queen who had a little daughter—"

Nova let her head fall onto his shoulder. She adored this story of the princess-turned-raven and the man who was no great hero, but persisted through his mistakes and difficulties to free her from the curse.

And she was exhausted. She couldn't protect Wyatt or anyone if she didn't give her body a chance to recover.

She picked up her sandwich and made herself eat the rest while Wyatt read to her in his smooth, soothing voice. When her eyelids began to droop, she allowed him to help her lie down. He wrapped his arms around her, and she snuggled into his warmth. She'd let herself have this. A few hours in his embrace would relax her and strengthen her. If she seized as much of him as possible right now, surely that would sustain her through their inevitable parting.

Soft lips brushed her temple. "Sleep well, love," he murmured.

Nova pressed closer.

*All of him. Just for a little while. Just for now.*

# 29

"Do a lap of the room. Slowly."

Nova gave Wyatt an exasperated look, but followed his instructions. He'd used his boot laces to lash her arm to her chest rather than sacrificing another article of his clothing. He wouldn't be able to run as well, but since Nova couldn't run either, that hardly mattered.

He watched her closely as she walked. Her arm didn't move, and he didn't spy any obvious signs of increased pain. He wouldn't say she was recovered—her cautious movements suggested she was still in some discomfort—but she was more her usual self.

Wyatt let out a breath of relief. She was going to be okay.

Nova had slept for more than three hours. Three hours in which he'd held her close, listening to her breathing and gazing at her beautiful face. Three hours fearing he hadn't done enough and her wound would reopen or she'd come down with a fever. But she was walking now, under her own power, with no signs of dizziness or weakness.

"How's everything feel?"

"Good enough to get us out of here." She finished the loop, halting at his side. "Are you ready?"

He slung his bag over his head, then fished out a banana. "Eat this first. And maybe a cookie or two." When her eyes narrowed, he added, "I'll eat some too. We ought to be properly nourished before we attempt…" He waved a hand. "Whatever."

Nova took the banana and stared at it for an oddly long time before snapping the top to peel it. "Read me one more fairy tale while I eat this."

Wyatt happily obliged. The more relaxed they both were when they set out, the better.

After Nova finished her snack, she used her family motto to open the door to the tunnel leading up into the house. They walked side-by-side, Wyatt sticking close to Nova in case she faltered. The passage was narrow and dimly lit, with a noticeable upward slope. By the time they reached the opposite end, Nova was panting.

Wyatt grasped her good arm. "Take a drink, eat some cookies."

"You are so annoying," she griped, before stuffing half a cookie in her mouth.

Wyatt gave her a playful nudge. "You love it when I fuss over you. It gives you something to scowl about."

"Shut up and eat your own damn cookie."

Wyatt did. Nova was sliding back into mercenary mode, and he didn't want to disrupt that. Not when they were about to enter the home of the man who was sending hired killers after them.

The final door also used the same password. It opened into a wine cellar full of barrels large enough to hide a dead body in. Wyatt shivered. He did not want to become the next dead body Deimos had to hide.

"Follow me," Nova said, her voice entirely calm. "The stairs to the main house are around the corner."

"Shouldn't we be whispering?" Wyatt hissed.

Nova shrugged.

Wyatt stuck close behind her, keeping his drone on their vulnerable left side. Nova had her knife, and the gun she'd swiped from Zeller, but he didn't know how well she'd be able to wield either, given her injury.

Their footsteps thundered in his ears. Every creak or groan of the floorboards startled him. How could Nova be so nonchalant about all this? Yes, she knew the house, and yes, Deimos had piss poor security from everything Wyatt had seen thus far. But even a small amount of apprehension on her part would ease some of Wyatt's anxiety.

Because he was beginning to think she meant to fling herself into a hopeless fight to give him the chance to flee.

Which wasn't fucking happening. Not ever.

At the top of the stairs, Nova paused for a moment, listening. Then she waved him out into a long hall lined with gilded mirrors. Light from chandeliers overhead reflected off nearly every surface, making him squint.

Wyatt had been in the public areas of Deimos's mansion before, during his infrequent appearances at balls and other gatherings. He knew the foyer, the dining room, and the ballroom, and had thought himself immune to their opulence. But seeing the same extravagance in an ordinary corridor of a far-off wing set his teeth on edge.

"I like sparkles as much as the next man, but does everything here need to be gold and crystal? I'm going to get a migraine from the glare."

"My father has appalling taste," Nova replied. "Your ravens would decorate better."

"Also, I look like hell." Wyatt combed his fingers through

his hair, trying vainly to sweep it back into the cute wave from that morning. "I cried so much I look like a child forced to work in a coal mine." He rubbed a hand across one cheek, which only smeared the eye liner more. "A kohl mine? Please pardon my punning, I've been under a lot of stress."

"I can survive your questionable sense of humor. There are only two more hallways before we reach the library."

"The library? What then? Do we climb out a window or something?"

"If things go according to plan, we'll walk out the front door."

The infinite Wyatts in the mirrors all went wide-eyed, like startled deer. "Um…"

Nova held up a hand. "Wait here while I check the next hall. It's more likely to be occupied."

She hurried toward the end of the corridor at a pace much too rapid for Wyatt's liking. Ignoring her orders, he jogged after her. No way was he letting her overexert herself for his sake again.

"No running," he ordered.

She glared at him. "Don't use your lord voice on me."

"Then stop endangering yourself for my sake."

Her expression turned as cold and neutral as stone. "It's my job."

*Then get a new job.*

He swallowed the words. He needed to keep his mouth shut so they could get out of here, and arguing with her would only distract them both.

Nova peered around the corner. "It's clear, but this is a long and often-used hall. Either we can run or we can hide behind fake classical statues every few yards. Your choice."

Something thumped behind them.

"Run." Wyatt's legs were moving before he got the word out.

They dashed around the corner and down the hall, past dozens of life-sized marble nudes that Wyatt might have appreciated in any other context. About halfway down, Wyatt thought he heard voices, but Nova didn't stop or slow down and he didn't dare look back. He matched his pace exactly to hers, braced to catch her if she suffered even the smallest stumble.

A few yards later, she snatched hold of his sleeve and hauled him down a side corridor—she certainly didn't lack any strength in her right arm. Her breathing had grown ragged, but she kept running, and Wyatt couldn't think of any better option than sticking with her.

She finally slowed as they approached a set of double doors with curved iron handles. This must be the library. Wyatt grabbed a handle and pulled the door open. He made sure Nova and his drone were safely inside before entering and closing the door behind him.

Compared to most of the house, the library was modest. Bookshelves covered most of the walls, while couches and large chairs filled the open space between. A fire crackled in the hearth. It was cozy. Intimate. He would have loved to curl up here with a good book.

Nova sagged against a bookshelf, breathing heavily.

Another surge of fury at the people who had done this to her engulfed Wyatt, and he made an abrupt gesture at the closest chair. "Sit."

She shook her head. Wyatt had half a mind to pick up the stubborn woman and carry her to the chair himself.

"Who's there?"

Wyatt yelped and fell back against the door. A head peeked out from behind one of the chairs at the far end of the room. Fuck! They'd been caught! How the hell was he supposed to talk his way out of this?

"Nova?"

Wait. Wyatt knew that voice and that face.

James, Lord Metus, the duke's sole legitimate child, rose from his seat and started toward them. "And Windborne? What are you two doing here?"

Wyatt didn't quite relax, but his pulse began to slow. Metus was a reasonable man. He wouldn't harm them. They were still trespassing on his father's property, however, looking like escapees from a battlefield hospital. Wyatt wouldn't really blame him if he called for help.

Nova waved. "Hi, Jamie. We ran into a spot of trouble."

Lord Metus strolled closer. He was younger than Wyatt and Nova, in his mid- or late-twenties. He was dressed like a scholar, in a gray herringbone tweed suit. Dark eyes exactly the same as his sister's peered out from behind square, rimless glasses.

"I can see that," the young lord replied. His gaze caressed Wyatt from head to toe. "Since the only other possibility is that you're here to invite me to a sexy street urchin party."

"I'm afraid not. That sounds a lot more fun." Wyatt cocked a hip and gave Jamie a coy smile. "You'd make a cute urchin." He'd flirt his way out of here, if that's what it took.

Nova cleared her throat.

Wyatt turned. "We won't leave you out, darling. The two of you could sit on the floor side-by-side, gazing up at everyone with those big brown eyes." He looked back and forth between the siblings. "Your father might be a massive prick, but he did give both of you absolutely gorgeous eyes. You'd have everyone swooning."

Nova scowled at him. "You can stop this nonsense. You don't need to seduce Jamie to get him to help us."

"Not that I object to being seduced," Jamie added. "But it would be bad form to steal my sister's boyfriend, even if he is hot as hell. How can I help you instead?"

"We came through the emergency tunnel," Nova explained. "Now we need to get out without anyone realizing who we are or where we came from."

Her brother's face lit up. "I can do that! Wait right here."

Half an hour later, they walked straight out the front door, as Nova had predicted. Wyatt had a hideous cowboy hat shadowing his face and an overly large plaid shirt that smelled like a century's worth of mothballs hiding his clothes and his drone. His mostly empty bag dangled from one shoulder. Jamie hung on his arm, beaming up at him. Nova, dressed in footman's livery—complete with powdered wig—followed closely behind, carrying a stack of books tall enough to obscure her injured arm.

"I do hope you enjoy the books, Mr. Whittaker," Jamie cooed as they passed a bored-looking doorman. "Feel free to return them at any time. Or come by to borrow more, if you like. As many as you want."

A flush had crept up the young man's neck and he sounded bashful. Wyatt didn't think he was acting. He'd tensed up the moment they'd left the library.

Jamie walked them along the drive to the carriage house and gestured at a small motorcar. "Drop Mr. Whittaker off at the trolley stop," he said to Nova.

She executed an elegant bow, despite her arm and the books. She dropped the books into the rear seat, then slipped behind the wheel, while Jamie held the door for Wyatt, an awkward smile still plastered on his face.

"Good luck," he whispered. "And I do want to see you again. I want to hear about how this thing between you two happened."

Wyatt took Jamie's hand and kissed his knuckles. "I'll invite you to the sexy street urchin party."

Jamie turned red as a beet. "I don't actually like parties."

"Neither do I. It'll be, like, me and three people."

"Then it's a definite maybe." Jamie smiled at Nova. "Take care, big sis."

She started up the engine. "I always do."

As they rolled away from the house, Wyatt crossed his arms over his belly, pressing the drone against his skin. It poked uncomfortably, but kept him grounded. His entire body prickled, like a thousand pairs of eyes were on him.

In reality, no one had spared them a second glance. He was some weird bookish friend of Jamie's. Nova was a servant. They didn't matter to anyone.

The main gate parted for them.

"There. We're out," Nova said. "Do you feel better now?"

"A bit. Thank you. Your brother is a nice guy."

She nodded, her gaze straight ahead.

*Silent protector mode, activated.*

They rode the trolley downtown before dumping the borrowed clothing in a rubbish bin, then walked the rest of the way to the factory. Nova's silence had persisted and she'd also grown restless, hunching her shoulders and shifting her weight.

Wyatt stopped outside the entrance. "Are you okay? Not the arm. We'll get you more water and some painkillers and get you checked out by a doctor for that. But you're fidgety and that's not normal. If you're anxious about telling the others what happened, don't be. You were spectacular. No one can fault you for what happened or accuse you of failing at your job in any way."

Nova shook her head, blinking rapidly. Crap, was she crying? Wyatt put an arm around her, but she flinched away.

"Let's go inside." He opened the door and held it for her. "Fair's fair, remember? I'm going to get you some meds and some rest, and then you can go back to protecting me. How about you move in with me? Then we can watch over each other around-the-clock and no one will need to worry."

"You should date my brother," Nova blurted.

Wyatt's brow furrowed. He couldn't have heard that right. "Who should what?"

"You and Jamie. You make sense. You're both aristocrats, but you both want to make things better. You know fancy things like Latin and have lots of money. If you don't like something, you both walk away and make your own rules. You fit, like a circle in a round hole."

Wyatt took hold of Nova's right arm and steered her through the door. "Is this about the flirting? That wasn't serious. He's cute and nice, but he's not you. I'm dating *you*. I like *you*, Nova. I really like you and I want to find out where this relationship is going to take us."

A single tear ran down her cheek. "It takes us nowhere. It can't. I can't." She turned away from him. "We have to break up."

The words hit him like a gut punch, stealing all the breath from his lungs. He tried to speak, but only choked.

"I'm sorry," she mumbled.

Wyatt fought for composure. This wasn't happening. It couldn't be happening. It made no sense. He stepped closer to Nova, but didn't touch her.

"Nova, love, whatever the problem is, you can tell me. We'll figure it out. We can fix it."

"We *are* the problem!" She banged a fist against the wall. "*I* am the problem. We don't fit. I'm a square peg."

"No, you're not. You're perfect."

"Goddammit, Wyatt!" She whirled around. More tears

glittered in the corners of her eyes, but didn't fall. "I should have left before, but I was selfish. We have to break up. Before it gets worse." Her shoulders sagged and her gaze dropped to the floor. "I'm sorry. I didn't... I don't want to hurt you." She kicked the door open and ran out.

For a while, Wyatt could only stand frozen in place, trying to comprehend what had just happened. Eventually his feet began to move, carrying him upstairs. Voices drifted out from the vicinity of the kitchen. Wyatt followed the sounds in a daze, hoping someone might be able to pinch him and wake him up.

Leo leapt up from his barstool the moment Wyatt entered the room. "Where the hell have you been? Everyone is shouting about a shooting at the hippodrome. We've been out of our fucking minds with worry!"

Wyatt blinked at his friend. His eyes couldn't seem to focus and his legs felt suddenly unsteady.

"I think..." His tongue felt thick, his mind sluggish. "I think I got dumped."

# 30

## Viper Defanged?

After months of dedicated work by RMC Commander Alaric Connington, the scofflaw known as the Viper has gone silent.

"We knew we had him when he started slandering others to hide his sins," Connington said in an exclusive interview. "The heightened security the RMC has provided at the spaceport has ensured that all goods entering the country are fully inspected and taxed. He is desperate, and recent 'incidents' are the result."

The commander declined to elaborate further, but this reporter can only assume he refers to the rumors of criminal activity at the Victoria Regina National Hippodrome. Reports of gunfire in the crew areas have since been confirmed, as has the presence of a certain Lord W—, in the company of an alleged rogue mercenary. Both are wanted for further questioning. Lord W— has not appeared in public since.

Nova crumpled the paper in her fist and hurled it across the trolley car at Leo. "How can you subscribe to this heaping pile of bullshit?"

The duke didn't glance up from his own reading. "It's important to know what the other side is saying. It's more difficult to respond to rubbish accusations if I'm taken by surprise."

"You don't like to feel uncertain."

Leo lowered his newspaper. "Neither do you."

Nova couldn't argue with that. It was why she was here, riding in a luxurious private trolley car with a duke, instead of on public transport or her bicycle. It was why she continued to insist upon the security protocol she'd created. Her life had enough uncertainty these days without adding unnecessary worry about the safety of her boys.

And it was working. She had to remind herself of that every time she got annoyed by one aspect of the protocol or another. They were all well. A week had passed with no gunfire or explosions. She was doing the right thing.

True, it did feel at times like repeatedly jabbing herself with a needle, but sometimes wounds needed stitching before they could heal.

"How's your arm?"

Nova blinked at the non sequitur. "It's fine. The bruise is still a riot of colors, but it doesn't hurt unless I touch it."

"Ah. You were grimacing and I thought it might be bothering you." Leo returned his attention to his paper. "Glad to know it's not. I'd prefer Wyatt not berate me again for making you work 'unreasonably long hours.'"

"There's nothing unreasonable about escorting you to and from a meeting. All the other men there had security."

The paper rustled as Leo turned a page. "I agree. I've been quite pleased with your security protocol. Only Wyatt has voiced objections. Perhaps he requires an explanation from a trusted ally who is not me."

Nova huffed. "I sincerely doubt he'd want one from me, either."

"Oh?" Leo turned another page. He couldn't possibly be reading that fast. "Whyever not? I was under the impression he held you in high regard."

"He seems content to keep his own company of late." Nova's voice came out frostier than she'd intended. Despite spending most of her recent days cozied up with the Lords of Dystopia, she'd yet to master the political art of prevarication.

"Indeed." Leo folded his newspaper with great deliberation before reaching for another. "I'm sure he has his reasons."

"As long as he's at home, he's safe. That's what matters." Nova rose to fetch the paper Leo had set aside. She settled back in her chair and began to peruse a page of advertisements. She had nothing more to say on this topic. If Leo wanted to know why she and Wyatt had hardly even looked at one another in the past week, he could bloody well ask Wyatt. She had more important things to focus on.

She glowered at an ad for a new flavor of Lisa Luna lip gloss. *Passion Fruit Pop! With plenty of sparkle and a hint of red for that extra zing!*

Wyatt would like it. He'd carefully paint his lips, then offer her a kiss with a flirty, "Want to see how it tastes?"

Nova tossed the paper aside and turned to stare out the window. How long would it take before she stopped thinking about him? He'd hardly left his apartment all week. The few times they'd been in the same room, they hadn't spoken. She'd been plenty busy accompanying Leo, Rion, and Aubrey on various outings and making regular patrols through the neighborhood. Her mind ought to be fully occupied with work.

Yet seven days later, every little thing still reminded her

of Wyatt. A flash of blue made her picture his eyes. A beep or a buzz had her turning to look for one of his drones. She couldn't smell chocolate without thinking about how he'd made her a whole damned batch of cookies to cheer her up.

Fuck, she missed him. Right now she'd give almost anything to see his sunny smile or hear his musical laughter.

She had only herself to blame for this gaping hole in her heart. She never should have allowed him to take her on dates. Wyatt had taken her hand like a fairy godfather and led her straight out of reality, into a mythical land where she could be somebody's princess. Where she could sparkle and dance in the sunlight, knowing that no matter what dark forces arose, a prince would swoop in to cherish and protect her.

Nova was no princess. Not by birth, and not by nature. A duke's bastards were raised to protect and serve. For her siblings, this was merely a stepping stone, a way to take them closer to those they worked for. For Nova, it was a calling.

No amount of conditioning could turn her to evil. No amount of training could instill mindless obedience. She wasn't sworn to defend any particular man, or even a particular government. She was sworn to defend the people.

*Upon my honor, I pledge my life in service to the people of Utopia.*

Every mercenary spoke those words before they were certified to take contracts. Most treated it as a formality rather than a public declaration that you would never stab a client in the back or leave them to be killed while you fled to save yourself. But to Nova, those words were a contract, and one that trumped all others. It was the only vow she'd ever taken, and she would not break her word, even if the world broke her.

And so she would defend her boys, these brave young

men who had been fighting the system since childhood, kicking down walls brick by brick. She would protect them and help them as they built something better, where the people—her people—weren't used up and cast aside. She wasn't a princess. She was a warrior.

The thoughts rolled through her mind on repeat, as endless as the estates rolling by out the window. When she finally stepped off the trolley downtown, it was with a renewed sense of conviction.

*I am a warrior. I fight for good and I'm doing what's right.*

Nova walked Leo to the factory entrance and waited for him to enter.

"Join us for dinner?" he offered.

Nova ruthlessly quashed the butterflies of excitement in her belly. "No one else is going out tonight, correct?"

"Correct. But we'd love to have you regardless."

Nova shook her head. The cozy abode above the factory was her office, not her home. Distance helped her remember that. "It's better if I turn in early. I'll be back first thing in the morning." She could grab takeout from the Pie-Pass next to her building. It would be fine. An eel pie would be enough to sustain her.

"Very well."

It sounded like a rebuke, or at least a stern disapproval. Two little words to convey "I will not force you to do my bidding, but I am most displeased and will hold you responsible for any consequences of your poor decision." They probably devoted whole classes to the proper tone and expression in Duke School.

Leo stepped through the door, then looked back at her. "Goodnight, Nova." This time, his words and his half-smile weren't ducal, but brotherly.

"Goodnight, Your Grace."

Nova rushed off to her apartment. Pie-Pass was closing up for the night, so her eel pie was lukewarm, but since that suited her mood, she insisted on paying full price.

She arrived at her building's entrance at the same time as a pair of chatting people. The first—a petite and voluptuous woman with dark brown skin and curly brown hair haloing her pretty face—lived directly across from Nova. They'd met before, briefly, and Nova hated that she couldn't recall the woman's name.

"Hi!" The woman waved. "Nova, right? Marika, from across the hall."

"Hi, Marika. Good to see you again."

"And this is Janna." Marika indicated the second person, who had lighter brown skin and hair buzzed to a short fuzz. "She just got a new job at Central Manufactory, and she'll be staying with me while she looks for a place nearby."

Janna bounced on the balls of her feet. "Hi! Pleased to meet you."

Janna dressed like Wyatt, in a crop top and jeans. She was lean and fidgety and had a smile that could light up a whole city block. She even had rainbow-painted fingernails.

"Nice to meet you too, Janna. I'm Nova." *And you are exactly my type and I should be really into you right now, but instead I'm just missing Wyatt and it hurts so much I want to hit something. What the hell is wrong with me?*

Nova waved her pie. "I should, um, go eat. But I'll see you around?" Crap, she hadn't meant that to sound like a question.

"Yes, go," Marika urged. "I'm sure you need to eat. Maybe we could do breakfast if you're not too busy." She leaned toward Janna and added in a pseudo-whisper, "Nova works for the *Lords*."

Janna's eyes widened. "Oh! You'll want to see our latest

cartoon, then!" She dug into her pocket and produced a folded piece of paper. "No need to give it back. We have lots. You can pass it on to someone else who will appreciate it."

"Thank you." Nova nodded to the women and scurried up the stairs to her apartment.

She unfolded the cartoon on the table as she scooped up a bite of pie. The main figure of the piece was a caricature of her father, dressed to the nines and wearing a haughty sneer. Behind him, a person in a black uniform with "RMC" on the back pushed against a bulging door. Hand, arm, and leg bones poked out all around the door, and most of a skeleton was escaping between the mercenary's legs. The caption below read, "Nothing to see here."

Nova snorted. The snort morphed into a chuckle, and then into a full-fledged guffaw that had her eyes watering and her sides aching. The cartoon had to be the most accurate portrayal of the Duke of Deimos she'd ever seen. He would hate it. He would order some underling to track down every copy and burn them. The thought only made her laugh harder.

"There's not a damned thing you could give me to make me one of your minions, Father."

And it was true, for maybe the first time in her life. Not even the attention and affection she'd craved for so long could sway her. Not after he'd manipulated her into thinking Wyatt and the others were the bad guys. Not when she'd seen a few of those skeletons in his closet. He was her sire, but he was not and would never be her family.

Nova was a true Dystopian now. One who ate fast food and passed around cartoons lambasting aristocrats and thought downtown was a decent place to live after all.

She dug into her pie with enthusiasm.

Before she could finish, a scream pierced the air, followed

almost immediately by another. Nova dropped her fork and leapt to her feet so fast her chair went flying. She ran out the door, pulling her knife. No one would harm anyone in this building if she had anything to say about it.

The door across the hall burst open, and Marika stumbled out, her golden eyes round and fearful. "A rat!" she cried. "A rat got in! Call the police! Or the fire brigade, or—"

"The exterminator!" Janna shouted from inside the room. "Kill it!"

Something in the room crashed to the ground. A second later, a furry gray thing skittered out the door, right between Nova's legs and into her apartment.

Janna appeared a moment later. "I'm sorry!" She flinched when she spied Nova's knife, then smiled. "We'll kill it. We corner it, and then you stab it!"

"What? No!" Nova shoved the knife back into its sheath. "We can't kill it. It's a living creature. It doesn't mean us any harm."

Janna and Marika looked at one another in confusion.

"But it's a *rat*," Marika said. "Everyone knows rats are horrible and filthy. Aren't they?"

Janna gave a helpless shrug.

Nova spun around and stepped back into her apartment. "We'll catch it. And take it… elsewhere. Does anyone have a bucket?"

"I'll get one!" Marika ran off.

Janna followed Nova into the apartment. "I can hear it squeaking."

Nova paused to listen. "That way, I think. The poor thing is probably terrified."

*And I sound like Wyatt.*

She amended that statement as she tracked the rat. *No. I am like Wyatt.* Her experience with animals was limited, but they fascinated and delighted her. They were full of personality and interesting abilities. She knew at least a dozen people who deserved to be stabbed far more than this innocent rat did.

Nova and Janna came at the rat from opposite sides, eventually backing it into a corner. The rat's nose twitched as it searched for a way out.

"I'm here!" Marika shouted.

The rat darted to the left, but years of training had honed Nova's reflexes to a fine point. She kicked out a booted foot, and the rat squealed and reversed direction. Janna stepped toward it, and when it hesitated, Marika dropped the bucket over it.

Nova clapped a hand down on the bucket. "Nice teamwork. Now, we slide something under the bucket so we can turn it over and carry the rat out."

"Carry it where?" Marika asked.

Nova didn't like the answer to that question, but it was the only one she had.

A quarter of an hour later, she rapped on the door to Wyatt's apartment. When he opened it, he stumbled backward in surprise.

"Nova? W-what are you doing here?"

Nova held out the bucket, which had one of her jackets tied tightly around the top and smelled of the eel pie remnants she'd fed the rat to soothe it.

"I…" she spluttered. "I… brought you a rat."

# 31

*THIS IS LOVE, apparently,* Wyatt marveled. *Staring down into a bucket to watch a shaggy rat gobbling up some kind of fishy goop because you're afraid if you look into the eyes of the woman who brought you the rat, you'll start crying.*

"It got into my building," Nova explained, her words tumbling out. "They wanted to kill it, or call an exterminator to kill it. The women in the apartment across the hall, I mean. Everyone thinks rats are evil, I suppose. But it seemed so wrong. They helped me catch it instead, and then we had it and there wasn't really a place to take it, but I thought you might like it. As a pet, maybe? Or for your animal gardens?"

A tear escaped Wyatt's eye, falling into the bucket and splattering next to the rat. He rubbed a hand across his eyes to prevent it happening again.

"Thank you for rescuing it. And bringing it to me."

Another tear plopped into the bucket. Fuck. He was microseconds away from becoming a blubbery mess. No one had ever given him such a gift in his life. Even the men he loved like brothers had never given him a pet. They probably figured he acquired enough animals on his own.

"I hope it's safe to feed it eel pie." Nova rocked from one foot to the other. "I felt terrible that we'd scared it and trapped it. I thought perhaps food would help?"

"From Pie-Pass?" Wyatt grinned down at the motley rodent and its mushy meal. The rat was filthy and smelly and one of the most beautiful things he'd ever seen. "I love that place." He blinked again to clear his vision, then straightened up to look at Nova. "We'll have to take the rat to the rehabilitation center at the zoo. It'll need to be cleaned and tested for diseases. But then we'll make sure it gets a long and happy life."

Nova stilled, her shoulders relaxing into her customary posture. "That's good. I should go home, then." She neither moved nor looked away from him.

"That's against security protocol."

Nova's nose wrinkled. "Why?"

Wyatt lifted the bucket. "We can't leave little Flare in a bucket all night, and I don't have an appropriate enclosure. I'll have to go to the zoo."

"Oh." Nova's features settled into a neutral expression. "Yes. I will accompany you, of course." Her gaze dropped to the bucket. "Flare, you said? You've named it already?"

"Yep. Flare. Because it came from a Nova."

A flush burnished her cheeks, and she spun away. "Let's go, then."

Wyatt draped Nova's jacket over the top of the bucket again and followed her out of the apartment and down the stairs. God, she was magnificent. From the fierceness of her stride to the sway of her ponytail to the curve of her gorgeous ass, she was beautiful. She had a shell as strong as a tortoise and a heart as big as a whale. Always giving, his Nova.

It was about damned time someone gave to her in return. Wyatt would give her the moon, if she asked. Earth's big, pretty moon, not Mars's tiny lumpy ones. Although they had their own quirky beauty, so if that's what Nova preferred, she could have Phobos. Wyatt wouldn't give her anything that shared a name with her father.

"I'm a complete weirdo," he said aloud.

"For rescuing a rat?" Nova didn't glance back at him, but her pace slowed slightly. "That makes us both weirdos. I don't care. Let other people think what they want."

"Yes. I was thinking about moons, though. I'd love to take you to Earth someday and show you the moon. It's so big and bright. And you can walk around and breathe with nothing but the sky overhead and feel the sun on your skin." A wave of longing choked him. He closed his eyes for a second and drew in a slow breath. "Fuck, I miss it. I've been here more than half my life and it still doesn't feel like home."

Nova waited until one of Wyatt's drones was hovering over him before opening the door to the outside and stepping through. "Do you ever think about returning?"

"To Earth? Nah. I'd be miserable living under any of the corporate states. If I go back, it would be to release animals into the wild in some unpopulated area. A visit only. Nowhere near whatever ruins remain of my childhood. And I'm needed here. The Viper needs to keep poisoning the system with cheap schoolbooks and tax-free bananas while trying to source as many goods as possible from not-horrible people."

Nova whirled to face him. "Shh." She put a finger to her lips, making her look adorably like an angry librarian. "Don't say things like that out loud. There could be spies anywhere."

"Yeah?" Wyatt put a hand on his hip and adopted his

best insolent smirk. "Well, if they don't like me, they can come and say so to my face."

Nova seized his arm and tugged him toward the trolley stop. "This was much easier when you were sulking."

Understanding sparked in Wyatt's brain like a match lighting. "That's why you dumped me! You think I'm safer in the house nursing a broken heart, and you'll sacrifice your own—"

"Shut up." Her grip tightened. "We're not speaking to one another."

Wyatt grinned so hard his face almost hurt. "If you say so."

He could accept silence. He'd unlocked another piece of her puzzle. Between this and the rat, hope now burned inside him bright as a star. There was still the matter of Nova insisting they didn't "fit" together, but he could work on that. He'd woo her with everything he had. Because a life without her was as unimaginable as life without Leo, Rion, or Aubrey. She'd wormed her way into that space in his heart called Family. Now it was up to him to convince her that she belonged there.

Since Nova didn't want to talk—and Wyatt wanted her to understand that he loved her taciturn stubbornness as much as any other part of her—he talked to Flare while they waited for one of the sporadic nighttime trolleys.

"You'll love the zoo," he told the rat. "It'll be so much better than eating garbage and hiding in people's apartments. We'll build you a great habitat with good food and lots of things to do. Maybe we'll even make it interactive, so you can play with the visitors. People can learn how fun and smart and friendly rats are. And we can start a corresponding program to humanely capture rats in the city instead of killing them. You'll want other rats for company, of course, and those unsuited to a zoo environment can be released into one of the Ag sectors."

Wyatt didn't look at Nova during this speech, but he could feel her eyes on him. And when they boarded the trolley, they sat side-by-side, only inches apart, though most seats were vacant. God, it was so nice to just be near her again. Her absence had been like a splinter he couldn't get out, constantly poking at him. His concentration had been shit all week. The only time he'd managed to hyperfocus was when he'd gone on a wild cleaning spree, tidied up his entire office, finished every one of his little puzzles, and arranged all his nail polish in a scientifically-accurate color spectrum.

"I missed you," he said softly. "It's okay if dating isn't something you can do right now. But I missed having you around. So maybe we can, like, not avoid each other anymore?"

She took her time replying, but eventually said, "Maybe."

The flame of hope danced inside him. *Progress.*

He made more progress at the zoo, because Nova couldn't help asking about the tank he used to temporarily house Flare and if she—it turned out Flare was a female rat—would be comfortable and how did they test her health and so on.

By the time they departed, their interaction felt so normal Wyatt had to walk with his arms crossed to keep from reaching for her.

*One step at a time.*

The last thing he wanted to do was violate her boundaries. She would open up to him again someday. He had to keep believing that.

The return trolley arrived only a minute after they reached the stop. As it pulled up beside them, the door swung open and the interior lights turned on, revealing a space empty of all other passengers.

"Evening, miss," the driver said as they boarded. "My lord." He tipped his cap.

"Good evening," Wyatt replied. He and Nova took sideways-facing seats near the front of the vehicle, once again close without touching.

"Thanks for accompanying me," he said, giving Nova a smile he hoped didn't look overly flirtatious. "And thank you for Flare. She's wonderful and I'm really excited to give her a great new home."

"You're welcome." Nova met his gaze and didn't look away. "It seemed cruel to kill her for merely existing, and I knew you'd understand."

"I do."

She offered a slight smile before turning to look out the window.

*I really do.* Wyatt admired the curve of her cheek and the serious line of her jaw. *You're a paladin. A knight in shining armor. Like I can't help wanting to cuddle and feed my people or my pets, you can't help rushing to the rescue or throwing yourself in front of an enemy. We're so much alike, Nova. We do fit.*

Wyatt tapped out patterns on his thigh and stared off into the distance, not trusting himself to attempt any further conversation, even now that she'd relaxed. He was much too close to blurting out something he could never take back, such as, "I love you. I adore you. Please say you'll marry me and have my babies and be my family forever and ever." Because when he went in, he went all in.

For fuck's sake, he didn't even know if she wanted things like marriage and babies. His leg jiggled in time with his tapping. Ugh, this was going to be so damn hard. He needed someone to unburden his feelings to. Aubrey maybe. Not Rion, he'd blab to everyone.

"Why are we stopping?" Nova swiveled abruptly, her hand brushing Wyatt's thigh.

Wyatt blinked to refocus his vision. The ghost of her touch lingered. He wanted to stroke his finger over that spot, beg her to do it again.

The trolley came to a halt with a final squeak.

Nova's voice dropped to a growl. "There's no stop here." She edged forward in her seat, a lioness primed to pounce.

"What—" Wyatt began.

"End of the line, milord." The driver chuckled as he rose to his feet.

Wyatt's brain didn't even register the pistol until he was on the floor, Nova on top of him. A gunshot cracked. Glass shattered. A second gunshot, then a cry of pain.

"Nova!"

"I'm fine!" She was already scrambling off him. The trolley driver staggered. Nova rushed the villain, grabbed his arm, and wrestled the gun from him. He slumped to the ground, and she stood over him, a pistol in each hand.

"Can you drive a trolley?" she asked Wyatt.

Wyatt jumped to his feet, skittered around the fallen man, and hopped into the driver's seat. "I'll figure it out."

"Go as fast as you can. It's obvious they know where we are." She placed a booted foot on the enemy's chest. "And I'd like to ask this one some questions before he falls unconscious."

"You bloody shot me!" the man whined.

"And I'll do it again, if you so much as move. Put pressure on that wound. I don't want you bleeding out."

"Can I move or can't I?" Out of the corner of his eye,

Wyatt saw the man press a hand to his side. "Bloody bitch. I ain't getting paid enough for this."

Wyatt located the correct controls, and the trolley lurched into motion.

"Paid by whom?" Nova snarled.

"Fuck y— ow!"

"Paid. By. Whom?" Nova's voice was soft, but ice cold. "I have had a very long day, and you've just ruined my night, so I suggest you don't try my patience."

"Some bloke named…" The man grunted in pain. "Zeller."

Nova grumbled a string of curses. "Who gave him the order? Connington? The Duke of Deimos?"

"Dunno." He grunted again. "Fucking hurts. Why'd you have to shoot me?"

"Because she's my bodyguard and she's damned good at her job," Wyatt snapped. He'd employed his lordly voice so much recently it was starting to feel natural. And he didn't like that at all. "You're lucky she didn't put that bullet through your brain."

"I still might do," Nova said through clenched teeth.

The man stopped complaining.

Driving the trolley turned out to be so simple it was boring. The rails negated the need for any steering, and even at top speed, the trolley wasn't fast enough to be in danger of jumping the track. Wyatt stared out the window and fidgeted. They rolled on through the city, leaving disgruntled people in their wake as they breezed through trolley stops.

"Beg pardon, everyone." He sighed as they passed a lone adult with three small, restless children. "But you really don't want to ride with a bleeding scoundrel and the angry people he tried to kill."

Nova grunted in agreement.

At long last, the trolley stop near home came into view. Wyatt let the car roll right on by, then yanked on the brake when they came as close to the factory as they could get.

The wheels screeched in protest. The trolley shuddered to a stop, but Wyatt lurched forward, smashing his knees on the controls. Nova, in seeming defiance of the laws of physics, managed to remain standing over her captured foe, cool as ever.

"Very elegant," she murmured dryly.

"Sorry. Ow." Wyatt rubbed his smarting kneecap.

Nova handed him one of the pistols, then bent over and hauled their captive to his feet with one hand.

"Have I told you you're so fucking sexy?" The words were out of Wyatt's mouth before he could stop them.

Her only reply was a nod of her head toward the closed door.

"Oh, right." Wyatt located the control and opened the door.

Their attacker had gone pale, and seemed too woozy to hold himself upright, so Nova slung her arm around him and half-dragged him out to the street. He made only minimal noises of protest. Nova positioned herself to shield Wyatt between the trolley and her own body, so he sent his drone out to shield her.

"Why is it so dark here?" He glanced up at the streetlights that ought to be lighting their way.

"I don't like it. Stay close and stay quiet."

As they stepped out from the shelter of the trolley, Nova motioned for Wyatt to move to her other side, where he could use the walls of buildings as cover. He complied, since she was angry enough already, and the effort on his part was minimal. His drone, confused, lifted to hover over his head, the wind from its rotors mussing his hair.

Despite the lack of streetlights, the single yellow bulb above the factory entrance remained lit, and Wyatt used it as a beacon to guide him home. He was about to suggest they run the rest of the way, when something caught his eye.

He pulled up short. At the edge of the circle of light haloing the door lay a supine figure. Heart in his throat, Wyatt raced toward the body, ignoring Nova's command to stop.

It was probably a man, Wyatt determined as he drew nearer, dressed in a gray or grayish suit, and definitely not moving.

Wyatt's boots skidded on the pavement when he finally beheld a pair of sightless eyes and a pale, bloodless face.

"Lord Eberwhite," he gasped.

A mixture of relief and terror washed over him. No one he loved was hurt. Wyatt, however, was in deep, deep trouble.

Because the weapon that had punctured Eberwhite's heart was the sharpened rotor of a drone.

# 32

THE TWO ENORMOUS VIDSCREENS on the Chamber room wall winked to life, displaying the massive rooms of the First and Second Chambers, filled with lords in neat rows of leather chairs. Nova glared up at the nearest camera from her place in the corner, wondering if she was visible to all those faces. A part of her hoped she was, and that someone would voice an objection. She could use a target for her wrath today.

The boys were unusually solemn. The lack of smiles and laughter lent the room a funereal air, which was appropriate, given what they'd found on their doorstep the night before. Nova watched them rather than the screens. If she looked at her father, she might draw her pistol and put a bullet right through his image.

Leo sat front and center, as ducal as ever in one of his navy blue suits. To his left, Rion lounged with his arms crossed, exuding a casual menace, as if ripping limbs off were his daily exercise. Aubrey looked like a different person entirely, dressed in unrelenting black and sitting ramrod straight behind his cousin. If Nova hadn't known better, she might have thought him in genuine mourning for Lord Eberwhite.

Wyatt also sat stiffly in the chair to Leo's right. He wore his glasses, a white t-shirt that said "I ♥ Earth," and a pair of faded black pajama pants dotted with orange butterflies. Flurry hung curled against his chest, and Wyatt pet the bat absently with one hand while the other drummed on the armrest.

The speaker crackled. "Before we begin," came the voice of the Duke of Phobos, "I ask that everyone observe a moment of silence in memory of Alexander Winston, Earl of Eberwhite, who was tragically lost to us last night."

Silent seconds elapsed. Nova hardly breathed. The only motion in the room came from Wyatt's ever-busy fingers, and even those made no noise.

"Thank you." Phobos returned to his seat.

A slight murmur rose through the speakers as the other Chambers returned to their usual state, but the men in front of Nova remained soundless as statues, and nearly as still. Awareness of what was to come pressed down like a palpable force. Nova adjusted her position, simply to make certain she still could. Her limbs moved freely. Any additional weight came from her mind rather than an unnaturally thickening atmosphere.

She would have preferred the latter. Emergencies, she could handle.

"Good evening." Her father's voice rang through the space, easy and polished. "As head of the First Chamber, I thank you for paying your respects to one of our own. Though perhaps not all of us have given the occasion the solemnity it deserves." He stared into the camera, which was as close as he could get to directing his gaze at Wyatt.

Nova's fingers twitched. Wyatt, however, didn't react. He was hardly the only person not attired in mourning clothes, but he was the only one dressed so casually. What was so wrong with that? He was comfortable and his usual self.

His clothes were an armor of sorts, no different than her tactical garb.

"Can we forgo the veiled insults, Deimos?" Leo called out. "I'd rather not be here all night. If you have something to say, say it outright."

"Better yet, come here and say it in person," Rion goaded. "We can settle things like honorable gentlemen." He began to crack his knuckles, one by one.

Nova had to give her father some credit. He displayed no obvious signs of anger, only a slight narrowing of the eyebrows. When he replied, his tone remained even.

"I see some of us are impatient tonight. I suppose that can only be expected, given the company you keep. Very well, I shall skip the pleasantries and begin a vital matter of business: the inquest into the murder of Lord Eberwhite."

Several audible and not especially convincing gasps came through the microphone, while on the screen various members of the First Chamber clasped hands over hearts.

"Good gad," Aubrey drawled. "We all read the papers. No need to swoon like chorus girls in a cheap melodrama. The poor sod was dumped dead on our doorstep and you all know it. Let's get on with it."

"Dumped you say?" Deimos almost smiled. "An interesting word choice. What made you say it?"

"No evidence of murder at the scene," Rion spoke up. "No blood, no signs of a struggle, no reports of shouts or fighting from the hotel across the street."

"The brothel across the street," someone jeered.

"The duke has the floor," intoned whichever unfortunate fellow had been assigned as moderator for the meeting. "I believe his question was directed at Lord Wells."

Aubrey waved a lazy hand in Rion's direction. "Report said he was dumped. I'm no expert."

"Thank you, Lord Wells," Nova's father continued. "I am curious what report this was, as it did not cross my desk. It could not have come from an RMC investigator or the DPST."

Rion made a coughing noise that sounded suspiciously like "dipshit" and Nova nearly burst out laughing. Dystopians had been first to nickname the DPST dipshits, but the mercenaries had quickly adopted the epithet. From the expressions of suppressed laughter worn by many of the Chamber members, it appeared the aristocrats had too.

"It was a report from the Dystopian Constabulary," Aubrey replied breezily. "You must remember the vote last year officially recognizing the unarmed crisis response force?"

Deimos gave up any pretense and openly glowered. "I remember."

"Thirty-one out of forty equals what, again?" Wyatt tapped his right index finger against each finger of the opposite hand, as if counting. "Ah, yes, seventy-seven point five percent."

*Dammit, Wyatt, don't provoke him.*

Every person in the meeting knew that number. Hell, every person in the entire nation knew that number. Despite her father's vehement opposition, the Constabulary proposal had passed unanimously in the Second and Third Chambers, and delivered him an historic loss in his own Chamber, at thirty-one for to only nine against. Thirty-ones and seventy-seven point fives had sprung up everywhere. People had printed the numbers in newspapers and cartoons, painted them on walls, written them in icing on cakes. Someone had deposited seventy-seven and a half pennies on the duke's doorstep. Junior mercenaries had been hired to "clean up" the mess.

It was the only time in Nova's memory that the Duke of Deimos had suffered a true embarrassment.

The duke's expression morphed into a chilling smile. "Windborne. How nice of you to speak up. I have a great deal to say to you."

"Go ahead. But don't talk too loud. Flurry's still sleeping, and we don't want a cranky bat interrupting your villain's monologue."

"I do," Rion cut in.

"I enjoy a good gothic novel, myself," Aubrey added.

"The duke has the floor," said the moderator, his voice pained. He was in for a long night, at this rate.

"Lord Windborne." Nova's father smirked at the camera. "You have already been implicated in a number of crimes."

Wyatt went on petting Flurry in an impressive display of calm. "I see Your Grace has been reading the gossip rags. Very ducal of you. Morland likes those too. He reads us the silliest bits. You do have to admire the imaginations of the writers."

"You are suspected of theft, smuggling, and tax evasion," Deimos continued, undaunted. "You have been involved in multiple altercations with law enforcement personnel, tampered with security systems, trespassed on government and private property, engaged in unlawful surveillance, encouraged seditious publications, slandered peers of the realm, and employed an armed mercenary outside the authority of the RMC."

"He sounds sexy as hell."

The words flew from Nova's mouth, propelled by some irrepressible force inside her. The quip wasn't merely the sort of thing Wyatt would say. It *was* Wyatt, springing forth from a place inside her he'd claimed as his own. He'd altered that piece of her, freeing it to wield words the way she wielded her knife.

She'd released this part of herself before, when she'd put Connington in his place, but this time her voice rang out in front of every peer of the realm, including her father. This time, her voice was public, and even though she'd surprised herself with it, she had no regrets. She was proud. Defiant. And it felt damned good.

Wyatt spun in his seat, startling Flurry awake. The bat squeaked a protest and flapped his wings before settling once more.

Nova's gaze met Wyatt's. All the breath left her lungs. She wanted to turn away from the unabashed adoration in his eyes. She wanted to run and hide, somewhere she could pretend she hadn't seen anything. And, good God, how she wanted to stand there and bask in the glory of that beautiful smile forever.

"Is that you, daughter?" Her father's question broke the spell, and both she and Wyatt turned once more to look at the vidscreens. "I thought you might be lurking somewhere."

Nova strode across the room to stand behind Wyatt.

"I see it's true, then." The duke turned up his nose in perfect aristocratic condescension. "You've thrown in your lot with a criminal. You went rogue and accepted his illegal employment. Do you deny it?"

She held her chin high. "Vehemently."

Maybe it was the truth, maybe it was half a lie. It didn't matter. It was the right thing to do, her declaration that he could not force her from the honorable path.

Leo rose from his seat. "Ms. Pratt works for me, not for Lord Windborne. She is employed under a legal and binding contract that was made and has been carried out in good faith. Your information is incorrect. If you have any other facts of which you are uncertain, I ask that you refrain from speaking of them until you have ascertained their truth."

"I am quite sure of my facts, boy," Deimos replied coldly. "She is on record as a deserter from the RMC."

"I didn't desert, I quit," Nova snapped. "And I was already under contract with His Grace. There is no provision in the RMC charter that prevents me from continuing to fulfill an existing contract, only from taking on a new one."

This time, when Deimos stared directly into the camera, Nova knew she was his target. Those so-familiar dark brown eyes bore into her. She held her ground and glared back.

"You are a traitor and a disgrace to your profession and your family," he said.

Bastard. Why in the universe had she ever wanted anything from this man? His good opinion wasn't worth the gunk on the soles of her shoes.

"Family." She huffed a small laugh. "You think *I* bring shame on my family. You know nothing. Your irresponsible ejaculations may have made you my biological parent, but you are not my family. You can't even recognize a real family when it's staring you in the face."

The moderator began to bang a gavel. *Bam! Bam! Bam!* "Order! Order!" *Bam! Bam!*

"I'm finished," Nova announced. She found the camera and looked directly at it. "I've chosen my side. It's not yours." She executed a mocking curtsy. "You may have the floor, Your Grace."

"Brava," Aubrey applauded softly. "It's about time someone gave that man what for."

Wyatt looked over his shoulder at Nova, and her breath hitched again under the force of his devoted smile. "My hero," he whispered.

*Bam! Bam!*

"New rules," the moderator declared, speaking into a handheld microphone. "All Chamber room microphones are to be muted immediately. His Grace is invited to come forward and use this microphone. Anyone he addresses directly may reply from a handheld mic. Once His Grace has ceded the floor, another may come forward to speak."

Rion hopped up and switched off the room mics. "Much better. Now we can freely tell all those fucking fuckers to shove it up their bloody arses."

"Quiet," Leo ordered. "We need to hear this."

Deimos took the microphone and cleared his throat. "Despite the urging from certain individuals to 'get on with it,' it seems we have strayed off topic. Lord Eberwhite's murder. Lord Windborne, where were you at the time Eberwhite died?"

Wyatt touched his scar, and a drone flew down from the ceiling to hover beside him. He had to have some kind of device implanted. A button, perhaps. She should have asked when they were still together. Now she might never know.

Wyatt turned a knob on the drone and spoke. "I'm afraid I can't give you an answer, Your Grace, as I don't know when the man died."

"This is a serious inquiry, Windborne. I suggest you treat it as such."

Wyatt examined his shiny nails. "Do I need to summon an attorney?"

Nova grasped the back of his chair. She wanted to rail at him to stop taunting her father, to tone down his defiance. She couldn't. Wyatt was defiance personified. He'd been raised and educated to fit a particular role in a rigid system, and he'd rejected it. Everything about him, from the way he talked to the way he dressed to the people he associated with was an act of defiance. *This is me*, he proclaimed to the world. *You don't get to choose who I am. Only I decide that.*

*My hero*, Nova thought, smiling wryly. She'd never admired anyone more than Wyatt in this moment. No wonder she'd always thought him so shiny. He was more precious than arcanium.

"This is not an interrogation, Windborne." Deimos's smile and voice softened. "It is a hopefully congenial discussion to establish basic facts."

"Ah, I understand." Wyatt leaned toward the drone and stated slowly, "I did not murder Lord Eberwhite." He sat back. "Who's next? Are we going around the whole room?"

"Where were you last night?" the duke snarled.

Wyatt sighed. "I took an animal to the health center at my zoological gardens." He nudged the drone toward Nova.

"I was with him the entire time in my capacity as bodyguard for the Third Chamber," she said. "We found Lord Eberwhite together upon our return."

Deimos snapped his fingers, and a footman approached, carrying a silver tray. Atop it rested a drone's rotor. "This was the implement used in the murder. Can you tell us what it is, Lord Windborne?"

"I can." Wyatt returned to petting Flurry.

Several beats of silence elapsed before the duke demanded, "Well?"

"You might consider saying please if you want something."

Nova almost choked. Dukes did not say please. Even Leo looked moderately horrified.

*Stop. Wyatt, please stop. He'll never forgive you.*

But that didn't matter, did it? Wyatt was already the enemy. He had been since the moment he'd discovered the anomalies with the cargo ships. Deimos wanted him dead. Nothing would change that.

So now the Viper was showing his fangs.

"Wyatt," Leo murmured, "you're walking a tightrope. Try not to fall. I don't want to put my back out catching you."

"Explain the rotor, Windborne." Deimos motioned for the footman to hold up the murder weapon to the camera.

"I beg your pardon, Your Grace." Wyatt spoke into the drone again. "But I don't think you really want me to explain rotors. Fluid dynamics is extremely complicated and if I tried to get into all the math and science behind it, I think I would put all of Parliament to sleep."

Enough people laughed that the sound carried through the duke's microphone.

"Merely looking at the Navier-Stokes equations can make people swoon," Wyatt added. "I had to stop wearing the shirt I had one printed on. Too dangerous."

"Is this or is this not the rotor from a drone?" the duke demanded.

"It obviously is," Wyatt answered, this time without a trace of sarcasm. "It's not from any of my drones. They're all operable and accounted for." He lifted his left arm to display his wristwatch. "I could scroll through the list, but we already established that I probably shouldn't put everyone to sleep. I would guess that your rotor there belongs to a cleaning drone or other service drone from a private company. I hope that assists the investigation."

"Lord Windborne." Her father's voice was almost soothing. Nova's skin prickled. "You illegally brought drones into the hippodrome on the day of the highly suspicious car crash. Lord Eberwhite suffered a broken leg in the incident. You were then involved in an altercation with DPST officers at the site, while trying to cover up your crimes."

Those thugs had been DPST? Made sense.

"You also assaulted Captain Zeller of the RMC."

Nova leaned over Wyatt's chair to put herself in speaking range of the drone. "That was me, actually. He pulled a gun on Lord Windborne and I acted under my authority as bodyguard. But why is Zeller working with DPST goons? And for that matter, why is Zeller sending assassins after us? That was the purpose of the man who attacked us on the trolley last night, wasn't it? Or did you expect that we would escape so you sent him only as a distraction to occupy us while someone was placing Eberwhite's body outside Central Manufactory?"

Only after Nova completed her speech did she realize how close she was to Wyatt. Their cheeks were almost touching. Her ponytail had flopped over her shoulder and brushed the back of his neck. She could hear the quickening of his breath. The mingled scents of roses and cedar tickled her nose. Her heart began to race and she jerked upright.

"I shall deal with you and your disloyalty later, daughter," her father replied dispassionately. "For today, I wish only to present to the assembled Chambers the facts of Lord Windborne's recent erratic and suspicious behavior. He is clearly implicated in a number of crimes, including the murder of Lord Eberwhite, and it is my opinion, formed with the backing of the First Chamber, that Lord Windborne must turn himself in to law enforcement authorities for interrogation."

"Absolutely not!" Nova shouted in unison with the four men around her.

On the Second Chamber screen, the Duke of Phobos rose from his seat and picked up a handheld mic. "Speaking for my Chamber, it appears that any evidence against Lord Windborne is circumstantial at best. Even so, his name has appeared over and over in recent reports and news, and I do not think that fact should be ignored. I propose we put the matter to a vote. An aye vote means you are in favor of Lord Windborne voluntarily surrendering himself to qualified members of the Royal Mercenary Corps for a criminal investigation. He may, of course, retain legal counsel during this process, and will receive a fair trial should the evidence lead to such."

"Okay, but it's not really voluntary if you all vote that I have to do it," Wyatt pointed out.

Deimos talked over him. "I second Phobos's proposed vote. My vote is aye."

Leo jumped up and switched on the room microphone. "Chamber vote," he commanded.

Nova blinked. "What's that?"

Wyatt leaned back in his chair to whisper to her. "We vote by Chamber only. Two out of three. It's a method of balancing things out a bit because there are only four of us but forty in each other Chamber. Any Chamber head can call for one, but only once a season."

Nova scanned the faces of the men on the twin vidscreens. This was an act of desperation, then. They would receive no more than a vote or two from the First Chamber, meaning Wyatt would need almost full support from the Second Chamber for the vote to fail. Impossible. But with a Chamber vote, he could win with a simple majority in the Second Chamber.

"Very well." Deimos nodded to the camera, then turned to face his group. "Any nays?"

Two hands went up: Marcus and a haggard-looking man Nova thought might be one of Lord Eberwhite's gambling buddies. Interesting.

The duke turned back around. "First Chamber votes aye."

"Third Chamber votes nay." Leo's voice carried not only the authority of a duke, but the surety of a man who knew himself to be on the side of right.

Nova stared at the Second Chamber screen, where Phobos stood addressing his men. A servant came up to him with a notepad and began tallying votes. With their room microphone off, she could only guess at what was happening.

She began to formulate escape plans in her head. Maybe Wyatt could hide somewhere. Maybe he could take a trip to Earth until everything blew over. Maybe Zeller and Connington wouldn't be in charge of the interrogation and he could simply do it and get the matter dropped for lack of evidence.

Phobos switched on the handheld mic. "Second Chamber votes twenty-two to eighteen. Aye. Lord Windborne, please report to RMC headquarters by end of day tomorrow. Contracts will be written up tonight to designate your interrogators. It is my sincere hope that this is resolved quickly and without further violence."

Nova's hand dropped to Wyatt's shoulder. He placed his hand atop hers.

"I won't let them hurt you," she vowed.

"I know." He squeezed her hand. "That's one of the things I love about you."

# 33

Wyatt surveyed the array of odd-shaped metal sticks lying on Nova's palm and shook his head. Thirty yards ahead, the plain concrete facade of RMC headquarters loomed, its long shadow creeping inexorably closer as the sun dipped further toward the horizon. It was time.

"Sweetheart, I don't know how to shoot a gun or fight with a knife. I can't pick locks. Anything you give me would be useless. And where would I even hide it? They're going to search me. If I need to escape, it'll have to be a rescue. I'm okay with that. I trust you all not to abandon me."

"Well, I'm not okay with it!" Nova shoved the lockpicks back into her pocket. "If one thing goes wrong, you're dead! I swore that I'd protect you, goddammit!"

Wyatt started to reach for her, then stopped himself. They hadn't established boundaries for their not-dating-anymore relationship. He couldn't hug her, no matter how much he craved her touch. Her fears and his own would have to go unsoothed.

"Work on the escape plan," he suggested instead.

"Make it foolproof. If things get too hairy, I can summon my drones."

Nova's gaze dropped to his collarbone. His shirt hid the scar, but he knew she'd noticed the way he touched it.

"You have an implant."

"I do. It's small, so it can't do anything sophisticated." Wyatt absently rubbed his wrist where his watch should have been. No watch, no drones hovering nearby. His stomach lurched. "But I can set drones at protective distances around me, and I can summon them to me. I'll be fine."

Nova's eyes narrowed. "You have no drones in the mercenary compound. Will anything be in range of your device?"

"Remember Drone 23, from Ag Sector 3? He got a nice software upgrade this morning, and has invited a bunch of his buddies over for a party. They'll hear me if I call."

Wyatt wasn't certain of that, to be honest. He wasn't certain of anything. He'd barely been able to keep his breakfast down, and lunch had been entirely out of the question. Throwing himself into the hands of his enemies wasn't his idea of a good time. But running would be worse. It would be tantamount to an admission of guilt, and then Deimos would have an opening to call for a bounty on his head. It turned out being wanted dead or alive wasn't nearly as sexy as stories made it out to be.

"Okay," Nova acquiesced. "We'll do this. But I am staying with you until I see Garret for myself. They're decent and fair, and I trust them not to harm you. Stick with them and call for Irene if you need anything. Do you have the list of your legal rights Leo wrote down for you?"

"I left it sitting on my desk," Wyatt admitted. "But I remember them." *Mostly.*

Nova gritted her teeth.

"I don't have pockets," he argued.

Which was partly to make it easy for his jailers to search him and partly because if he was going to be treated like a criminal, he figured he ought to dress like one. Or rather, like his own interpretation of one: black tee, black leggings, tiny black pleated skirt that barely covered his crotch, black work boots, black lipstick, black eye liner, and black nail polish. By the time he'd replaced his gold earrings with black studs he'd been starting to regret ever buying anything black.

*I am the Viper. I live in the shadows. I really miss colors.*

Nova turned her gaze on the building ahead. "Let's get on with it. The sooner we do this, the sooner I can break you out."

Wyatt truly smiled for the first time all day. "You've come a long way since we met. Soon you'll be a criminal mastermind. We'll have to think up a sexy nickname for you."

He expected her to snap at him with a biting remark, but she only sighed. "When the legal path to justice and virtue is barred, one must fight however one can."

She sounded sad. Fuck.

Wyatt again stopped himself from reaching for her. She was right, they needed to get this over with before they both broke down. He started toward the entrance and Nova fell into step beside him.

Inside, at the front of a small lobby, a bored teenager slumped against a podium, playing a colorful puzzle game on a vidscreen. They couldn't have been more than sixteen, still lanky and awkward. They barely took their eyes off the screen when Wyatt and Nova entered.

"You Windborne?" they mumbled. "I'll call Mx. Garret." The kid pulled their cap lower over their eyes, flicked a switch on the podium, and returned to their game.

While he waited, Wyatt leaned against the wall and studied the security cameras. The constant surveillance would be a problem if he needed to flee. The lack of a drone was starting to feel like an itch he couldn't scratch. Even a mini could block a camera or send a message. Some of his drones could even pick locks. He hugged himself and tapped an unusually rapid pattern.

Garret arrived mercifully soon, greeting Nova and Wyatt with a smile before ushering them out of earshot of the kid at the podium.

"Lord Windborne." They bowed, as if addressing him in a formal capacity and not as a jailer. "I am pleased to meet you and sorry it has to be under these circumstances. I'm Mx. Garret, and I've been assigned as lead interrogator for your case. I'm sure you must have questions regarding the process, so please feel free to ask me at any time."

Wyatt gaped. He had expected coolness from his interrogator. Perhaps even coldness. He'd definitely prepared himself for anger, suspicion, condescension, and cruelty. Friendliness had not been on the list.

"Uh, hi," he managed.

Garret smiled. They had a nice smile, one that caused creases around their mouth and crinkles at the corner of their eyes. They smiled often, apparently. They wore a gray jacket and trousers much like Nova's, and had a similar athletic build. Their skin was a rich cream, their hair curly and gray-brown. If Wyatt had seen them on the street he might have guessed they worked as a masseuse or a flower arranger.

"I'm not here to make you uncomfortable, if that's what you were expecting," Garret continued. "On the contrary, I want you to feel as comfortable as possible. My job is to get to the truth, not to bully you into saying what you think I want to hear."

"Yeah." Wyatt's fidgeting didn't slow, despite this reassurance. "Great. I appreciate that."

"You have an attorney, I presume?"

Leo had a man on retainer, naturally. "Yeah. He'll be here first thing in the morning."

"Excellent. Tonight we'll cover the basics: name, background information, time of arrival, and so forth. And I'll go through the list of charges against you so you understand exactly what we're dealing with. My primary contracts for the past ten years have all been in investigation, and I've done many interrogations during that time, for both innocent and guilty parties. I try my best to begin with no assumptions. Is there anything else you wish to know about me before we head upstairs and check you in?"

Wyatt glanced at Nova, but she was too busy glowering at Garret to notice.

"I want your word of honor that he will not come to any harm," she demanded.

Garret arched one eyebrow. "You know I would do no such thing."

"But you're hardly the only one here."

"True," Garret admitted. "Lord Windborne's case is to be handled by myself and my team: Shaw, Burnside, and Whelan. They've never been physical with any interviewee, and I have no reason to think they would behave otherwise in this case. Does that satisfy you?"

"No, but nothing will unless you let us turn around and leave with the case declared closed. I trust you and your team will do their best, so thank you for that."

Garret shook their head slowly. "People here don't understand you, Pratt. Calling you 'disloyal.' Hah. That's the exact opposite of what you are. Now get going before someone like that sees you. You shouldn't be here. Not that I would expect someone else's rules to stop you."

Nova frowned at that, but quickly shook it off and turned to Wyatt. "Be careful. Call for Irene if you need help."

"I promise." This time he couldn't resist opening his arms to her. "Hug? If it's okay w— Oof!"

Nova crushed him against her chest in a hug as fierce as her soul. Wyatt let his head fall onto her shoulder, content for her to hold him as long as she wanted. As long as she needed. He needed forever. Since that was impossible, he'd simply linger in this moment, absorbing all he could of her heart, her spirit, and her goodness.

"Be safe," she murmured in his ear. "Come back to me." And then she released him and stepped away.

"Would you like some coffee?" Garret rose and walked to the sideboard, which held a silver urn and a stack of ceramic mugs.

"No, thanks." Wyatt rocked his chair onto the back legs, then let it down slowly. He was plenty jittery without adding caffeine on an empty stomach.

He looked around the little meeting room while Garret filled a mug. He couldn't call it nice. The chairs weren't great and the walls were bare, but it did have a window. If asked to describe it in one word, he'd have to say, "beige."

But it wasn't a prison. He wasn't handcuffed, no big, bruising jailers loomed over him, and no one spied on him from behind a two-way mirror. Vid-dramas lied, it seemed. Or maybe his title afforded him preferential treatment in this situation, despite the fact that many of his fellow aristocrats seemed to consider him the social equivalent of a clump of mud.

"Last thing for tonight is the official charges against you." Garret sat and pulled a piece of paper to the top of their stack. They sipped their coffee and began to read.

Wyatt lost track halfway through the list of the different types of murder, when his brain snagged on the word "degree." Perhaps murders could come in angles. A ninety-degree murder would be worse than a forty-five degree murder. Or maybe vice versa, because ninety degrees was a right angle, and a right murder would be self-defense, or a similarly justified killing. Or perhaps degrees meant Celsius, and a zero-degree murder was one done in cold blood, while a forty-degree murder was one done in the heat of the moment. Did a killer who got away with their crime have a doctorate degree in murder? While those who were caught in the act were the students who had been sent down from University?

As usual, his mind wandered further, contriving increasingly improbable ways to escape from high security prison after he was inevitably convicted of murder in the nth degree.

"Do you understand?" Garret asked.

Wyatt's vision refocused on his interrogator. *What was the question?* He avoided direct eye contact and mumbled, "Sure."

"Let's call it a night, then." Garret downed the last dregs of coffee, then left the empty mug sitting atop the stack of papers. "We have a long day tomorrow, and you'll want a clear head when you talk with your attorney. Let me show you to your room."

Garret locked the meeting room, then led Wyatt down a long series of hallways, chatting as they walked.

"You'll have a private room with facilities, so it should be quite comfortable. You will be locked in for the night, of course, but you'll have a call bell in case of emergency." They stumbled and put a hand to their forehead. "Whew. Guess the coffee didn't help as much as I hoped. My body thinks it's bedtime. I'll save the reports from the autopsy and the Constabulary who were first on the scene for the morning. Your lawyer will wish to read them, but you don't have to if you think the details might upset you."

Wyatt only nodded. He doubted a technically written description of the matter could be worse than actually finding the man dead on his doorstep.

If Garret's intention was to get Wyatt completely lost, they did an excellent job of it. None of the halls had windows, every wall and floor was identical, and they had taken so many left turns they surely ought to have gone in a circle and ended up back where they started.

At length, Garret paused at a door and unlocked it.

"Here we are." They held the door for Wyatt, and he entered.

The small room had the same beige and gray color scheme as the rest of the building. Wyatt fiddled with the hem of his skirt. He really, really should have worn something colorful. He was pretty certain this wasn't actually hell, but he was also starting to think that hell probably looked like you'd stepped into a daguerreotype portrait.

"That's the washroom, there." Garret pointed at the narrow door to one side of the single bed. "It should be stocked with everything you need. The trunk over here has—" They swayed suddenly.

Wyatt threw out a hand to catch them. "You okay?"

"Light-headed," they replied groggily.

"Here, sit down." Wyatt helped them to the bed.

"Thanks. I'll just—" They slumped over in a dead faint.

"Garret? Shit."

Wyatt put two fingers to Garret's neck. Their pulse beat a steady rhythm that seemed reasonable. It wasn't far off from his own heartbeat, at least. So that was good. And they looked to be breathing okay. He tugged their legs up onto the bed, one-by-one, and adjusted their position so they could lie comfortably.

"Garret?" Wyatt clasped their hand in one of his and patted it, trying to wake them. "Can you hear me? Can you open your eyes?"

"I'm afraid Garret is temporarily indisposed," purred a sinuous voice.

Wyatt dropped Garret's hand and whirled around. A young woman stood in the doorway, pistol in hand. She was shorter and paler than Nova, but with a similar facial structure and the same dark mahogany eyes. Another Pratt?

She surveyed him for a moment, a condescending smile playing on her lips. "What *does* my sister see in you? You look as though you might break in a strong breeze."

"You must be the evil sister." Wyatt studied his nails, half out of spite, and half to avoid looking at the gun. "Nova mentioned you once."

"Once?" She huffed. "I'm surprised the bitch acknowledges me at all. The prim and proper princess thinks she's so much better than the rest of us."

Wyatt lifted his head to meet her gaze. "Wrong. Nova greatly underestimates how much better she is than you." He waved a hand dismissively. "But you wouldn't understand."

She rolled her eyes. "This would have been so much easier if you'd drunk the coffee like you were supposed to. Ah, well. Needs must."

She pulled the trigger.

Wyatt flinched, but there was no gunshot, only a soft *thwick*. For a second he wondered if he really was in hell. Maybe guns didn't work there, since he was already dead. Then a sharp pain registered, and he glanced to the side to see a small dart sticking out of his shoulder. The room began to spin.

"Good evening, Lord Windborne." The serpentine voice swirled around him, fading with each word. "I'm Enid Pratt, and I'll be your new interrogator."

"Bloody bi—"

The world went dark.

"Wyatt's missing." Leo threw up both hands as Nova raced across the conference room. "Don't panic yet. We're just now getting the facts."

Nova stopped behind Leo and looked over his shoulder. He, Aubrey, and Rion sat crowded together at the short end of the table, watching a small vidscreen. On the display, Garret and a portly, bespectacled Black man sat together in one of the mercenary compound's small meeting rooms.

She fingered her knife. "I'm not panicking. I'm deciding who needs to be killed."

*Liar.*

Her heart beat double-time in her chest and she swore she could feel the adrenaline rushing through her bloodstream. Goddammit all to hell. She should have trusted her gut. She should never have left Wyatt alone.

Rion cracked his knuckles. "I call first dibs on anyone who hurts him."

"Let's not be hasty," Leo said. His voice held a tiny tremor, but it was so small Nova couldn't tell whether it was rage or fear. "First, we all need to know exactly what happened. Nova, the man with Mx. Garret is Charles Nolan, my attorney. Chuck, this is Nova Pratt, our friend and security agent. Please go ahead and share your information."

Nolan looked into the camera as he spoke. "I arrived as planned to speak with Mx. Garret and Lord Windborne. Garret did not respond when first summoned, but eventually arrived twenty minutes late, rumpled and groggy. Lord Windborne was nowhere to be seen, and a search of the building did not locate him. Garret?"

The mercenary turned their face to the camera. Dark circles lined their eyes, and their usually-neat hair was mussed. "The last thing I remember was escorting Lord Windborne to his room yesterday night. I felt light-headed. I woke this morning on the bed in that room, alone and unharmed, but not feeling my best. I was locked in the room, which was otherwise empty. The official report states that Lord Windborne drugged me and escaped, but that does not match his prior behavior. He was entirely cooperative and polite last evening, and he was in possession of no weapons or drugs."

"If he'd wanted to run, he wouldn't have turned himself in in the first place," Nova growled. "The whole bloody point was to prove his innocence!"

She uncurled her fingers before she did anything foolish, like pounding her fist on the table. Red marks lined her palm where her nails had dug into the skin.

She took a steadying breath. She had to keep a clear head. Wyatt needed her at her best.

"Precisely," Garret replied. They rubbed the back of their neck. "We reviewed the security footage, naturally. There was a twenty-minute break in the recording shortly after Lord Windborne and I arrived at the room."

"Time enough for someone to slip in and kidnap him the moment you passed out," Aubrey mused. "If Wyatt was also drugged, they could simply drag or carry him away.

And then claim he ran. What about the outdoor cameras? Did they have a similar 'malfunction'?"

"No," Garret answered. "The outdoor footage shows no abnormalities. There is no indication that Lord Windborne left the premises by any means."

Nova's stomach lurched. "He's in the Underground."

Aubrey, Leo, and Rion all turned to look at her.

"What's the Underground?" Rion asked. "It's bad, isn't it? Shit, you sound freaked out and you're really pale. Do you need to sit down?" He pushed his chair back from the table. "Here, sit on my lap."

He took Nova's arm in a gentle grip. When he tugged her down, she sat. It should have been weird, sitting sprawled across his thighs. She had no sexual intentions toward Rion. They weren't related. But when his arms came around her, she relaxed into the embrace. It was right. Comfortable. And at the moment she didn't have the spoons to consider the matter more deeply.

"The Underground is a dungeon," she explained. "Beneath the RMC campus. A secret detention and interrogation center. A place where the laws of the land don't apply."

"It's a myth," Garret insisted. "It doesn't really exist. It's a stupid story made up to scare the junior mercs."

"That's what I used to think. I scoffed at the kids who wanted to find it. 'It couldn't be there. We wouldn't do that.' God, I was so naive." Nova rubbed her forehead where a headache was beginning to form. "I knew some of us cared less about helping people and doing our job than about jockeying for position. But it goes further, doesn't it? It's about working for certain people. Not because that brings prestige, or even money, but because it brings power. It brings the ability to circumvent the rules oneself, while imposing ever stricter rules on everyone else. That's what they want, and that's why I no longer doubt the Underground exists." She pushed to her feet, sad to leave the comfort of Rion's lap, but unable to sit another second. "Garret, go find Dr. Irene Castelbury. She can suggest some trustworthy people to assist. Assemble a team and start searching for a possible entrance to the Underground. I'll be there as soon as I can."

Rion leapt to his feet. "I'm going with you."

"No, don't. Stay here and guard the others. Do political stuff."

"I am already making notes about the violation of my client's legal rights," Nolan stated gruffly. "I suggest we keep this line of communication open, if you have no objections, Morland?"

"None whatsoever," Leo replied. He held up a hand to prevent anyone from running off. "Stop a moment, all of you."

Rion kicked his chair. "Wyatt might not have a fucking moment, shithead!"

"C'mon, Ri," Aubrey began, "Insults won't—"

"Shut up!" Leo snarled. "We need a plan."

Rion glared at him. "We need to—"

"I'm in charge, damn you!"

"Fuck you, Your Dukeness."

Nova pounded her fist on the table, jarring the others out of their squabbling. All eyes turned to her. She opened her mouth to scold them, then snapped it shut.

*Channel Wyatt. How would Wyatt soothe them? He's good at that, and they need it more than usual right now. Think.*

She gestured at the door. "There are leftover cookies in the kitchen. Go eat some. It'll help you feel better."

The boys blinked at her.

"Well, it will. And turn on some lights. It's dark and gray in here. We need to brighten things up. I know none of us are sunshine, but we can still make an effort until we get him back."

"I like cookies," Rion growled. He stalked from the room.

Nova followed. "You can't come with me. You need to stay here with Leo."

"I agree," said Leo, from behind her. "Aubrey will go with you."

Nova didn't want any of the boys trailing after her, but she wasn't going to waste time arguing. Especially when Aubrey's private trolley car would be the fastest method of transportation. "Acceptable."

No one argued further. They ate their cookies in solemn silence.

· · 🦇 · ·

Okay, he wasn't dead. Or probably not dead.

Wyatt squirmed sluggishly. His limbs weighed too much, and his head was stuffed with cotton. His arms were stuck behind him somehow, and whatever lay beneath him was cold and hard. He couldn't see much in the dark... room? Place? Box? There was something hard down near his feet, too, preventing him from stretching out.

Also, he might have been spinning. Or falling? No, he couldn't be falling because he was lying on a floor. Unless the floor was falling.

Maybe this was a dream. Not much of a dream, though. His good dreams featured Nova.

"Ah," murmured a distant voice. "Are you waking up?"

Wyatt tried to place the voice. It could have been an

imaginary person. Dreams were like that. But this voice sounded like one he'd heard before.

Muffled scraping noises joined the voice. Also familiar but unnamable in his current state.

"Wugh." His tongue tripped as he tried to reply. "Aah… I…"

"Do speak up," the voice purred. It belonged to a woman, he thought, and an unfriendly one. "No one will hear you in here." The scraping noises grew louder. "In fact, no one will even notice your screaming. We have excellent soundproofing."

"Wer'm I?"

*Scrish, scrish, scrish.*

Enough of his mind cleared to identify the sound. Someone sharpening a knife. An enemy. What was her name?

"Wha'd'you want w'me?"

"Me? Nothing."

Enid. That was her name. Enid Pratt. Nova's evil sister.

"You're merely a bit of fun and a way to please my father," she said. There was a small clatter as she set down the knife. Then the sharpening noises began again, at a slightly different pitch. "Not for his sake, you understand."

Wyatt grunted and left her to interpret that however she wanted.

"He's a means to an end, is all."

Enid fell silent while she finished sharpening the knife. A while later an electrical hum began to swell.

"Ooh, this looks like a fun toy."

Wyatt didn't reply. His body was still slow to respond and the room still seemed to be going around in circles.

"You're a terrible conversationalist, you know," Enid said. Whatever she was playing with went *zap.* "How am I supposed to Villain Monologue without a captive audience? Heh. Do you see what I did there?"

"Sod off," Wyatt managed.

Enid ignored this. "What is my end game, you ask? Why, I aim to be Duchess of Deimos, naturally. The men in the family are so short-sighted. All that money, all that power. So underutilized."

The electrical buzzing stopped, and a chair scraped across the floor. Enid moved toward Wyatt, each footstep louder than the last. His stomach heaved, and he wasn't sure if that was the drugs or fear he'd be chopped into tiny pieces.

"I have a vision," Enid continued. "None of this Utopia nonsense. With the duchy in my possession, I could build a conquering army. Mars would be mine. The solar system. The galaxy." She laughed. "Move over, Victoria. Empress Enid intends to rule more than one meager planet."

She was close now. On the other side of whatever box or cage held him. Wyatt tried to sit up, tried to force his blurry vision into focus.

"Oh, and don't expect to remember this conversation."

A sharp needle pierced Wyatt's thigh.

*Another fucking druggg…*

# 35

AUBREY MADE A DECENT COMPANION. The marquess neither lagged behind nor tried to make conversation during their ride to RMC headquarters. Nova spent the time checking over her weapons and mentally walking through fighting moves.

*I'm coming, Wyatt. Hold on.*

The teenager who'd been watching the door last time Nova had been here was gone. Six armed guards snapped to attention the moment she stepped into the lobby.

"Halt!" one demanded as they all raised their guns. "Nova Pratt, you are on record as a deserter and are banned from the premises. Any attempt to enter will result in your arrest."

Aubrey stepped in front of Nova. "How dare you wave such vile things in my face? Lower your weapons and stand aside at once! My God, the disrespect! I will be speaking to the Commander about this," he waved disdainfully at the men around them, "uncivilized behavior."

The guards glanced at one another in bafflement.

"Go on." Aubrey made a shooing motion. "Off with you." He looked over his shoulder at Nova. "Honestly, it is *so hard* to find quality help these days. One would *think* they would

276

know not to greet a marquess with *guns*. And not a single bow from the lot of them. How vulgar."

"Y-your lordship," one of the guards protested. "She's not supposed—"

Aubrey made an abrupt zipping motion in front of his mouth. "*Zzzt*. Not another word. Come along, Ms. Pratt."

Nova kept close on his heels as he stormed through the line of guards and down the hall.

"Where are we going?" he whispered.

"Medical. Irene can tell us where the others are. I'll lead the way, unless we need to flummox anyone else with your 'I'm a prissy, entitled prick' character."

They raced down the halls, ignoring anyone who called out to them, and managed to reach the med unit without encountering any more open hostilities.

"In there," said a redheaded orderly, pointing at the closed door to Irene's office. "They're expecting you."

Nova put a hand on her pistol—anything could be a trap, and she wasn't taking any risks—and pushed the door open.

The room was packed. Nearly a dozen people stood crowded around Irene's desk, staring down at something. Nova and Aubrey hurried inside, and Nova closed the door behind them. The group shuffled around to make room at the table.

Nova squeezed in between Irene and Garret. Garret's friends were here too, along with several junior mercs that Nova recognized but didn't know by name—most of them women. Her one-time partner, Cameron, was bent over the desk, running a finger along a blueprint of the building.

He glanced up. "Hey, Nova. We've narrowed our search to these two areas. I've been working on some calculations to estimate where they could hide a space big enough for a subterranean lair."

Nova nodded. "Math whiz. I remember you getting excited about the algebra books."

"Yep. Figure Lord Windborne's not gonna be murdering people when he spends his days helping kids learn maths. So I'm on your side. We're still guessing about the secret room, though. If it's buried deep underground…" He shrugged.

Aubrey pointed to one of the two locations Cameron had indicated. "If those were my choices, I'd put it here. There's enough space between the foundation walls, but the area isn't so big that you have much worry about cleaning or maintenance. It's away from any place like the medical facility or the kitchens, where you might run into extra piping or utilities. And the rooms above all look like private offices. No worries that you might have to put the entrance in a public space. You can restrict it to only the people in the know."

Nova tried to match the blueprint to the rooms and hallways she knew. Private or semi-private rooms of that size on the ground floor would probably belong to Connington's inner circle, and—

She snapped her fingers. "The officers' card room."

"Of course!" Garret smacked their hand to the side of their head. "That whole fiasco two years ago, when the carpets were replaced, and they insisted on buying and installing something special?"

Nova was already moving toward the door. "Several men pitched in to pay for it, and none of them were the sort to happily spend their money for the communal good." She flung the door wide. "It should have been obvious they were hiding something."

She flew out of the med unit. A junior merc jumped into her path, attempting to bar the way, but she shoved him aside with a single hand. If they wanted to stop her, they'd have to do a hell of a lot better than sending awkward kids who weighed less than she did.

The overhead alarms began to blare.

"Attention, attention." Connington's voice echoed from every direction. "Former RMC member Nova Pratt is in violation of Section 244(b) of the Code of Conduct. All personnel are authorized to apprehend her and anyone attempting to assist her will be subject to immediate suspension."

Nova extended her middle finger toward the nearest security camera. "Section 244(b) isn't even a thing, you turnip-faced fuckwit!"

"You tell 'im, Nova!" called a feminine voice from behind her.

Good. She still had some support. The instant her enemies figured out where she was headed, she'd be swarmed.

She sprinted up the next staircase she came to, hoping to throw them off track. Alarms continued to sound, and now and then, Connington's recorded voice would repeat his message. Nova bloodied a few noses along the way, always striking while she had the advantage of surprise.

A *ding* announced the arrival of an elevator, but she charged past on her way to the stairs. No fucking way was she stepping inside anything without a clear way out.

Armed guards—possibly the same men from the lobby—rushed out of the elevator, tangling with the group of friends that had stuck with Nova thus far.

"Go!" Aubrey shouted. "We'll hold them off!"

As Nova turned toward the stairs, she saw him take down a man via an elbow to the solar plexus. *Make that a 'prissy, entitled prick who can fight.'*

She took the staircase in a handful of reckless leaps, each

time hitting the floor hard enough to jar her legs. She'd pay for that later. After she'd found Wyatt later.

More adversaries blocked the path to the officers' card room, but these, thankfully, didn't have any guns in hand. Nova lowered her shoulder like a goddamned rugby player and plowed right through them. Hands grasped for her, but she punched and kicked, and even bit one finger that got too close to her face. When that particular merc yowled in pain, the rest backed off.

*Thank God for mercenaries. You don't pay them, they won't stick their necks out.*

But she would. She kicked away the man she'd bit, dodged another who made a final half-hearted grab for her, and sprinted the rest of the way to the card room door. She planted her left foot and swung her right leg up, landing the full force of her kick right below the doorknob. The door flew inward and splinters of wood sprayed across the threshold.

Despite the alarms and announcements, four men sat around a baize-topped table, cards in hand. Nova didn't even try to process their cries of surprise. She ran to the table, grabbed a corner, and upended it. Cards and chips sailed through the air and one of the men crashed to the floor. The other three scrambled from their chairs, but Nova already had a grip on the faux-antique carpet. She flung it up to expose the floor beneath.

The trapdoor wasn't even disguised. A simple inset handle gleamed silver against the surrounding wood planks. One firm tug and the door lifted, exposing the top of a ladder and a dark shaft.

"Wyatt!" she shouted down into the darkness. "Wyatt, can you hear me?"

The click of a cocking revolver sent a bolt of terror straight to Nova's heart. No! She was too close to fail now.

"Wyatt!"

Another revolver clicked, then a third. She was surrounded.

"Surrender now," one of the card-players threatened. "Or we shoot."

A faint voice drifted up to her. "N-nova?"

*Wyatt!* Her heart skipped in relief. He was alive. Thank the Universe. She took a deep breath and jumped through the trapdoor.

# 36

NOVA DROPPED FROM THE SKY like an avenging angel. The damned wire mesh surrounding the wooden cage obscured Wyatt's view, but even as a shadowy outline, her fluid grace was unmistakable. She turned what could have been a crash landing into a skillful tuck-and-roll, and sprang to her feet with the ease of an acrobat.

Wyatt picked himself up from the floor in much less elegant fashion, rolling first to his knees, then staggering upright, one leg at a time. His head swam and his stomach roiled. He wasn't sure which was worse, the lingering aftereffects of the drug, or the handcuffs pinning his arms behind his back and biting into his wrists.

Two halting steps brought him up against the rough two-by-fours of his prison walls. He tried to wedge a shoulder between the slats. No good. He was skinny, but not that skinny. He tried an elbow instead, and let out a cry of triumph when his skin hit the scratchy metal of the cage's exterior. They'd been smart to lock him in a Faraday cage, but mesh tight enough to block any signal to and from his drones was also thin enough to break through.

Wyatt jabbed as hard as he could manage with his hands cuffed. The mesh bowed outward, but didn't break. Damn.

Outside the cage, Nova danced back and forth in a sparring match with another silhouetted figure. A gunshot rang out, followed by the ping of a bullet ricocheting off metal.

Wyatt's heart stuttered. Too close. He jabbed again at the mesh, but the flexible metal only deformed further. Fucking hell. The woman he loved was in danger on his behalf, and he was trapped here like a swooning damsel.

"Break, dammit!" It was no use. He simply didn't have enough leverage in this position.

"I'll be right there, Wyatt," Nova called. She spun and kicked, and her opponent let out a low grunt of pain. A second blow sent them toppling to the floor.

"Well done, sister," Enid Pratt's chilly voice cooed. "These men really ought to know better than to fight with a Pratt."

"You." Nova darted away, disappearing from Wyatt's view. "I should have known. A hidden torture dungeon is exactly the sort of thing you would love."

"Because I'm 'evil'? Don't tell me you still believe in fairy tales?" Enid's laugh was a high, tinkling thing, much better suited to a happy girl than a villain. It made Wyatt's insides turn to ice. "But of course you do. That's why you're here to rescue your sweetheart."

The two women moved almost silently through the dimly lit room, one predator stalking another. Wyatt strained to hear their faint shuffling, but it was lost beneath the muffled shouts and thundering footsteps of a scuffle overhead.

*Please, please be reinforcements.*

"Let him go, Enid." Nova's voice came from behind

Wyatt now. She was circling, keeping out of her sister's sight. "If I have to shoot you to free him, I will."

"How dramatic. And to think you're doing all this for a man. He can't be *that* good in bed. Now step away from that cage or I'll shoot *him*."

Wyatt dropped to the floor to make himself a smaller target. A gun barked, but whatever the target was, it wasn't him. His cage remained undamaged.

"Nova, stay down!" he shouted.

Another gunshot sounded, from a different direction, and he thought his heart might beat right out of his chest. He couldn't see anything, couldn't do anything.

"Fucking Viper." Wyatt wormed his way into a seated position and began to wriggle his bound hands beneath his ass. "Whole damned drone army." A bit more squirming and his hands were under his thighs. "Some bloody good it does me when I need it." He tucked his legs up to his chest and slipped the cuffs past his feet. Being slender and flexible was good for something, thank God.

His arms ached from wrist to shoulder, but that was a problem for another time. Still on the floor, he lunged for the nearest gap between bars and pushed. The mesh peeled away from the floor.

"Hey, Enid!" he shouted. "Why aren't you shooting at me?"

Her gun fired, but he didn't even flinch this time. It was a bluff. She wasn't going to put holes in his prison.

"Are you afraid of damaging my Faraday cage? Afraid of what I might do?"

"Wyatt, shut up!" Nova commanded. She was to his left now. How the hell had she got over there? She was damned sneaky.

A distant gunshot added to the general melee above.

Shit. Nova's friends were in danger too. If these fuckers hurt any of them—if they hurt her—he was burning down the fucking world and taking them all with him.

Wyatt got a finger beneath the mesh, then another, then his whole hand. The jagged edge bit into his palm, but he dug his nails into the soft metal and yanked as hard as he could. Outside, the gunfire continued, punctuated by Enid's taunts.

"I can do this all day, sister. I have plenty of ammunition. What do you have? Three shots left? Four?"

Wyatt yanked again, biting his lip against the pain. The mesh shifted.

*Come on, come on.*

One more tug, and he felt the wire give. A section of the mesh bowed outward and tore free, leaving one entire side of the cage uncovered. Wyatt leapt to his feet and pressed a finger to his scar, angling his body so his transceiver faced the square of light in the ceiling. The implant pulsed beneath his skin, but he didn't lift his finger. Five seconds. Ten. Fifteen. *Buzz, buzz, buzz.*

*Hear me. Come to me. Nova needs you.*

"Stay down, Nova!" he called again. "She's not going to kill me. If she wanted that she'd already have done it."

It was somewhat true. Clearly the orders from on high were to capture him, presumably to torture him into telling them everything he knew of Deimos's schemes. Did he think Enid would obey those orders if it became inconvenient? Not at all.

But he had to keep her attention. He had to buy time for the drones to travel here. Ag Sector 3 was ten minutes away at top speed.

A bullet whizzed by Wyatt's head, close enough to ruffle his hair. He dropped to the floor, curling into a ball in the corner of the cage.

"Get away from him!"

Nova! She was close. Nearly on top of him. She fired her own gun, and he heard Enid scrambling for cover. He lifted his head to curse Nova's reckless bravery, but she was already running around to the back of the cage.

The shouting upstairs had become a chaotic roar. What in hell was happening up there? Surely anyone on their side would have been overwhelmed by now.

*Please don't be hurt. Not for me.*

Wyatt crawled slowly to the opposite side of the cage. The mesh still clouded his view, but he could see Nova crouched near the floor.

"Nova," he whispered. He slipped his bound hands between two slats and pressed until the mesh bowed outward.

Nova placed a hand opposite his. The warmth of her palm seeped through the thin material separating them. Together. They were going to get through this mess together. Though fuck if he knew how.

"Your friends aren't coming for you," Enid sneered. "I intended to hand over you and your boy-toy as a special gift, but I can settle for displaying your dead bodies."

She fired again and Wyatt ducked instinctively. When he glanced back up, he found a bullet hole mere inches from where his and Nova's hands had been moments ago.

"The only question is…" Enid materialized out of the shadows. Light from the trap door above illuminated her feral grin as she stepped up to the cage where the mesh had fallen away. She aimed her pistol directly at Wyatt. "Who should I kill first?"

Nova sprang to her feet, as Wyatt knew she would. He jumped up too, ready to reach through the bars and try to knock the gun away, if that's what it took. He was no warrior, but he'd fight the devil in hell rather than allow his love to be hurt.

Before any of them could act, a discordant hum filled the air. Round shapes blotted out the square of light in the ceiling. The hum grew louder and louder as first one then a dozen drones flew down the shaft into the underground room. Little drones darted through the slats of the cage to shield Wyatt. Larger ones surrounded Nova. Drones poured in by the dozen, then by the score, battering Enid as they fought their way to their general's side.

His army had arrived.

# 37

AND TO THINK, *I used to hate having drones around.*

Nova peered around the whirring machine shielding her. This one was bigger than she was accustomed to, nearly the size of the trapdoor in the ceiling. She guessed it to be a work drone from one of the Ag sectors, from the dirt smears on its body and the appendages meant to dig, cut, or spray. Already it had sliced through the wire mesh around Wyatt's cage, trying to get to him. She wanted to pat it on the head—or whatever passed for a head—and say, "Good boy."

Across the room, Enid growled a curse.

"Get her, 100 Series!" Wyatt cheered. "That's it!"

"Should've fucking killed you," Enid snarled. "Won't make that mistake again. Connington can clean up his own mess." She ran off into a dark corner of the room. A door slammed.

Nova tore away a panel of mesh. "I'm getting you out of here. How does this thing open?"

"There're hinges here." Wyatt pointed through the swarm of mini drones at the corner nearest him. "There must be a latch in the next corner somewhere."

Nova ran there, pulling away what remained of the mesh wrapping to expose the wooden bars. "Shit. It's padlocked. Take cover in the opposite corner. I'm going to blast it off."

She backed away, and the big drones went with her, circling to protect her from all sides. She swatted at one of them with her pistol. "I appreciate the cover, but aren't you supposed to be protecting Wyatt?"

If he'd reprogrammed them to shield her, she was going to scream at him for the rest of his life.

She raised her weapon, shaking off the thought. That wasn't possible. She didn't have an implant. The drones couldn't have any idea who she was.

"Stay down," she called, then aimed and pulled the trigger.

The impact sent pieces of the lock flying in all directions, but it remained stubbornly fastened. Even though she'd scored a direct hit to the body of the lock, it was too strong for her small caliber bullets.

"One more," she promised Wyatt. She took aim again. This shot needed to hit the shackle. Her ammunition was limited, and they still had to get up the ladder and out of the building. From the noises upstairs, she didn't expect a casual stroll. Calling on all her professional calm, she took the shot.

The bullet tore through the shackle. Bullseye.

"Got it!" Nova ran to the cage and gave the damaged padlock a firm tug. It broke off, and she flung the pieces aside.

Wyatt sprang to his feet. "Great shot! Let's get the hell out of here."

Nova threw the door open. Wyatt dashed toward her, and for a split second, she thought he would fling himself into her arms. When he didn't, a pang of disappointment speared through her.

She flinched. *Don't be a fool, Pratt. You shouldn't even be thinking about hugging him in the middle of an escape. Keep your head on straight and do your fucking job.*

"Up the ladder," she ordered. "Drones first. I'll watch your back."

Wyatt jogged toward the exit, his steps faltering now and again. Damn Enid and Connington and all their cohorts. If she ever saw any of them again, they'd be sorry they'd touched even a single hair on his head.

Despite the cuffs around his wrists, Wyatt started up the ladder. He moved slower than he otherwise might have, but he didn't wobble, and after a few rungs, Nova began to breathe easier. The mini drones followed him loyally, clustering around him as he ascended. Nova's own protective squad continued to surround her, the Ag worker leading the way.

"What the heck, big guy? Go up there with him!"

The drone ignored her. A smaller one buzzed past, circled around Wyatt, then back to Nova in a figure-eight pattern. Cursed machines! She couldn't even push them away, or she'd risk losing a finger to the rotors. She'd be of no use to Wyatt bleeding out on the floor.

The first few drones passed through the trap door, blotting out areas of light like artificial solar eclipses. When no gunfire erupted, Wyatt grasped the edge of the opening and began to haul himself up.

He froze half-way out. Nova scrambled higher, her brain already weighing the best ways to haul him down atop her without killing them both.

"Aubrey?" Wyatt's tone held no fear, only surprise, and Nova stopped with her hand inches from his boot.

"Wyatt! Are you okay? Is Nova with you?"

"Right behind me." Wyatt's legs dangled in the air for a moment, then he disappeared into the room.

Nova hauled herself up and out, scrambling to her feet before Wyatt could even get himself off the floor. The card room resembled one of those vid-dramas where machines rose up and destroyed civilization. Drones filled the air. What had once been the card table was now a heap of boards and splinters. Two unconscious men lay sprawled on the floor amid the wreckage, along with several broken drones.

"Poor baby," Wyatt cried, reaching toward one as he pushed himself up. "Look what they've done to you."

Aubrey picked up the mangled drone and tucked it under one arm. "Let's get you out of here."

Wyatt held out his bound hands to Aubrey. "C'mon." The drone guards slid aside as Wyatt guided the other man into the protective circle. Wyatt glanced at the downed enemies. "Did you do that?"

"Nope. That was your drones." Aubrey led Wyatt into the hallway, stepping over the prone body of another incapacitated mercenary lying just outside the door. "I did that one, though. Bastard has a skull like iron. I'm going to have to find a different pair of gloves to wear to the ball tonight."

"Pratt! Milords!" Garret waved to them from down the hall, then flattened themself against the wall to avoid a speeding drone. "This way!"

Nova jogged to them and imitated what Wyatt had done with Aubrey, extending a hand and bringing Garret inside the drone shield.

"You have mechanical guards too?" they asked.

"They won't leave me. I don't have time to worry about it right now."

"They're still filing into the building." Garret set a brisk pace toward the exit. "It's chaos."

Nova checked behind her. Wyatt's complexion was sallow, and his strides weren't entirely steady. But he was keeping pace and he had Aubrey to support him if needed.

"How many hostiles between us and the door?" she asked.

"Not sure," Garret responded. "Everything went tits up when the drones arrived. I'm not sure anyone remembers who was fighting who, so this is our best chance to get you out of here. And maybe don't come back again."

Nova barked a mirthless laugh. "Not planning on it."

No way. No how. By-the-books Nova was going fully rogue. She was taking Wyatt and going into hiding, and not even her friends could stop her. She'd steal a spaceship and take him home to Earth, if that's what it took.

Garret was right about the chaos. Bits of glass and metal from smashed light fixtures littered the floor. Doors had been battered open, and windows shattered. Scratches and holes marred the walls. Incoming drones joined Wyatt's protective force, clogging the hall until they all had to walk single-file. Mercenaries scattered at the sight of them, loyal to themselves above all.

"Maybe creating a pay-for-hire system for security and law enforcement wasn't the smartest decision ever." Aubrey chuckled. "Who would have guessed?"

"Should've used drones!"

Wyatt's cheerful tone buoyed Nova's spirits. He would be okay. She hadn't failed him.

Minutes later, they were crunching through the remains of the front entrance, entirely unmolested. Nova stepped outside without a second glance, knowing in her gut that she would never set foot in the building again. She expected a pang of loss or at least nostalgia for her old, orderly life. It never came. She felt freer. Lighter.

"This is where I say farewell." Garret crawled beneath Nova's ring of mechanical escorts, not rising until they were well away from the drones. "I have a report to write up and a long conversation to have with Lord Windborne's attorney. Good luck to you all."

"Thank you," Wyatt said. "If you could have any broken drones you find sent to Central Manufactory, we'll make sure you are well compensated for the trouble. They at least deserve proper recycling for their heroics."

Garret bowed. "Of course, my lord. Godspeed." They jogged back into the building.

Nova, Wyatt, and Aubrey headed straight for the trolley tracks, where Aubrey's driver patiently awaited them.

"Can't you get these damned drones off me?" Nova griped. "We can't take them in the trolley, and they're supposed to be guarding *you*!"

Wyatt tapped his chest, and the drones expanded their circle from nearly on top of them to a few meters away.

"I won't send them away yet. And I don't know why they're around you. I don't even know how so many got here so fast. It should have taken longer."

"Leo, probably," Aubrey guessed. "Harriet almost certainly has a backdoor into your system. He probably told her to send help."

Nova glared at the large Ag drone that still sniffed around her like a guard dog. "They should still be protecting Wyatt, not me."

Wyatt grimaced. "Leo better not have fucked up my system. I can't check it or change anything without a terminal. If I had my watch, I could—"

"Oh. Here." Nova dug into her pocket and produced the watch. "I thought you might want it back." She tossed it to him.

Wyatt caught the watch in his cupped hands. For a long moment, he stared at it, not moving. The drones that had guarded Nova began to fall into place around him.

"Oh!" She grinned at the now-cooperative drones. "They thought I was you. I should have—"

Wyatt nearly knocked her off her feet with a heart-stopping smile. "Damn, I love you, Nova Pratt."

Her world upended. The ground beneath her lost all solidity and the air became too thick to enter her lungs. The edges of her vision blurred, until all she could see was Wyatt's face, alight with admiration and love. The humming of the drones faded to nothing beneath the rush of blood in her ears and the pounding of her heart.

Moisture gathered in the corners of her eyes. He was alive. He was alive and safe and he loved her.

And damn her stupid, foolish heart, she loved him too. It wasn't merely lust. It wasn't only her protective nature. She wanted to see him every day. To laugh and talk and coo over his animals. She wanted to feel the blossoming joy in her chest whenever he smiled at her and the warmth of his touch on her skin. Fuck, she even wanted to let him fuss over her and feed her and wrap his arms around her.

Her futile attempt to stay away from him only reinforced the truth that now seemed mortifyingly obvious: she'd been bewitched the moment she'd first seen him dancing in his office. She'd never stood a chance.

Nova set her mouth in her customary scowl, and the world seemed to shift back into focus. The abrupt gesture she made at the trolley car felt normal, comfortable. Thank God. She might have lost her heart, but she hadn't lost her head.

"Get in the trolley," she barked. "We're getting the hell out of here."

# 38

"SUGAR BEET?" Wyatt brushed dirt off the lumpy white root vegetable and held it out.

Nova leaned away from the grimy bulb. "No. Thank you. You're the one who needs food, not me."

"Mmm-hmm." He took a bite, chewed, and swallowed. "They're tasty. We can dig up a few more for dinner."

He hadn't called her out for her lack of a response to his love confession, thank God. It hovered in the back of her mind like a pesky gnat she couldn't shoo away, but she chose not to let it distract her. Not now. She needed all her professionalism to keep him safe.

Nova scanned the acres of beet leaves. She hadn't known this many beets even existed. Beets beneath her feet. Beets in every direction. Ag Sector 3 was an unending carpet of beets. It must have supplied the sugar for every bite of candy she'd eaten in her entire life.

Her parasitic worker drone—she was calling it Minion from now on—plucked a beet from the soil, turned it this way and that in front of its camera, then held it out to her.

Sighing, Nova accepted the beet, and the drone sped ahead to attend to its next incomprehensible task.

"You really can't do anything about Minion?"

Wyatt swallowed another bite. "Minion? Oh, you mean

W405? Something's broken. It wants to do its job, but it wants to do it for you. I think it got confused when you had the watch and went into video-tracking mode. I'll never find the bug without a terminal. I could disable its cameras, but then it might go around poking at everything, trying to find you."

Nova flung the beet like a baseball, and it sailed a satisfying thirty-ish meters before disappearing among its brethren.

"It's slowing us down. Anyone could see us walking out here, and I don't like it. Sending most of the drones with Aubrey and the trolley won't fool Connington for long. You need to get out of sight ASAP."

Wyatt flashed that damned adorable grin again. "I'm fine. But it's sweet that you're still worried about me."

"Yes, I can be sweet sometimes," she grumbled. "And yes, I'm worried. Now walk faster."

Admitting to her internal struggles did nothing to ease the knot in her gut. If this was how talking about feelings always felt, it was a wonder anyone ever did it. Yet Wyatt went blurting out I-love-yous in the midst of mortal peril. Earthlings were bizarre. Earth earls, most incomprehensible of all.

"What's that machine off in the distance?" she asked. "It looks big."

Wyatt tapped his watch. "Harvester. I can call it over. We should be able to shelter underneath so we'll stay dry when the irrigators go off."

"Do it. We'll meet it halfway."

Wyatt fiddled with his watch for a bit. Bright red scrapes and dark bruises ringed his wrists where the handcuffs had been.

Hot rage flared in Nova's chest. Wyatt was a beautiful,

happy, generous, *good* person. How dare anyone hurt him like that! How dare anyone try to destroy someone who made the world a better, brighter place!

"The farmers are going to hate me for screwing up all their routines," Wyatt quipped, then went back to gnawing on the sugar beet.

"The farmers can go fly into a star," Nova snarled.

He mumbled something around his mouthful of beet.

"What?"

"You can shout at me, if you want," he said again. "Or at the Universe. Like, to get out all your emotions. I know you're angry and upset and whatever. I am too, but it's kinda hanging out in the back of my brain right now. I might cry when the adrenaline rush fades."

Plants snapped beneath Nova's boots as she quickened her pace toward the harvester. "Did you study feelings in Earth school?"

"Oh, no. I just discovered when I was a teenager that expressing all my emotions flustered Leo, and it had the added benefit of making me feel better."

"I see." Nova's every stride grew longer, which wasn't good for Wyatt, but the only command her body would heed was *faster*! "I currently have neither the time nor the mental processing power to waste on expressing emotions."

*Not until you're safe. Not until you're hidden. Not until I can rip off every stitch of your clothing and be certain that you're unharmed. Or else catalog every cut and bruise in order to inflict them one hundred times onto anyone who laid a finger on you.*

"Except being grumpy," she clarified. "I am very, very grumpy right now."

Wyatt began to jog. "We should run, then. Because

according to Drone 23, the rain will begin in…" He checked his watch. "Seven minutes."

Nova matched Wyatt's pace, watching for signs of difficulty, but he ran steadily enough. In fact, he soon pulled ahead, falling into his runner's stride. The few small drones he'd brought along flew overhead. Minion, meanwhile, continued to zip here and there, probing the dirt and offering Nova samples.

In the end, Wyatt beat her to the harvester by an embarrassing fifty meters. When she reached him, she found him smiling and red-cheeked, eyes alight with mischief.

"Nice to know I can beat you at something." He gestured to the space behind the five-foot tall wheels. "Your shelter, milady."

"You're the aristo, not me. You go first."

His gaze caught hers and held it. "Is that still how you see us? Noble and common, like we're different species? You know there's no strict line between good and evil, between him and her, between strength and weakness. You've read the fairy tales. Pauper marries royal through character and heart. If that's the qualification for a title, you're a goddamned empress." He held out a hand. "Together?"

This man! Not only could Nova not resist him, she no longer wanted to.

She clasped his hand and they crawled beneath the harvester. The space underneath was large enough to sit upright, and by the time the irrigation began to drum down, they were settled comfortably. The flashlights on Wyatt's three utility drones lit up their small shelter. Minion circled outside the harvester, checking the dirt and the beets in its misguided desire to please her.

*Safe.* At least temporarily.

Nova studied Wyatt beneath the white lights of the

drones. He looked better than he had earlier. His coloring was normal, and while he appeared rumpled and tired, exhaustion didn't weigh on him as it had during their race from RMC HQ.

"How are you feeling?" She tugged aimlessly on the leaf of a plant beside her. "Do you need another beet? Water? Anything?"

"I'm fine. Whatever your sister drugged me with has worn off, and my stomach's not growling anymore. And if I get thirsty, well…" He stretched a hand out of their shelter and held it there for a few seconds before pulling it back. Crystal-clear droplets beaded on his skin. He lifted the hand to his mouth, licking the water from each finger in turn.

Nova's simmering desire flared into a white-hot torrent. Her stomach clenched and her breathing faltered. All those feelings packed tightly inside her began to uncoil. Rage. Fear. Relief. Hope. Uncertainty. Love. Need. If she opened her mouth, she was certain she would scream.

Instead, she lunged at Wyatt, grabbed the hem of his shirt and yanked it up.

"Whoa!" He caught her wrists to slow her. "What are you doing?"

She forced the words out through her tight jaw. "I need to see that you're not injured."

"I just said I was fine."

Nova looked directly at the livid marks around his wrists. "*That* is not fine."

"Those are the only marks on me, I promise." He released her wrists and his expression softened. Slowly, gently, he brushed a single finger across her cheek. "I'm okay, love."

The endearment broke her. She pushed him down into the carpet of greenery and straddled his hips. "Prove it." She lowered herself atop him until her lips were within an inch of his. "Prove you're alive. Show me you're real."

Wyatt's lips parted on a soundless gasp. Bloody hell, he looked like a feast laid out for her, his pupils blown and his skin flushed. If she didn't get her mouth on him soon, she was going to explode.

"I need to taste you." She would beg if she had to. Offer him anything he desired.

The tip of his tongue wet his lower lip and she groaned.

"Please," he rasped. "Yes, please."

"Thank fucking God." Nova sealed her mouth to his, wasting not even a second before thrusting between his lips.

He relaxed beneath her, his arms lifting to lightly encircle her, allowing her the freedom to take what she needed. Her hands grabbed at his clothing while her tongue plunged in and out of him, exploring the depths of his mouth and the contours of his lips.

Wyatt met each greedy, possessive kiss with a soft sigh. He was soft everywhere, despite the sharp angles of his lean body. His lips were cloud-like in their gentle plumpness, moving across hers in the lightest of breezes in response to her long licks and the nip of her teeth. His skin felt like silk wherever it glided against hers, and even the stubble along his jaw left only the merest of scratches as she nuzzled his cheek and dragged her kisses lower.

Nova kissed her way down his neck, reveling in each tiny shiver she drew from him. He was deliciously sensitive here, where his pulse pounded so close to the surface she could catch each heartbeat between her lips. She peppered his throat with delicate sucks and nibbles, his every helpless tremor eliciting a corresponding flicker of heat in her belly.

He called out her name, a desperate half-sob so thick with emotion that her breath stuttered. Her chest felt suddenly, oddly tight, and moisture pooled in the corners of her eyes. It was too much. Like a burst of fire slicing through the darkness. If she touched him, she would burn to ash. And yet, she couldn't resist the lure of the warm, dancing flames.

She yanked the collar of his shirt down, exposing the jut of his clavicle and the small scar beneath. He'd marked himself there. Tied himself to his flock of mechanical guardians. But for all their uses, they were still only machines. They could never provide all he needed.

Nova sank her teeth into his skin, gently at first, then harder when he arched into her, seeking more. She was his champion now, and he would wear her mark.

*Mine.* She traced the small, red indents with the tip of her tongue. *All mine.*

Hers to protect. Hers to touch. Hers to claim.

She grasped the hem of his shirt and pushed it up to bare his torso to her sight. A gorgeous pink flush of arousal colored his pale skin. She spent some time licking and sucking his nipples, while her fingers traced lazy patterns down his ribs and across his belly. When she found a ticklish spot on his side he squirmed and giggled, and she couldn't help answering with a laugh of her own.

"You're fucking adorable, you know that?"

"It's one of my—" He broke off with a groan as Nova explored his navel with her tongue. "My best qualities," he finished breathlessly.

Nova almost snorted. "You're far more than just adorable." Infinitely more. Wyatt was kind, loyal, brave, determined, intelligent, gentle, passionate, loving, and a whole host of other good traits. Those were what made him adorable. His pretty face and his wriggling hips were a mere bonus.

"What am I, then?"

"You're Lord Windborne." She grasped his hips, holding him still and pinning him down as her mouth inched toward his low-slung waistband. "You're the Viper. You're a flirt and a lover and a brother and a friend."

She licked down his treasure trail, eliciting a needy moan. His fingers clenched around the leaves of the beet plants to either side of him.

"And you're *mine*," Nova finished. "Every bit of you. You and your drones and your enormous heart and this fucking miniskirt that's been taunting me." She flipped the skirt up and tugged his leggings down, exposing his rigid cock to her gaze. She swiped her tongue across the tip, tasting the slight tang of precum.

Wyatt's hips jerked. "Shit, Nova. Oh, God."

Ah, yes. This was what she needed. A banquet for her senses. He was hot and hard beneath her fingers, sweet and salty on her tongue as she licked him down to the root, then back up again. She breathed in the scent of sweat and sex, and the earthiness of the plants beneath them.

Nova pleasured him at her leisure, lingering on each new discovery. A cluster of freckles decorated his left thigh where leg met pelvis. He would hold still when she stroked him with her hand, but he couldn't help twitching every time she put her mouth on him. And when she sucked with the right amount of pressure, his breath would hitch in tiny, almost inaudible hics.

She took him deeper into her mouth, increasing her pace slowly, not willing to miss even the tiniest of his reactions. Her body hummed like one of his drones. He was so fucking real, so alive. She could feel him with every part of herself, heat and hunger filling every cell, every atom. She, too, was alive. More gloriously alive than she could ever remember.

She paused to catch her breath, removing her hands

from Wyatt's body long enough to unzip her trousers and shove them down to her knees.

"Do you want—"

"Hush." Nova caught Wyatt's gaze and held it. "I'm in charge here."

He lowered his lashes. "Yes, Mistress Nova."

*Holy shit.*

Thank God she'd gotten her trousers down, because she needed to touch herself *now*. Fuck, she was going to combust if he kept looking at her like that—meek with a hint of defiance. She slipped a hand between her legs, planting the other one firmly on Wyatt's abdomen.

"You are going to hold still and you are going to be quiet," she commanded. "You're going to take whatever I give you."

"Yes, Mistress Nova." His voice was hoarse, and he twitched beneath her hand.

"And you will tell me to stop if I do anything you don't want, do you understand?"

He stared up at her through his lashes, eyes so dark with desire that only the thinnest ring of blue remained. "Yes, Mistress Nova."

"Good boy."

Wyatt let out a strangled moan. Already disobedient, the rogue. She was going to thoroughly enjoy this.

Nova slicked her fingers with her own arousal and rubbed her aching clit in slow, light circles. Part of her screamed for hard and fast, but she needed this to last more than she needed release.

She teased Wyatt mercilessly with lips and tongue, dragging him close to the edge, but gentling her ministrations and starting over every time he cursed or wiggled or arched up into her. Her own body burned like the surface of Io, half-melted by forces too powerful to escape. Without the pauses to shush Wyatt, she would have been torn to pieces within minutes.

"You are not holding still," she scolded. "And I heard that noise you made."

"S-sorry," Wyatt gasped. It was obviously a lie, because the moment Nova closed her lips over the crown of his cock, his back bowed and he cried out an agonized, "Fuuuuck!"

She groaned around him and redoubled her efforts. He was going to kill her with that combination of willing submission and inability to control himself. Her hips made an involuntary jerk. Fuck, she was getting close. So close. Too close.

She forced herself to slow, even as Wyatt began to writhe beneath her. He swore again and moaned her name. Her abs tightened and her toes curled, caught somewhere between trying to stave off orgasm and urging it on.

*Wyatt, oh, God, oh yes.*

Her control was breaking. She sucked him hard, with little finesse. Anything more was beyond her ability. Her own fingers wouldn't even obey her commands, moving faster and faster, increasing the pressure on her clit until she was rocking helplessly against her own hand.

"P-p-please," Wyatt whimpered. "P-please. I can—can't—" He bucked beneath her, shouting out his climax.

Nova drank down his bitter spend, drawing out his orgasm until he fell still and silent. Triumph surged through her veins. Wyatt was all hers. Conquered and claimed. It was all she needed to let herself go. She rose up off him, throwing her head back and stroking herself up over the edge and down, down, down, tumbling again and again until her legs were quaking and her brow damp with perspiration.

"Fucking hell," she gasped, and let herself crumple atop him.

Wyatt's arms came around her as she lay panting against his chest. He began to stroke her hair. "You are magnificent."

"Mmm." It took her several seconds to find her voice. "You're a disobedient little brat."

"I'm sorry, Mistress Nova," he replied, not at all sincerely.

"But I suppose I already knew that."

He flashed her a wicked grin. "Feel free to punish me at any time."

Nova laughed and held him tight. For now, for a time, her worries were behind her and she could simply exist in this space, happy and content with the man she adored.

She had nearly nodded off when he asked, "Does this mean we're not broken up anymore?"

# 39

A FURIOUS BEEPING shook Wyatt from his dreamy sex-and-sugar-fueled doze. He tried to swat at the noise, only to find his arm pinned beneath Nova's sleeping body. She shifted and mumbled something incomprehensible. The movement was enough to awaken the nerves in his trapped limb, which rudely responded with a thousand needles of sharp pain.

"Ow!" Wyatt squirmed free of his lover's embrace and shook his arm, trying to ease the tingling. "Bloody stupid body. Full of bugs that we can't fix." His watch—the source of the alarm—screamed in time with his arm. "Yes, yes, I hear you."

"What did you forget this time?" Nova asked, not lifting her head.

Wyatt silenced the alarm. "Nothing. It's an alert from 23." He scanned the notification as he tugged his clothing back into some semblance of order. "Shit! We've got company."

Nova bolted upright, immediately at full alert. "Where? How many?" She scrambled to  do up her trouser buttons.

"Not sure." The watch was too small for any detailed video, but he swiped rapidly through a series of still photographs from 23's feed. "Two small clusters of people, looks like. I think they're on motorbikes and they're moving in opposite directions."

Nova leaned over his shoulder to look. "They're looking to flank us. They've guessed we're using the harvester as cover. Those must be the lightweight dirt bikes or else we'd be able to hear them coming. Go back to the beginning and scroll slower this time."

Wyatt held his arm out and let her swipe the photos at her own pace.

"Three hostiles on bikes heading west northwest. Second group of three heading northeast. Dress reminiscent of RMC, likely armed. Current trajectories indicate flanking maneuver." Nova paused and cocked an ear. "Small numbers and stealth of approach suggest targeted assassination attempt. Expect squad one to flush us out into the fire of squad two."

Thank God for Nova's absolute professionalism. The words "assassination attempt" shrieked in Wyatt's brain like an angry wasp invading his beehive, and he could sense his pulse quickening in response. Weary as he was from one ordeal after another, he could easily have slipped into a full-blown panic attack. Nova's brisk tone soothed him, however, as did the hard set of her mouth. Nothing would ever stop her from charging into battle for him. And that left him no choice but to throw himself into the fray alongside her.

"Which group is squad one?"

"No way to know," Nova answered. She pulled her revolver from beneath her jacket and swung the chamber open. "I have two bullets left. I wish I'd checked Zeller's pockets for extra ammo when I took this off him. All I could find at home were small caliber bullets."

Wyatt's heart leapt at her casual reference to "home."

He would never forget the way she'd looked when she'd bossed him around and growled the word "mine," her eyes afire with hunger and need. Whatever had held her back or scared her off in the past, it wasn't enough to break them. He certainly wouldn't be holding back any longer. He was going to tell her he loved her every day for the rest of his life, in as many ways as he could. In this imagined future, she'd never have cause to doubt him or herself.

Step one to achieving said future: stay alive.

"The bullets at home are for the security bots that guard the factory," he explained. "We don't use weapons otherwise. Well, Rion has knives, and Aubrey might have poisonous plants in his conservatory, but we don't use firearms."

Nova put a hand on his arm. "You don't have to. It's not a fault, merely an observation. I'll have to take particular care with how I use the shots I have. Let's say I take two of them down with the revolver. That leaves four armed men against two of us."

"And four drones." Wyatt held out a hand and the closest utility drone floated down onto his palm. "These guys got me out of the handcuffs easily enough. They could do some damage."

"How many can you control at a time?"

"One. If I had a keyboard I could whip out commands, but I'm limited here."

Nova rubbed her chin thoughtfully. "Ranged weapons: two bullets, three small drones with cutting tools. Melee weapons: one knife, my hand-to-hand skills, Minion. We need an ETA on the hostiles. Let me see your watch again."

Wyatt loaded an updated set of photos and stuck his arm out.

"Trajectories still the same," Nova concluded. "Moving steadily, but slowly. I can't hear them yet, can you?"

Wyatt held his breath for a moment, listening hard, but couldn't detect anything beyond the faint whine of the utility drones. He shook his head.

"Then they likely believe us unaware of their presence." Nova drew her knife and jabbed it into the ground. "This is us. They're moving in like this." She sketched lines in the air with both hands. "If they turn to converge sometime in the next few minutes, we'll know we're right about their intent." She angled her hands so her fingers pointed at the knife. "I think our best strategy is a surprise attack. If you can take one down with a drone and I take two down with the gun, we'll no longer be flanked. We'll have two more drones even if the first is disabled, and I can take any weapons off our fallen enemies. We can use the harvester for cover, so the other squad will have to go around it to get to us."

"And if you miss a shot or the drones can't do enough damage to stop an attacker?"

Nova's lips turned upward, but Wyatt couldn't think of the grim expression as a smile. "Plan B is you take cover between the wheels where you're most shielded and Minion and I charge any remaining enemies. But I don't think you'll go along with that plan."

"Would you hide while I put myself in danger?" Wyatt countered. "What's plan C?"

Her composure faltered and she threw up her hands in despair. "I don't have one. And we haven't much time. The moment those bikes are close enough to risk us hearing them, they'll come at us full speed."

Wyatt didn't know the odds of accurately hitting a target moving at full speed on a motorbike, but he guessed it wasn't good, even for a trained markswoman like Nova. He trusted his accuracy steering a utility drone even less.

"I'd estimate a seventy percent chance of failure." His

brain was whirring so fast his words gushed out with hardly a breath in between. "Maybe as high as ninety. I'd summon more drones, but if the enemy is smart they'll have sealed off the entrance to the sector. And we can't keep doing this. People rely on those drones. This has to end. We need to cut the head off the monster and we need to do it now."

Wyatt's fingers, which had been drumming rapidly on the beet plants, curled into fists. He yanked on one of the plants, snapping the stem off and leaving the beetroot buried in the ground. The bees in his brain went suddenly still.

"We're sitting on thousands of projectile weapons!" He tossed the beet greens at Nova. "The diggy thing at the front of the harvester pulls up the beets, shakes the dirt off them, and then dumps them right here!" He banged a fist against the belly of the harvester directly above him. It echoed with a hollow clang. "*And* it spits them out the back so they can be taken for processing or whatever!"

Nova's face lit up. "Can we get inside?"

"Yeah. The top should open."

She seized his hand. "Quickly. Before they're close enough to shoot."

They crawled from beneath the harvester, and Wyatt scanned the field for any sign of their enemies. When he found them, he jumped.

"Shit! They're closer than I thought." Close enough to distinguish three figures atop three bikes, at least one of them with a rifle slung across the handlebars.

"Up," Nova ordered. "Get in the tank and get it started up."

Wyatt climbed up the knobby tire, and from there hauled himself onto the roof. The harvester hadn't been designed with a driver or passenger in mind, but someone had thankfully given consideration to cleaning the thing.

The top of the storage compartment had simple latches, and swung open on well-oiled hinges when he and Nova pulled on it.

They dropped down inside. A layer of beets lined the floor, making footing awkward. Wyatt kicked beets aside until he could stand flat. Or flat-ish, as the floor sloped slightly toward the back of the machine so the beets could tumble into the lift that would carry them up and dump them into crates.

Nova was back in full mercenary mode. "Ammo comes in here, out there. We have two positions: gunner and driver. Can we split them? How fast can this tank go? How fast can it shoot?"

Wyatt already had a connection to the harvester called up on his watch, and he sent it a startup command. The vehicle rumbled and began to vibrate underfoot. He scrolled quickly through its specs.

"It's got a lot of torque, big engine. If we can bypass the safety controls, maybe fifty kph? I can crank up the speed of the lift, but it'll put stress on the motor and the moving parts. We'll have a limited time before it shakes itself to pieces. As for controlling it…" He scrolled back to the details about the offloading lift. His heart sank. "Crap. Looks like it hooks to a machine in a barn or warehouse and that manually moves it side-to-side or up and down. Even if we climbed out onto it, I don't think we could aim it ourselves."

"Can Minion do it?"

"Probably. It can definitely grab on, and if you could—" The sound of multiple engines caused Wyatt's words to break off with a squeak. The noise swelled to a roar, drowning out the low purr of the harvester. Wyatt jolted in alarm, stepped on a loose beet, and crashed to the floor.

Panic flooded him. He was failing. Failing Nova, who'd

come to his rescue at her own peril. He'd changed her plan and now she was going to pay for it. And he was dressed all in black and he'd never said goodbye to Flurry or the ravens and the squirrels and his brothers would be heartbroken…

"Wyatt!"

He blinked. Nova knelt beside him, hands clamped on his shoulders. "I need three things from you. Only three. One, call Minion to grab the beet cannon. Two, have one of those little drones cut a hole so Minion and I can see each other. Three, drive the tank." She leaned back. "You can do that. Look at you, all dark and disheveled and sexy. You're the Viper and you command half the machines on Mars."

"Not half." His fingers moved with renewed purpose, sending commands to all three utility drones in quick succession. "Seventeen point six percent of machines in the country are part of my network. Two thirds of those come from Dystopia. The rest are in Ag sectors owned by the Third Chamber."

A gunshot rang out and Wyatt instinctively ducked.

"Keep talking," Nova commanded. "Tell me what you're doing."

He unstrapped his watch, pushing buttons, tapping, and swiping with both hands, as if he were playing a vid game. "Ute drones are cutting you some view holes. They're easy because they're simple and full of pre-programed tasks. Minion is waiting outside with cameras pointed this direction, trying to find you. It's not happy."

Gunfire continued as Wyatt tried command after command. Minion stubbornly ignored him. No bullets penetrated the harvester's walls, but it was only a matter of time before that changed. No one built farm equipment to be bulletproof.

"C'mon, c'mon." He glared at the watch screen. Three

alerts flashed simultaneously. The ute drones had finished their slicing. "We're through!"

Nova punched at the wall to open the holes and a flood of messages filled Wyatt's vision. Minion could see Nova again. With its primary problem solved, it ran through every command Wyatt had tried, eager to be of service. It flashed and whirred happily, finally clamping itself to the beet shooter.

"Wave your hands," Wyatt instructed. "Up, down, left, right. It should understand as long as it can see you."

"Got it. Now drive. Full speed."

*Yes, Mistress Nova. Anything for you. All for you.*

In an instant, Wyatt slipped into hyperfocus the way he did at the keyboard, losing all sense of time and blocking out everything but the harvester's movements and Nova's commands. The vehicle lumbered at first, but once his overrides kicked in it chugged along like a locomotive. Beets flew up into the compartment, battering his shins and thighs. He idly pushed the vegetables aside as he worked. Something whistled overhead, and it took him several seconds to realize that a gunshot had penetrated their defenses.

"Stay down and start the cannon on my mark!" Nova ordered.

Wyatt crouched lower into the growing pile of beets. He pressed the top right button to call up Minion's rear camera. The video flickered and blurred, but it was enough to get his bearings. The two groups of bikers had merged and were rapidly closing in on the slower harvester. At least two of them had rifles raised.

"Three." Nova waved a hand, directing Minion. "Two."

Wyatt switched back to the harvester controls.

"One. Mark!"

The lift howled to life. Through Nova's spy holes, Wyatt

caught a glimpse of the massive chains, spinning faster than even the most foolhardy engineer would have recommended. Beets tumbled into the chute, filling their makeshift gun with ammunition.

"Here it comes, Connington, you fucking bastard," Nova shouted. She looked like Boudica, ready to stand against the Roman Empire, fierce and determined and glorious.

"I'd follow you all the way to hell, love," Wyatt vowed.

She snarled. "And I'd carry you back out again, you bloody fool!"

If she said anything else, it was lost beneath the screams of men and the crunching and twisting of metal.

# 40

Two in one blow. Weaponized beets was definitely an idea worthy of The Brave Little Tailor.

*That's my Wyatt.* Nova moved her right hand and Minion followed the motion. *Fighting with his brains and his heart.*

The two mercs who had crashed stayed down. The others veered away from the stream of beets. Nova felt a grim smile tugging at her lips. Connington had underestimated her for years, and despite his failures to take her down, that hadn't changed.

She gestured sharply to the left and down. Minion responded in seconds, changing the trajectory of Nova's attack. The machine whined in protest. Wyatt had been right to warn her that it wouldn't hold forever.

"Missed me, bitch!" Even through the clamor, Nova recognized Zeller's voice.

*That's because I wasn't aiming at you, asshole.*

"Hard left!" she called to Wyatt.

The harvester spun, its movements more agile than Nova had expected. The four remaining attackers swerved and slammed on their brakes to avoid a collision. One lost traction and skittered out of control.

"Hard right!"

Nova gestured to Minion, adjusting her cannon as her

enemies tried to recover. She caught Zeller's front wheel with the full force of her spray, sending him flying over the handlebars.

"Take that, *bitch*!"

The other rider who had lost control was on his feet again, attempting to remount his bike. Nova pulled the cannon up into a high arc, raining beets down on the man. One large specimen hit him squarely on the head and he crumpled.

"Four down." The beet cannon trembled, and a piece flew off, pinging against the harvester's exterior. "Do a u-turn. This thing isn't going to last much longer and we need to get our hands on those bikes and guns."

"Don't tell me you're going out there," Wyatt protested. He obeyed her order regardless, turning the harvester in a tidy arc. "I'm shutting down the lift. Tell me if they come within range again."

"Not likely." Connigton was smarter than that. He'd adjust quickly. And Zeller wasn't down for good. They were still outnumbered. She clambered across the pile of beets and poked her head out through the still-open hatch. "Correct course to one o-clock."

"Get down!" Wyatt hissed.

Nova crouched and turned to him. "I need you to get me to where those bikes are." She drew her revolver and checked it again. "Don't worry, I've got Minion and two bullets."

Wyatt kicked a beet. "I can't not worry!"

Nova trailed her fingers down his arm. "And I have you. We're ending this. Today." She lunged in for a quick, fierce kiss before rising once more to check their progress.

A quick sweep of the area told her everything she needed to know. This was her chance. Connington and his remaining goon were to the left, the crashed bikes to the right. Zeller's bike lay dead ahead, the man himself nowhere in sight.

She dropped down an instant before a burst of rifle fire peppered the harvester's left side. When she glanced up, her gaze snagged on a pair of neat holes in the metal. Right where her torso had been a split second ago. Connington had always been a braggart, but he hadn't overexaggerated his marksmanship.

"Be prepared for some bumps." Nova shoved beets into a defensive pile on Wyatt's left side. "I'm going out for a bike and weapons. You're my cover. If I bang once, turn left, twice turn right."

"Nova." This time when he spoke his voice was neither angry nor worried, but deadly serious. His eyes bored into hers, afire with purpose. "Don't die."

"I won't. I have things to say to you later." She rolled her shoulders to loosen up, then sprang to her feet and hauled herself over the wall and into the fray.

Her landing was less elegant than she preferred, but the cushion of the beet leaves helped soften her roll. She'd be sore later, but no real damage. At the moment, she didn't have time for pain.

The goon who'd been clonked with a beet lay closest. Nova sprinted over and grabbed his bike. It appeared intact and responded when she thumbed the controls. She scanned the area for his rifle, but it was either lost among the beets or someone else had grabbed it.

*Zeller? Shit.*

Nova swung herself onto the bike and spun it in a slow circle. No sign of Zeller. The bike's front tire felt a little wonky, but nothing she couldn't handle. Nearby, the harvester rolled onward, still taking fire from the far side.

*Stay safe, Wyatt. We can do this.*

She sped the short distance to the pair of bikes that had crashed first. Neither appeared salvageable. One of the men lay face down and unmoving. The other moaned, clutching his leg. The good news was they wouldn't be getting up any time soon. The bad news: this pair had also been relieved of their rifles.

"Fuck!"

The revolver it was, then. Nova kicked the bike up to speed and pulled alongside the harvester. She thumped it once and moved with Wyatt into a left turn. Her faithful Minion flew to her side.

"Cover my back." Nova gestured behind her, and the drone obeyed. "Thank you. You can be annoying as shit, but you're a good friend."

Friend? What had happened to her these past months? First she talked to animals, now she talked to machines. She opened the throttle, easing the bike toward the digging apparatus at the front of the harvester. Wyatt. Wyatt had happened to her and she was damned glad of it.

"Here we go, Minion. We've only got two shots, so let's make the best of them."

With the drone at her back, Nova powered forward, holding the wobbly front wheel steady with her left hand and cocking the revolver with her right. She rested her right forearm atop her left to give her some stability. Aiming across her body while on a moving vehicle was the opposite of an ideal shooting position, but needs must. Her firearms instructor would suffer an apoplexy if he saw her like this.

The thought was oddly heartening. She'd been the type of student he hated, always asking questions and contemplating increasingly implausible scenarios under which she might be called to shoot accurately. Maybe she'd never been quite as orderly as she'd believed herself.

The ping of a ricocheting bullet revealed Connington's location. Nova revved the bike up to full speed and roared ahead of the harvester. She executed a sharp turn, found the last of Connington's mercs, and fired. The man dropped like a stone.

Without a second's pause, Nova wheeled around, ducking low and waving Minion to cover her. Fragments of metal sprayed as the drone took a direct hit from Connington's rifle. Minion emitted a chorus of displeased beeps, but didn't fall. Nova veered around the front of the harvester, narrowly avoiding its churning blades. Connington was the better shot, but she was the better cyclist. She could play cat and mouse with him for a long time with her two machines to aid her.

She spun the motorbike in another tight circle, drawing alongside the harvester as she'd done before. A flash of movement in her peripheral vision made her glance up. Her blood froze. Zeller was climbing her beet cannon.

As she stared in horror, he pulled himself onto the harvester's roof. The three rifles of the fallen mercenaries were slung across his back, and a pistol lay holstered at his hip.

Wyatt's name tore from Nova's throat. She pounded frantically on the harvester's wall with the butt of her revolver, denting the metal and sending shivers of pain up her arm.

"Minion! Get him!" She released the handlebars to point at Zeller. The bike slewed beneath her. She flailed and grabbed hold, wrangling the vehicle into control by a hair's breadth. "Wyatt! Wyatt, above you!"

*Oh, God, oh, God, oh, God.*

She hadn't told him she loved him. She hadn't said a word and now she was going to lose him and her heart would shatter like so many shards of glass. She'd never find all the pieces, let alone put them back together.

"Zeller!" The primal scream tore at her vocal chords. "It's me you want, you steaming pile of horse dung!"

He paid her cry no heed. Cool as the polar caps, he reached behind his back for one of the rifles. Minion flew toward him, but it wouldn't get there in time. The damage had slowed it, and its primary directive was to protect her, not Wyatt.

Nova cocked her revolver again. One last shot. One last chance.

Her angle was terrible. Only the luckiest of shots would strike him from here, and she'd surely used up her share of good luck over the past twenty-four hours.

Her body reacted without conscious thought. In a move even her teenage self would have thought foolhardy, Nova rose up and jumped onto the bike seat like a stunt driver.

Time shifted from a raging river to a slow ooze. Nova found her footing. Her hands gripped the revolver. She sighted the target. Pulled the trigger.

Through the dream-like haze she saw everything: the impact of the bullet, the spray of blood, the slow fall of the body. She hung in the air for an eternity—suspended, weightless—until the dam burst and time rushed back in, sweeping her away.

The force of the impact with the ground knocked all the air from Nova's lungs. Pain exploded through her, and her mouth gaped in a soundless cry. For agonizing seconds, she gasped helplessly, unable to draw breath. Minion peered down at her, chirping its own powerlessness.

At long last, Nova's body unfroze from the shock and she gulped a lungful of air. She hurt all over, but she focused on her breathing: in, out, in out. The pain began to ebb.

Her heart rate crept toward normal. She eased herself into a sitting position, taking stock of her battered body. Nothing broken, but she'd have bruises for weeks.

Assuming she survived the day. Connington was still after her, and now he sped toward her on his motorbike, skidding into a stop that sprayed dirt and bits of leaves across her.

Minion darted in to shield her.

Connington dismounted and stalked closer. He carried his rifle strapped across his back and made no attempt to draw it. A few feet from the drone, he stopped, crossed his arms, and smirked.

"You can't really think that toy is going to protect you."

Nova reached for her knife, only to find the sheath empty. Her eyes darted back and forth, searching the ground for the weapon.

Connington bent and picked something off the ground. "Looking for this?" He twirled the knife in his fingers. "Nice blade. Perhaps I'll kill you with it. It would be fitting."

Nova beckoned Minion closer. Maybe she could snap off a tool and club Connington with it. She scowled up at her nemesis. "If you're going to kill me, then get on with it. I'm not in the mood for a villain monologue."

He turned his head to look at the harvester, which rolled across the field in a straight line. Too far away to hear her shouts. Too far away to protect.

"Perhaps I'll save your knife for a special occasion," Connington mused. He tested the point on the pad of a finger. "There is still the matter of the Viper, after all."

Nova shifted to a kneeling position. Every movement hurt, but she would rip Connington's throat out with her teeth before she would let him touch a hair on Wyatt's head.

She struggled to her feet.

*The stalwart warrior to the end. I should have known I was meant to die in a heroic last stand.*

"If you kill either of us," she spat, "the Lords of Dystopia will tear you into so many pieces they'll need a microscope to find your body."

Connington threw back his head and laughed. Then he lashed out with a vicious kick, sending Minion toppling. The drone crashed into the ground and stuck, beeping mournfully.

"No more worthless gadgets from your pathetic Earthling boy," Connington mocked. "I'm going to enjoy cutting him to pieces. But first, you." He adopted a fighting stance. "Try to stop me, little girl."

Nova took up a defensive position, years of training shutting out the pain in her body and the rage in her heart. Her eyes sharpened and her ears pricked up. Her mind took it all in: her enemy, her body, the surrounding terrain.

A familiar whirr caught her attention, but before she could locate the source, Connington lunged. Nova dove for the ground and rolled away from the attack.

He ran at her, knife poised for a downward slash. The moment he raised his arm to strike, a medium-sized drone swooped down, smashing into the side of his head. As he reeled from the blow, a figure sprang up from the ground and rushed him.

Nova's heart skipped a beat. "Wyatt!"

He was caked in dirt and leaves, and he threw himself at Connington with all the lethal agility of his serpentine nickname. He grabbed Connington's arm, twisting until the mercenary commander yelped in pain and released the knife.

Wyatt snatched the blade out of midair and plunged it deep into Connington's abdomen. "This pathetic Earthling will see you in hell before you touch his beloved." He yanked the knife free and stabbed again, this time directly into the mercenary's icy heart.

Connington only had time to gape in shock before gravity carried his dead weight to the ground.

Wyatt took a few stumbling steps backward, then dropped the knife. "Oh, shit, I just killed a man." He swayed, but held up a hand to stop Nova from rushing to his side. "Give me a sec."

Nova walked to him slowly, the aches and pains of her body reasserting themselves now that the danger had passed. Her right ankle throbbed with every step. Sprained, probably, but not terribly so.

Wyatt's shakiness vanished in an instant and he reached for her. "You're limping! Are you okay?"

"Sore. Bruised. Nothing that won't heal." She clasped his hand. "Thank you."

He squeezed her fingers gently. "Thank *you*."

Nova nearly choked as a wave of emotion swept over her. Tears pooled in her eyes. They were alive. They were together. And, dammit all, this time she was going to keep it that way.

She dropped Wyatt's hand. "Call your drones. I'll free Minion and then we can hop on the motorbike. I think we should head straight for the spaceport. We'll board the first flight to Earth, sleep with the cargo, whatever we have to. I'll find you a nice, safe place to live. Build you a cabin in the wilderness, where you can pet animals to your heart's content."

Wyatt reached out and tucked a flyaway lock of hair behind her ear. "Nova, love, we're not going to Earth. We're going home. Where we both belong."

The tears began to fall.

# 41

THE REMAINDER OF THE DAY passed in a haze. Wyatt hardly remembered getting onto the motorbike behind Nova and riding downtown. He had a vague recollection of meeting a soot-covered Aubrey at the factory door and listening to him rant about how difficult it would be to get the smell of smoke out of his upholstery.

Mostly, he remembered the shower. He'd been certain he'd never felt anything so good as that warm, clean water pouring down on his achy and filthy body. Until he stumbled into bed and realized that his sheets and pillow outdid the shower by at least a factor of ten.

Fourteen hours later, Wyatt woke to a rumbling stomach and an extra rumpled pillow beside him. Nova had been there, and he'd slept right through it.

Dammit.

He flung the sheets aside. If she was already up and about, he needed to get moving. He took another quick shower, then dressed in the most colorful clothing he could find: lime green jeans, a rainbow tie-dye t-shirt, and shiny red boots. He repainted his nails in assorted colors, and gelled his hair to emphasize the bright green tips. He used purple eyeliner instead of black, and finished with tinted glittery lip gloss that tasted like raspberries.

Today, he would slay the world with cuteness.

The smell of frying bacon lured him into the kitchen. Rion stood by the stove, poking at sizzling strips of meat. A tray of freshly fried eggs sat on the counter nearby.

"Humanely raised delicacies from one of Aubrey's farm sectors," he said. "Grab a plate and eat up."

Before Wyatt could reach for a dish, Leo sprang from his seat and enveloped him in a crushing embrace. "I should never have let you go alone to that place. Christ, Wyatt, I'm so sorry."

Wyatt gave Leo a quick squeeze, then squirmed free. Very little was more unsettling than Leo getting emotional, and Wyatt didn't need to start crying and ruin his makeup.

"I'm fine. The decision made sense at the time. Tell Harriet thanks for mobilizing the drones." He glanced around the room. "Where's Nova?"

Aubrey waved his fork. "Leo made her go see the doctor to assess her injuries. You're next, so grab some food while you can. He made me do it yesterday after those fucksters firebombed my trolley, and I completely missed dinner. I had to eat eel pie from a street vendor, like a plebeian."

"Uh, yeah. Thanks." Since Wyatt wasn't certain whether Aubrey was joking or not, he let the matter drop and grabbed a plate.

"After you are declared fit by the physician, there will be a briefing," Leo said, his usual authoritative demeanor returning. "I've called in a special investigator from the Constabulary. She's already taken statements from several witnesses to yesterday's events. You and Nova will give yours today, including everything that happened in Ag sector 3."

"Drone 23 has video footage."

"Good. Share that with the investigator, please. Finally, be prepared for an emergency Chamber meeting tonight at five p.m." Leo's voice turned icy. "Deimos apparently has some things to say, and I have a few choice words for him as well."

Wyatt gazed mournfully at his plate of eggs. All he'd wanted was some time alone with Nova. He wasn't sure how things stood between them. And he'd never fully quell the butterflies in his stomach until he saw with his own eyes that she was alive and well.

It was four-fifty-nine p.m. before that happened. Wyatt had alternated hours of meetings and appointments with solitary work cleaning Flurry's enclosure. His brothers never minded feeding the bat or letting him in and out when Wyatt wasn't home. But they all drew the line at scooping guano. So Wyatt cleaned and talked, and never once did Nova's appointment schedule line up with his own.

She was already in the Chamber room when he arrived—last, as usual. Someone had brought an extra chair in for her and placed it with the others, as if she were an official member of Parliament. Wyatt paused to look her over before sitting. She wore her usual military-style garb, and appeared comfortable, though she did have her right ankle wrapped and resting atop a padded footstool.

Wyatt dropped into the empty chair beside her. "How are you?" he murmured, darting a quick glance at the cameras. Steady red lights showed they were already live. "Any injuries?"

"The ankle needs a few days' rest." Nova nodded at a pair of crutches propped near the door. "Some aches and pains otherwise, but nothing serious." She looked him up and down. "You look like a ray of sunshine today. Any injuries to report?"

"None." His left shoulder still smarted from when he'd jumped from the harvester after hearing Nova's crash, and he'd collected a few other bruises and scrapes while rolling through the dirt and crawling through the beets to get to her. But the doctor had deemed him fit for his usual activities.

Nova raised a skeptical brow and started to reach for him. A booming voice calling the meeting to order intruded on the moment, and she and Wyatt both straightened in their seats and faced the screens.

"His Grace, the Duke of Deimos," the emcee announced.

On the screen, Nova's father rose from his seat and walked to the front of the room. He glared into the camera. "Third Chamber, this is a closed meeting. Why is there a commoner seated among you?"

Leo stood. "Prospective members of a Chamber are permitted to attend all meetings. As Ms. Pratt is daughter of a duke, she is an ideal candidate to fill one of our many vacancies."

Rion's hand shot up. "I vote aye."

"Aye," Aubrey agreed.

Wyatt raised a hand as well. "Fuck, yeah!"

Nova flashed him one of her rare incomparable smiles before sobering and turning her attention to the man on the screen.

Deimos looked ready to protest, but behind him, Marcus hopped to their feet and began to speak.

"Before anyone objects further, I should like to state that you all have both acknowledged and accepted that I am not a man. With this as a precedent, it cannot be denied that clear reform to the rules of inheritance is needed. I will be co-sponsoring a new proposal of this act with Lord Brandt, to be presented at our next regular meeting. As this act addresses not only the outdated notion of birth-assigned gender requirements, but also those of birth order and parental marital status, I believe the wisest course of action is to allow Ms. Nova Pratt to observe today's proceedings as a prospective member. Thank you." They sat.

"Well said!" shouted someone in the Second Chamber.

Deimos smiled a toothy smile. "Very well. We shall proceed. I have called this meeting as a vital update to the matters of the Viper smuggling and the murder of Lord Eberwhite. Recent incidents and new discoveries have revealed much. I would ask Investigators Garret of the RMC and Jain of the downtown Constabulary to come forth and present their findings."

Wyatt exchanged a glance with Nova.

She shrugged. "She seemed honest when I spoke with her," she whispered.

"Same."

Jain stepped to the center of the room. "As you may or may not know, Commander Connington of the Royal Mercenary Corps was killed yesterday during an altercation in an agricultural sector. After interviews with witnesses and a review of the video footage of the incident, I have concluded that Commander Connington and his deputy Captain Zeller led an unauthorized, armed attack against two citizens, one of whom is a peer of the realm. The deaths of Connington, Zeller, and their compatriots have been ruled to be self-defense and the investigation is closed. One of the surviving perpetrators has offered a full confession, including an admission that he was ordered by Connington to place the body of Lord Eberwhite outside Central Manufactory in order to implicate Lord Windborne in his death. Commander Connington was named as Lord

Eberwhite's killer, and that investigation is also closed. My full written report may be reviewed upon request. Thank you for your time." She bowed and departed.

*What the fuck?* Wyatt mouthed to Nova.

She extended her hand in response, and this time he took it. With Investigator Jain's report, he would no longer be under suspicion of murder, but he didn't believe Deimos would roll over so easily. Something more was happening here.

Wyatt hadn't realized how hard he was squeezing Nova's hand until she flexed her fingers, forcing him to relax his grip.

She leaned closer. "Hey. It's going to be all right. We'll go to the zoo after and you can hug some animals."

Wyatt blinked away a stray tear. He raised Nova's hand to his lips and kissed her knuckles. He had so much more he wanted to say, but Garret had come forward to present their findings.

"Good evening. I am Investigator Garret. I will be brief, but my written reports will also be available to you after the meeting, should you wish to review them. Lord Windborne was brought to me for questioning at the behest of you all, whereupon he was kidnapped and detained in an illegal interrogation chamber. Two members of the RMC have separately given written confessions stating that they knew of this chamber. Both have independently asserted that Commander Connington knew of the room and occasionally authorized its use to detain his personal enemies. It is my conclusion that the room be immediately emptied and permanently sealed off. All charges against Lord Windborne have been dropped, and the RMC is working with his attorney to determine if any further investigation into his mistreatment is necessary. That is all I have for you at this moment. Thank you."

Nova's father shook Garret's hand, then addressed the assembly once more.

"I am deeply saddened to learn of the treachery of a man whom many of us considered to be an ally." Deimos placed a hand over his heart. "Connington's abuse of his position of power has caused much suffering, including that of our esteemed colleague, Lord Windborne—"

Rion snorted audibly enough that the duke faltered.

"*Ahem.* And the family and friends of dearly departed Lord Eberwhite, who I fear also fell afoul of the commander's schemes." Deimos withdrew a folded stack of papers from his inner coat pocket. "I received some additional information, discovered among Connington's papers by those clearing his office. Among them were receipts for the purchase of identical ships from Eberwhite's fleet, and a detailed timetable of these same ships passing through the J-M splice, with many anomalies marked."

Wyatt dropped Nova's hand. He let his head fall against the back of the chair and stared up at the ceiling. "You bloody bastard," he groaned.

The duke continued on about how thankful he was that the smuggling had been discovered and stopped and various other nonsense, but Wyatt tuned most of it out. All his research was now nothing but so much space dust. Deimos had retreated from one battle in order to win another. The war was still on.

Nova touched his arm. "You're still ahead," she said softly. "He has to start over. He's lost Connington and his influence over the RMC. You've made new allies and you've lost no one."

Wyatt sat up straighter, a smile returning to his lips. He

ought to have known his warrior princess would have a good grasp on the big picture. He leaned over and pressed a kiss to her cheek, in full view of all of Parliament.

"I found you," he murmured against her skin. "That's what matters most."

# 42

*YOU HAD ALL DAY*, Nova scolded herself as she swung down the hall towards Wyatt's suite. *You had all day to come up with an appropriate way to express your feelings.*

Every dull *thud* of the crutches on the floor carried her closer to the inevitable conversation. One she was sure to botch, even if she had one hundred years to practice for it.

It didn't help that the Chamber meeting had thrown several more emotions into the mix. She felt both embarrassed and delighted by how the boys had championed her and welcomed her as one of their own. Her father's manipulations infuriated her, but they'd made Wyatt less of a threat to him, and she couldn't regret that. Her relief was so great, in fact, that she'd sailed from the room as if she were floating on a cloud, despite her crutches.

Until Wyatt had rushed ahead so he could open his door for her and she'd remembered they needed to have A Talk.

Ugh.

When he'd asked about their relationship status after they'd made love in the beet field, she really should have answered with more than a vague grunt and a sleepy cuddle.

"My lady." Wyatt welcomed her into his sitting room with a graceful sweep of his hand.

"Thank you."

He shut the door behind her. "How is your leg feeling? Is there anything I can get you?"

"I'm fine. How are you?" Nova eyed his wrists. The marks left by the handcuffs were fading already. That was good, at least.

"Also fine." He chuckled. "I like how we both keep worrying about each other. Maybe we should make a chart to track it. First person who worries a hundred times gets treated to a bubble bath or massage or however you like to relax."

"Bare-knuckle cage matches to the death."

"One-on-one, or battle royale? I'd like to know ahead of time how many bodies will need to be hauled away. It'll affect the janitorial fees." He cocked his hip and gave her a flirtatious smile.

God, he was so fucking cute.

"I love you." The words just fell out, without any sort of thought or preparation. They hung in the air for a split second, as if she might be able to reach out and snatch them back.

But then Wyatt's smile broadened, his face lighting up with a joy so powerful it knocked the planet from its orbit.

"I love you too."

Nova had to look away to quell the tears gathering in her eyes. "I should have said it before. Before the attack. If anything had happened to one of us, it would have been my fault that you didn't know."

"Sweetheart." He moved closer and laid a gentle hand to her cheek. "You have risked your life for me over and over. You have thrown yourself into chaos and walked away from the life you knew. If that's not love, I don't know what the hell is. Maybe I wasn't certain if you loved me in quite the same way that I love you, but that doesn't matter. I knew you loved me as yourself in whatever way worked for your life. And that's enough. If you want to be friends, that's enough. If you want to be lovers but not live together, that's enough. Even if you want nothing. You've given me a piece of your heart, and whatever shape and size that comes in, I will treasure it for eternity."

He leaned in for a kiss, but she pushed him away.

"Oh, fuck you, Wyatt Hartforrd," she growled without wrath. "I can't be all romantic and poetical like you. You're fucking sunshine and baby animals and happiness. You make me laugh and smile, even though I'm a grumpy bitch. It's goddamned sorcery, is what it is! Now get in the bedroom so I can show you my feelings with sex instead of words."

"That was wonderfully romantic!" Wyatt laughed as he bounced toward the bedroom. "And I believe I promised you a dance."

The music started the moment Nova entered the room, a chipper Earth-pop tune that made her body want to twitch in time to the beat. Wyatt swayed his hips and dragged a finger down his chest to the waistband of his jeans.

"I need you," he sang. "My starlight. My supernova."

Nova sucked in a ragged breath. Shit, he was really doing this. She propped her crutches against the wall and hopped to the bed to sit.

"My supernova," he crooned again, catching the hem of his shirt and pulling it up just past his navel.

"Higher."

He spun in a circle in perfect time to the music, then began to inch the shirt upward with every downbeat. Each new reveal of skin sent pulses of heat through Nova's body. Her fingers itched to touch him, her mouth hungered for his taste. But his voice and his movements held her frozen in thrall.

The music crescendoed, and Wyatt yanked his shirt over his head and cast it aside. The grin he bestowed on her was pure, wicked delight. "This working for you?"

Nova shifted, trying to get comfortable in clothes that were too tight, too warm. "So much," she rasped.

"Good." He zigzagged a finger across his chest. "Because I have more for— Uh, hang on. I don't know how to do sexy boot removal."

Nova laughed as he scrambled to shed his boots and socks. By the time the chorus came around again, he had resumed his sultry sway.

"My starlight. My supernova." Wyatt moved his hips in a slow, sensuous arc as he undid the button of his jeans.

"Sexy to silly to sexy in nine point six seconds." Not something she would have expected to consider perfect, but it was. Because it was Wyatt and she loved both the silly and the sexy. She loved him when he was awkward and when he was lordly. When he was all smiles and in his rare moments of anger. She loved the entire complex package because with him she could be her best, most authentic self.

Nova began to remove her own clothes as she watched him slither out of his trousers. As the last strains of music sounded, he tugged his tight briefs past his hips and let them slide to the floor. His cock was hard, his skin was flushed, and he looked at her as if she was his universe.

She patted the bed. "Come over here." Maybe she'd never find the words to explain how thoroughly he'd stolen her heart, but she'd keep on showing him, today and all the days to come.

Wyatt walked to the bedside table and opened the drawer. He withdrew two narrow lengths of silk, which he deposited in Nova's lap. Only then did he stretch out on the bed beside her.

Nova slid one of the ribbons between her fingers. "What am I supposed to do with these?"

Wyatt's brow furrowed. "Tie me to the bed, obviously. Why else would I have this pretty brass headboard with all its lovely poles?" He curled his fingers around one of those poles and stroked up and down, the way he might stroke himself.

Nova rolled onto her knees so she could frown down at him. "You were recently kidnapped, locked in a cage, and handcuffed. You're sure you won't mind being restrained?"

"No." The confusion in his expression smoothed out into a smile. "I trust you."

And there he went, sending arrows straight to her heart again. "Stop being all romantic. If you make me cry…" She shook a finger at him.

"What will you do? Tie me to the bed?"

"You brat." Nova seized his wrist and pinned it to the headboard. With swift, military precision, she tied his wrist in place, taking care not to make the binding too snug around his still-healing skin. "We're going to do this, but that means *you* have to be the one in charge. If you want something, you have to tell me. Got it?"

He smirked at her. "Yes, Mistress Nova."

She captured his other wrist and secured it in the same manner. "Feel okay?"

"Yep."

Nova straightened up and admired her handiwork. God, she couldn't wait to rub her body all over his. She tore off her remaining layers of clothing, cursing when her trouser leg caught on the ankle wrap and she had to slow down.

"You don't have to rush," Wyatt said. "We have all night. We have the rest of our lives, if you want."

"My life isn't going to last much longer if I don't get to

touch you soon." The cuff of her trousers finally slid over her heel, and she grunted in satisfaction. "I feel like I'm about to explode."

"Is that so? How 'bout you come up here and sit on my face and I'll give you an explosion worthy of your name."

Nova groaned and scrambled up to straddle his thighs. "Can I kiss you first?"

"Absolutely."

She kissed him hard and hungry, rubbing her body against his to soothe her aching skin. Wyatt tasted of raspberries and honey and rainbows.

"I love you." She kissed his stubbly jaw and down his neck. "I adore you. I love when you talk dirty and when you let me boss you around. I love your animals and your drones and your colors, and, fuck, Wyatt, I can't get enough of you."

She kissed back up his neck, slower this time, licking and sucking until he whimpered.

"I thought… I was in charge," he gasped.

"In charge-ish."

Wyatt's throat vibrated under her lips as he laughed. Nova rocked her hips against his hard cock, and the sound turned into a moan.

"You… cheat," he panted.

She pressed a swift kiss to his lips. "Do I?"

"Yes." He took a deep breath, then said in his most aristocratic voice, "Now get up here so I can taste your hot, slick quim and suck your clit until you scream my name."

Nova had never obeyed a command so eagerly. Not only was she aching and dripping with need, but Wyatt was making demands for *her* pleasure. Maybe she was a princess after all—one who fought for and protected her people. And Wyatt was her hero, 'who saw all of her and made sure she would be cared for too.

She scrambled up his body and planted her knees to either side of his raised arms. The position spread her wide, with plenty of room to adjust for the perfect angle. She wrapped her hands around Wyatt's bound wrists, then lowered herself until she felt the swipe of his tongue.

"Please." She almost lost her breath as he licked over her in a long, firm swipe. "God, Wyatt, please."

He repeated the motion, making a noise of satisfaction when she trembled. Nova's eyes squeezed shut. Pleasure robbed her of her wits and seized control of her body. Her back arched and her hips began to gyrate. Wyatt was music, and she was a dancer, caught in his rhythm.

"Yes. Oh—" She pressed down harder, rocked faster. "More."

Wyatt's lips closed around her clit and Nova nearly screamed. Her hands clenched around his wrists, her knees squeezing his torso. The music they created swelled as he sucked harder, the tempo accelerating until each note of pleasure crashed atop the next in a chord of brilliant chaos.

"Love. You." Nova fucked his mouth in wild, desperate jerks, losing her rhythm. "L-love—" The word ended on a soundless cry.

The climax tore her apart, scattering pieces of her in every direction. Only once the explosion had consumed every last drop of energy in her body, did the dust begin to settle, coalescing bit by bit into flesh and blood.

Nova's eyes fluttered open. She released her grip on Wyatt and sagged against the headboard. "Bloody hell."

Wyatt's lips brushed her inner thigh. "I love you too."

Nova gave herself a moment to catch her breath and bask in the feeling of perfect peace. Yes, her father was evil. Yes, the world sucked sometimes. But she'd found a place where she could seize moments of unfettered joy. Where she belonged.

"I want to be part of your family," she vowed. "Permanently."

Wyatt kissed her thigh again. "Love, you already are. For as long as you want."

"Good." She rolled off him. "What's next?"

Wyatt beamed at his bedraggled, lust-drunk lover. "Next you get the lube and the strap-on and you fuck me until I'm as wrung-out as you are." He pulled against his bindings, but Nova's knots didn't budge. "I'm afraid you'll have to do all the work. Terribly sorry."

Nova sat up and scowled at him. "You really are a brat."

"Maybe next time I can tie you up and you can be the snarky one."

Her lips pursed. "I'll think about it."

Nova climbed off the bed, but instead of going to the bedside table, she hopped on her one uninjured leg all the way into the bathroom. A short time later, she returned with a moist cloth and crawled back up the bed to wipe Wyatt's face clean.

"Aww. You didn't have—"

"Hush." She finished her cleaning and patted him dry with the opposite end of the cloth. "It's my turn. If you want to take care of me, you can make me a sandwich after we're done."

"Grilled cheese? I can do grilled cheese."

"I'd like that." She set the cloth aside and went to rummage through Wyatt's drawer of toys. Her voice dropped to a husky purr. "Hot. Melty. Mouthwatering."

Wyatt's too long ignored cock throbbed. When Nova finally pulled out the strap-on harness, he groaned, "Please."

"Which do you like?" She held up a pair of dildos.

"The purple." It was a bit smaller than the other, but more anatomically lifelike. "It's my favorite."

Nova fastened it in place, then wriggled into the harness, taking care not to put weight on her ankle. "We should get you a rainbow colored one."

"I like the purple. It matches your hair."

She ran a hand over the colored lock of hair in an unusually self-conscious gesture. God, she was beautiful. Sexy and smart and strong. Life had made her a soldier, but she'd made herself a champion for others. A goddamned hero.

"Come here, my blazing star," Wyatt commanded. "I'm still in charge, remember?"

Nova finished adjusting the harness, then knelt between his legs, one hand on the base of the dildo, the other tight around the jar of lubricant. "I've never pegged anyone before."

"You'll be brilliant. Wedge a pillow under my hips, then have at it. I promise to tell you if I don't like something."

He couldn't imagine a scenario under which she'd do something he didn't like. Not his Nova. He let his gaze rove up and down her body. Her biceps bulged and flexed as she maneuvered herself over him. So powerful. She could tear him apart, especially tied as he was.

He adored that about her. Nova was so hard and strong, but soft too, with lush, round breasts and a gently curving belly. Exactly as she was on the inside, a perfect, intoxicating mix.

A slick finger circled his entrance, and he jerked at the sudden, electric thrill.

"Oh, shit," he gasped. "Don't touch my cock or I won't last long."

Nova sprinkled light kisses over his chest and abdomen, while her finger continued its gentle exploration. "Thank you for the warning."

Another slow circle, and then she pushed in, only a fingertip, but it was enough to make Wyatt's back arch.

"More. All of it."

She took her time, easing him wider, sliding carefully in and out before daring to repeat the process with a second finger.

Wyatt's head fell back against the headboard. Fuck, she was killing him. His arms were twitching, his fingers clenching into fists. He couldn't touch himself, couldn't ease the mounting pressure twisting inside him. All he could do was beg.

"Please. Fuck, Nova, more."

She straightened up and applied a generous amount of lube to the dildo. Grinning like a predator, she teased his entrance with the tip until he whimpered the way she liked so much.

"That's a good boy." Her voice was breathy with desire, her eyes dark. She wiggled her hips to get friction against her clit, making herself sigh.

And, holy hell, Wyatt had never needed anything in his life as much as he needed her right now. He rasped out another "please," and then she was pushing in, filling him the way he craved. He made an inarticulate noise, and she pulled out and thrust in again, a bit harder.

"Yes, God, just like that."

She drove in a third time, the angle exactly right to stroke his prostate, and he lost the ability to do anything but moan. His eyes fluttered closed as pleasure swamped him, but he could feel her in every part of himself. Her hands pressed down on his hips, holding him still as she quickened her pace, taking him in faster, firmer stokes. Her breaths came as rapidly as his own, growing more ragged the quicker they moved.

Wyatt rocked into every thrust, trying to say with his body the words his mouth couldn't form. *More, more, harder, faster, please, God, yes, please.*

Nova let out a squeak and her rhythm faltered. She moved a hand to his cock, squeezing him tight, her fingers still wet with lube.

He forced his eyes open. "Yes, Nova, that's it." He wasn't sure she could understand his garbled words, but he kept talking. "Yes, that's my girl, that's my supernova, oh, fuck."

All her thrusts were imprecise now, her hand on his cock erratic as her own pleasure neared. Wyatt couldn't have asked for anything better. His own orgasm rushed onward, nearer with every wild movement of their intwined bodies.

"Nova, y-yes. Take it, take your pleasure. Please, I c-can't—"

She cried out in ecstasy as she thrust hard into him, catching him in her climax and sweeping him along until he was writhing and keening and spending into her fingers in long, hot pulses. The universe came to a standstill, freezing them together in a moment of shared rapture.

Drip by tiny drip, time thawed. There was no sound but their panting, no movement save for the exhausted slump of their sated bodies. Wyatt could have happily fallen asleep right there, except he knew his arms and neck would hate him if he did.

"If you untie me," he said, "I'll hold you for a while before I make that grilled cheese."

Nova moved with her usual fluid efficiency, and in

seconds, they were wrapped in each others' arms, a sweaty, sticky mess of sex and joy.

And for the first time in twenty years, Wyatt knew, with a deep, abiding certainty, where his home was. Here. There. Anyplace at all where he was loved.

# 43

Dr. Cass Garner tapped their security code onto the keypad. The cargo box beeped once, then popped open to reveal dozens of small sample tins, each neatly labeled with a series of letters and numbers.

"You're going to do that tonight?" asked Dr. Miles Stanton, Cass's colleague at the Royal Jovian Resources Commission.

Cass had once hoped that the Commission's laboratory, with all its gleaming machines and fascinating astrological specimens, would be their happy place, but the job hadn't quite lived up to expectations. Stanton—who questioned everything Cass did, from sample analysis to duration of lunch breaks—was one of the reasons.

"Yep." Cass slotted the first tin into the analyzer.

"Waste of time. We got three surveyor reports from that sad little moon. You know they all came back as unprofitable."

And there was the other main reason this job was lacking: the money-hungry corporate hierarchy.

*As if the only value in a celestial body can be measured in pounds sterling.*

Cass kept their eyes fixed on the analyzer. An image of the sample popped up on the screen, alongside the blank database entry corresponding to the sample's ID number.

"You know how I like to be thorough," they said.

Stanton only sniffed and walked out. Ass.

Cass flipped the switch to start the analysis, then turned to the attached keyboard to type up some visual observations on the sample while the machine hummed. Finally, they could have a second to fully relax. If only it could be like this every day: a quiet lab, interesting research, no interruptions.

The first several samples produced nothing but ice and rock—the "unprofitable" things people like Stanton hated. Cass made copious notes anyway. Someday, a young scientist would want to know about the compositions of the small moons and asteroids Cass had meticulously recorded. Perhaps a particular detail would lead to new understanding of the Jovian system or the formation of rings and moons.

Cass inserted another sample into the machine. "What kind of rock do you have for me to— Holy shit!"

They jumped so hard they nearly toppled off their stool. The sample on the display screen, while mostly gray rock, was flecked with droplets of liquid gold.

Cass zoomed in on the image. "It can't be."

*Arcanium.* Cass had never seen the rare, precious metal in person before. It gleamed like liquid fire, the light dancing off the surface of each tiny bead in sparkles of red and gold. The golden equivalent of quicksilver. It fit every description they'd ever read.

Cass set the analysis running. Their fingers flew over the keyboard, inputting every detail they could think of. Number of droplets. Location. Size. Estimated volume. They could hardly breathe. Civilization as they knew it wouldn't even exist without arcanium. No other fuel was compact and powerful enough to keep such a massive fleet of spaceships running. And even more vital were the atmosphere and gravity drives that created Earth-like living spaces on Mars and here in the mining colonies. Without arcanium, humans would still be stuck on an overpopulated Earth, dying of hunger and disease, or wiped out entirely due to their own folly.

The analyzer beeped and spit out its results. High percentages of silicate rock, as usual. But there, near the bottom of the list, in clear digital text was the word Cass had been hoping for. Arcanium.

They pumped their fist. "Suck it, Stanton! Unprofitable, my ass!" They hopped off the stool and danced a jig. They had Irish ancestry; it worked. Kinda.

"Oh, my God, oh, my God." Cass took a deep breath, then sat back down and grabbed the next sample.

Arcanium. What a find! This could be revolutionary. Every new deposit of the vital material meant easier availability and lower costs. A tiny bit more power dragged from the hands of the ruling class.

Cass bounced excitedly as the next sample appeared on the screen. No obvious gold droplets on this one, but that wasn't anything to fret about. There could be traces here. And they had dozens of samples to go. More would contain arcanium. They knew it in their soul.

When the analyzer beeped this time, it was accompanied by a flashing red light. Contamination warning.

"What?" Cass scanned the data. Machine oil. Normally any contamination came from the drone taking the samples. But the Commission's drones didn't use this type of oil. This was the sort of heavy-duty stuff used by mining equipment.

*Mining equipment.*

A knot of dread twisted in Cass's gut. Someone was

mining a supposedly untouched, inconsequential moon. The surveyor reports should have caught any illegal mining. Unless someone had falsified them. And if that someone had a secret cache of arcanium…

"Shit, shit, shit."

Cass scurried to their small office attached to the laboratory and flicked on their personal vidscreen. They had to tell someone. No one here would do. The higher-ups were too focused on money, and the fake reports meant they were all under suspicion. Someone in government, then.

Cass's jaw tightened. The bloody aristocracy. A bunch of pretentious old men like Grandfather, patting one another on the back for each new exploitation of the people. Maybe there were a few good ones among the offal, but Cass couldn't risk trusting the wrong person. Not with something like this.

They pulled open their desk drawer and rummaged around for the latest edition—several weeks old—of their favorite Dystopian newspaper. The Lords of Dystopia could be trusted, according to the paper, but they were still aristos. Morland was out, for sure, and Wells had questionable alliances. Windborne was a mystery, and tied up in a lot of recent misadventures.

That left Brandt. He owned this newspaper. He'd publicly stated his disdain for the government, including his own title. He was the closest Cass would find to an authority who would be on their side.

They reached for the vidscreen and began to type.

# EPILOGUE

Nova peeled off the last of the tape, revealing the pristine edge of the massive rainbow that now arced across the wall behind their bed.

"Ta-da!"

Wyatt turned from his work on the adjacent space-themed wall to admire her handiwork. "I love it. It's so even and perfect. I'll think of you every time I see it." He grinned. "As if I don't already think of you every time I walk into this room."

He returned to his project, dipping his fingertips into a paint bucket, then flicking the paint onto the blue-black background. A nearby drone blew a steady stream of air, preventing the paint spots from dripping.

"No wonder you're a mess," Nova said. "And don't you think it's covered enough?"

Wyatt flicked more paint onto the wall. "I don't mind the mess. And it's the universe. There are supposed to be trillions of stars. Or quadrillions or whatever." He wiped his fingers on his trousers, adding a pale blue smear to the myriad of other colors splattered up and down his legs.

"That's never going to come out, you know."

Wyatt turned to face her. His black crop top and trousers bore dots and splotches in every color of the rainbow and more besides. He had paint on his belly, paint in his hair, even a streak of red paint down his cheek that could have been mistaken for blood if it weren't glittery.

"It's not supposed to come out. That's why I wore these clothes. I don't ever want to wear all black again in my life."

"Ah." Nova motioned for him to turn in a circle, and he did. "Your backside needs more color. Stay right there."

While he waited, she cracked open the can of purple paint. She dipped a brush in, then spread an even layer of the paint over her entire hand. Satisfied with the result, she walked over to Wyatt and planted her hand firmly on his ass. She gave him a little squeeze for good measure, then stepped back.

"I like it."

Wyatt tried to look over his shoulder. "I need a mirror. But I bet these are now going to be my favorite pair of pants."

"Good. Everyone will see you wearing them and know you're mine."

"Should I scrap the plan to get a dagger tattooed on my arm, then?"

She poked him. "No. You're supposed to get that done when I get my viper. Now finish your trillions of stars so we can clean up and start prepping to paint the office next."

"What about your office?" Wyatt shot her an impish smile.

After officially moving in with Wyatt, Nova had turned her apartment into an office for her new private investigation business. It was still technically illegal, but the people of Dystopia needed someone they could hire for security and detective work. The majority of them couldn't afford the RMC fees. They *could* afford Nova. In all probability, she'd barely make enough to cover rent. But she'd be helping people, which would make her happy, and Wyatt would get to be the provider of food and shelter, which would make *him* happy.

"You are not touching my office." Nova held out her paint-coated hand in a *stop* gesture. Her office was the opposite of Wyatt's chaos haven—sleek black desk and shelves, an armchair of dark red leather, blue-gray walls with subtle cream trim, and a large, shiny file cabinet to keep everything tidy—and it was staying that way.

He laughed. "Fair enough. And I'm almost done. I just need to find the most beautiful spot."

Nova crossed her arms and waited silently while Wyatt scrutinized every galaxy and nebula of his space mural. After what seemed an eternity, he nodded. Then he picked up a tray covered in assorted mixtures of paint colors. He smeared some blue and purple and silver together until they formed a shimmery pale violet. Then he dipped one finger into the paint, reached up into a swirling nebula high on the wall, and created a single bright star.

"A nova inside a nebula," he declared. "Rare and spectacular."

Nova pulled him close and kissed him, not giving a damn about the paint he was getting on her clothes. "If anyone asks, it's called the Wyatt nebula."

He rocked his pelvis into hers. "Because you want to be inside me all the time?"

She laughed. "Yes, that. But mostly because we belong together."

Wyatt joined her laughter, and for a moment they simply held each other, free and happy. When their lips met again, the kiss was soft and lingering, as if they had all the time and space in the universe. Maybe they did.

# THE END

# THANK YOU

Special thanks to the backers of the *Earth Earls Are Easy* Kickstarter campaign for helping make distribution of this book possible in digital, print, and audio formats.

A. Lee Welles

Alexandra Vasti

Alison

Andie Wood

Andrew Betrix Jr.

Bethany Bennett

Ch. N. Heinzl

CherylSR

E. McAuley

Elizabeth Schechter

girvinias_books

Glori Medina

Isaac 'Will It Work' Dansicker

Jossi B.

Julia Zwicker

Kate Lane

Katherine Grant

Kimberley Stafford

Kyle M.

Lisa Cody

Mandy Tufail

Megan Struttmann

michelle@betahelix

Megan

PunkARTchick "Ruthenia"

Robyn Douglas

Sarah Weitman

SomersSketch

Tea

# ABOUT THE AUTHOR

Award-winning author Catherine Stein believes that everyone deserves love and that Happily Ever After has the power to help, to heal, and to comfort. She writes sassy, sexy romance set during the Victorian and Edwardian eras. Her stories are full of action, adventure, magic, and fantastic technologies.

Catherine lives in Michigan with her husband and three rambunctious kids. She loves steampunk and Oxford commas, and can often be found dressed in Renaissance festival clothing, drinking copious amounts of tea.

Visit Catherine online at
**www.catsteinbooks.com**
Join her VIP mailing list for a free short story.

Instagram
**@catsteinbooks**

Facebook
**@catsteinbooks**

# ALSO BY
# Catherine Stein

## Potions and Passions

*The Earl on the Train* - Book 0.5

*How to Seduce a Spy* - Book 1

*Mishaps & Mistletoe -*
A Holiday Novella -Book 1.5

*Not a Mourning Person* - Book 2

*Once a Rake, Always a Rogue* - Book 3

*Love at Second Sight* - Book 4

## Sass and Steam

*Love is in the Airship* - Book 0.5

*A Shot to the Heart* - Book 0.75

*Eden's Voice* - Book 1

*What Are You Doing New Year's Eve? -*
A Holiday Novella - Book 1.5

*Priceless* - Book 2

## Sass and Steam (cont.)

*Dead Dukes Tell No Tales* - Book 3

*Beyond Repair* - Book 4

*Luck Be a Lady Pirate* - Book 5

## Arcane Tales

*The Scoundrel's New Con* - Book 1

*The Spinster's Swindle* - Book 2

## Mad Scientists Society

*The Courtesan and Mr. Hyde* - Book 1

*The Electrical Affairs of Dr. Victor Franklin* - Book 2

## Other Books

*Mating Habits* - Book 1

*Idle Nature* - Book 2

*My Heiress, 'Tis of Thee*

Available at your favorite online retailer.
**www.catsteinbooks.com**

# Thank you so much for reading!

If you enjoyed the book and are so inclined,
I would love for you to leave a review.
Happy readers make an author's day!

I love hearing from readers, so feel free
to contact me on social media, or email:

## catherine@catsteinbooks.com